Blue Sun, Yellow Sky

by Jamie Jo Hoang

HEYJAMIE

HJ Publishing
Available wherever you request a copy.

Published by
HJ Publishing
Los Angeles, CA 90064

a division of
HeyJamie.com

First paperback edition, HJ Publishing, March 2015.
Printed in the United States of America.
Design by Jamie Hoang
Cover illustration by Ryan Eslinger

Library of Congress Cataloging-in-Publication Data
Hoang, Jamie Jo
Blue Sun, Yellow Sky: a novel / by Jamie Jo Hoang.—1st ed.

ISBN: 1-63443-371
ISBN-13: 978-1-63443-371-6

This book is dedicated to my sister,
Dr. Kimberly Kay Hoang, who supported
me throughout this journey. Thanks
for making my pipe dream a reality sis.

Contents

"From the moment I held the box of colors in my hands, I knew this was my life. I threw myself into it like a beast that plunges towards the thing it loves."

—Henri Matisse

CHAPTER ONE

Color

Have you ever noticed that fire hydrants are rarely alike in shape or color? I have. Most people associate them with the color red, but that's not always true. For example, looking around my neighborhood of Venice Beach, California, I can tell you the majority of them are, in fact, white.

Before I knew their function, I thought these oddly shaped, metal objects bolted down into the sidewalk were street art. I grew up in Houston, Texas, and at the tender age of three my dad took me to an opening at the Rothko Chapel. Located in the Museum District, the chapel sat just off the main strip of museums, so it was more like being in a neighborhood than the center of a city. Nestled inside quaint, single story homes, the grassy area surrounding the chapel made it easily mistaken for a community center, and rightfully so. In honor of whatever they were celebrating, a team of local artists had gotten together at night and painted every hydrant in the town black. My dad noticed them first as he walked me to one and said, "Look honey, it's a Rothko fire hydrant." He meant the artists had painted the hydrants black as a tribute to Rothko, but being three, I thought he meant the physical hydrant was for Rothko. I remember growing more and more fascinated as I noticed them on every street.

Taking an immediate interest in what I imagined to be a worldwide phenomenon, I spent hours scouring our library of coffee table books at home (known to me at the time as 'picture books') for photos of international monuments. It was a "Where's Waldo" type search for fire hydrants in iconic places. I looked for hours and hours and when I didn't find a single hydrant within the covers of my books, I drew them in myself. My mom was furious when she found out, yelling at me and slapping my hand to get me to understand what I did was wrong. Meanwhile, my dad stood in the background cackling so hysterically that his laughter became contagious and my mom couldn't help but join in. She didn't so much care about our books, even though they were quite expensive. With the start of preschool the next day she was afraid I might deface all of the books in the classroom. Which I did.

Years passed before I realized the two-foot high objects bolted into the sidewalk were lifesaving water pumps used to put out fires. But by then, I'd already spent so much time studying fire hydrants that it was impossible to pass one by without taking notice, and on the rare occasion I came across one decorated like Super Mario or engineered to double as a drinking fountain, I'd take a picture and send it as a postcard to my dad. Our inside joke became a small-scale version of what later emerged as Banksy or Space Invader art pieces, a duly oxymoronic sense of community amongst art enthusiasts who found unity in bearing witness to a public secret. I personally wasn't the trespassing or graffiti type artist, so my subtle form of artistic expression with the hydrants was to include them in every single one of my paintings. They were hidden in plain sight as part of the landscape; like trees in a forest, viewers just expected them to be there. I'd only ever had one person recognize the black fire hydrants in my work, and he happened to also have been at the Rothko celebration that day.

At my gallery openings, nearly two decades later, I made a habit of wandering about the room and listening to see if anyone ever recognized the motif. Not many did, and even if they took notice of one, they never thought to look for another. People rarely notice fire hydrants.

On the night of my biggest gallery showcase to date, I nervously stood in the back room of the Michael Sanders Gallery watching the event from afar. Typically at openings I moved around, studying the expressions of strangers as they connected with or dismissed my work, but this night was different. Champagne and bite-sized quiches floated about the room on large platters, carried by waiters who deftly weaved in and out unnoticed by the clusters of patrons gathered to examine my creations. My paintings had shown in galleries before, but this was the first time an entire space was reserved solely for me.

The layout was strategic, designed to move the viewer

from one painting to the next and a break in sequence was delineated via a wall separating the rooms. Weeks of interior design, light installation, bulb testing, and precise placement of the artwork all culminated in this one evening. But as I stood watching people, both familiar and strange, my pinky finger strummed the ridge of a dime-sized, shallow hole, where someone had nicked the doorframe chipping the paint. All I could think about was the imperfect floor-to-ceiling crack in the wall behind Dr. Rostin's diploma from UC Irvine. *Retinitis Pigmentosa* (RP)—those words were the last thing I remembered him saying. I stopped listening after he said there was no cure, and my body numbed as it felt everything and nothing, all at once.

"Aubs," Michael Sanders called, in a slightly-too-loud, perhaps intoxicated, greeting.

He was the gallery owner and my biggest supporter. From across the room he motioned for me to come over. I took a deep breath, lifted the hem of my long black chiffon dress and moved toward him with a glass of now-warm champagne. As I approached, he began the introductions: "Aubrey, you remember Mr. and Mrs. Gibson?"

"Of course," I replied as we shook hands.

"So tell me. Is this a love story?" Mr. Gibson asked, cutting right to the chase.

Being that art was subjective, no right or wrong answers existed, yet people wanted affirmation that their interpretation was the same as that of the artist. Michael explained to me some time ago that people bought art that spoke to them, so if the artist was available, why not double-check that you "heard correctly," so to speak? "If I dropped

$7,000 on a painting, I'd want to know that what appeared to be a symbol of unity was not simply a walrus," he'd said, making me laugh.

"Depends on your definition of love," I said to Mr. Gibson.

"I love your use of color here. The painting simply exudes romance. But there is a darkness to it too, a foreboding shadow if you will," Mrs. Gibson chimed in.

The Gibsons were looking at one of my favorite paintings, *Midnight in Paris*—an abstract cityscape with a couple dancing underneath the Eiffel Tower. I'd never actually been to Paris, but my mother often talked about dancing underneath the iconic symbol of love with my dad on their honeymoon.

"I painted this in honor of my parents, on their 20th anniversary," I said. I knew better than to say, *On what would have been their 20th anniversary*. Not many people want paintings that have any kind of connection, however remotely, to death, and so for good measure I added, "If you come at it from the angle of love, then the darkness symbolizes marital struggles, but you'll notice that the dark is only on the periphery, never seeping into the core. On the other hand, the argument could be made that couples cripple themselves by disengaging with what's on the periphery in exchange for each other."

Mrs. Gibson squeezed her husband's elbow and I knew I had sold them this painting. Couples who had been together as long as the Gibsons, or my parents, knew that in a relationship, one kind of love did not exist without the other.

Just behind them, I caught a glimpse of one of the first paintings I created in graduate school at Columbia

University. A juxtaposition between poverty and gluttony, the piece was aptly named *Poverty and Gluttony*. The scene took place at night in the back alleyway of a row of high-end restaurants, where every night, high-quality food was thrown out. In a corner, curled up in a ball, was a little boy exhausted from starvation. I painted *Poverty and Gluttony* not long after my parents' death. It was the darkest time in my life.

Drawing from the pain in Picasso's Blue Period, more specifically *The Old Guitarist*, I mimicked Picasso's technique of bodily distortion to convey loneliness and isolation. My painting hung in the Michael Sanders Gallery for two years before the San Francisco Museum of Modern Art asked to display it in a traveling exhibit showcasing emerging artists. Too dark a subject matter to be hung in someone's home, the painting never sold, but it had a tremendous museum and gallery run because it directed the viewer to a place of uncomfortable contemplation.

It's rare to see signs of it this young.

The words rang like deafening bells in my ears as my smile stiffened and I started walking to another piece of art, with the Gibsons following closely behind. What started as occasional blurred vision and patchy peripherals had culminated in a diagnosis with no treatment.

Six to eight weeks…a genetic disorder affecting the retina.

I had only recently started to gain recognition in the art community. "You're sitting at the tipping point, Aubrey," Michael had said to me on numerous occasions. I remember being on cloud nine and wishing the clock would start ticking at half-pace so I could enjoy the moment. But I no longer wanted time to simply slow down. I wanted it to stop.

I remained aware of the people moving around me, but in my own thoughts time moved at a rapid pace. No one knew what was happening to me and even if they did they probably wouldn't care. In the art world, save for the select few who were lucky enough to die before their time, artists moved in and out faster than the fashion trends of the New York Runway. Michael stood less than three feet away from me discussing how my paintings were a juxtaposition of life's many facets—precisely the reason he found my work so fascinating—but his words registered as faint and far away.

I looked at him and smiled, unable to stop myself from reminiscing about the first time we met. I was in a low place when Michael stumbled upon me. Stunned by the sudden passing of my parents, I had dropped out of graduate school after only one semester and obtained a permit from the city to be a street vendor. Weeks went by with tourists asking me to paint them New York City skylines, which I refused to do until my landlord squashed my pride with an eviction notice. If catering to the lowest common denominator meant being able to pay the bills, then I wasn't above it. Michael had just made a small fortune buying up the re-make rights of Southeast Asian horror films and selling them to the major motion picture studios in Hollywood. Atypical of a gallery owner, Michael was a jeans and zip-up sweater entrepreneur first and a suit-and-tie art enthusiast second.

At the time we met, my body of work included: ballerinas on skid row; cityscapes with churches next to brothels; a boy dressed in a suit sitting on a bench reading the newspaper; and a homeless woman carrying a Birkin bag—images that offered multiple meanings depending on what the viewer brought to the conversation. For instance, on a normal day, seeing the boy sitting in a suit, reading a newspaper might evoke laughter at its absurdity. But look at the painting on an especially trying day and the boy becomes a symbol for the end of youth and loss of innocence… or something like that.

I often wondered if I had missed the mark because no one ever paid attention to those pieces, even though I made a point to display them in front of the cityscapes. On especially slow days, I'd dream about a bigwig executive buying a piece for his penthouse office in the financial district. Michael was not that guy. At least, I didn't think so. New York was a business-suit city and Michael's casual attire suggested he was either a tourist or vagabond. So when he offered me $500 cash for *Ballerinas on Skid Row*, I laughed at him. He gave me a confused look, handed me the money, and asked for my number.

"I have a boyfriend," I lied. I was 23 and certain he had just propositioned me for sex.

"I'm happy for you," he said, dryly. He handed me his business card. "I just bought a gallery in California. Call if you're interested in how this piece does."

Just shy of two weeks later (ten days to be exact), I called to find that the painting sold. That call marked the single greatest leap in my career and was how I ended up driving 3,096 miles to a new residence in Venice, California.

Had it already been four years? The time passed so quickly that I wondered if I had taken it for granted. Looking right at the Gibsons, who were talking to me, I smiled in blind acknowledgment of compliments I didn't hear. I knew I wasn't dreaming—the champagne glass and Michael's hand on the small of my back leading me to another painting were proof of that—but I wanted to rewind and reverse the news I'd received earlier. I wanted to go back to not knowing. It didn't matter that the disease was genetic, predetermined before I'd even had a chance to fight it. I simply wanted to get out of this phase of excruciatingly slow acceptance.

Unfortunately, there is no cure.

Other than an experimental vitamin A palmitate, a drug that could, at best, slow the process, I saw no reason for regular office visits. Short of a miracle or divine intervention, it seemed the battle had already been lost. When the thoughts in my head calmed, I realized the Gibsons had begun negotiations for *Midnight in Paris* and excused myself.

I spotted Jeff Anderson, an old friend who was both familiar and strange, in a far corner looking pensively at a painting I'd entitled *Home*. One of the few paintings in my collection with no subtext, it was literally a painting of my childhood home, only instead of a frontal view it showed an obscure angle from outside our kitchen window looking into our 1970s-style living room. A home void of its people, it remained the only still life in my collection.

As I approached him I said, "You actually came."

Jeff dressed up for the occasion in a suit and tie, but the look didn't fit his personality and I wished I'd just told him to wear jeans.

"I did," he smiled.

"Nice boots," I said, looking down at the black cowboy boots he wore beneath his cuffed dress pants. The boots gave him a rugged demeanor closer to the guy I remembered from high school.

"Just keepin' it real," he smiled.

"Are you having a horrible time?"

"No, but I did overhear a conversation that could've come straight out of a Daniel Clowes comic," he said. Of course he did. I smiled.

That Jeff showed up at all to an event he probably considered pretentious, playing the part of an interested patron, was a whole new level of maturity. He was never a fan of art. In fact, in a heated debate about the value of art, I remembered him saying he thought collecting art was a wealthy person's game of who could pay the most for the least comprehensible painting. Being around him was familiar and distant all at the same time. Jeff had always been my forever friend, the one I thought I'd never lose. But time and distance changed us and now our relationship was just a shadow of the childhood friendship we once shared.

There was a bit of an awkward silence until Jeff said, "Where's the fire hydrant?"

I grinned, thrilled that he remembered. "It's there," I said. "Look closely at the texture of the exterior wall."

Jeff stepped forward and squinted. "No kidding," he said, as he searched until he found it.

"Do you mind if I borrow her?" Michael asked, coming up beside me.

"No, of course not," Jeff said.

"I'll be right back," I said to Jeff.

"Want to grab lunch tomorrow?" he asked, as I walked away.

"Sure," I said, turning back to him with a smile.

"Who's that?" Michael asked me.

"Just an old friend," I said. "How are we doing?"

"Eight! Eight of your paintings have minimum bids placed on them and three have multiple bidders. You're going to be up there with the likes of Mike Kelly and Douglas Gordon in no time," he said. And I couldn't help but think, *If he only knew how quickly.*

"If you're lucky, they might even include your name next to mine in the history books," Rusty Coal said, breaking into our conversation. A slender five-foot ten inches, he sported a tailor-made, gray Dolce & Gabbana skinny suit and black tie. Sleeves rolled up to show his mural of tattoos, he looked more like a rogue runway model than an artist.

Michael rolled his eyes. "I knew that line in the New York Times about being the perfect blend of Warhol and Jasper Johns was going to go to your head."

"Ah yes, if only I could be so lucky," I added, giving my favorite arch nemesis a hug. "How are you?"

Rusty was my contemporary—an artist who broke out onto the art scene alongside me. Reviewers often pitted us against each other like horses in a race to the finish line. But our relationship was more akin to that of siblings; we were competitive, but at the end of the day we always looked out for each other. I loved him because he was one of those people who constantly broke the mold of stereotypes placed upon skinny hipsters covered in tattoos.

"I'm good. Working on a series for MOMA in New York," he said.

"Holy shit Rusty, that's awesome. Congratulations!"

"Pshh, what kind of traffic does MOMA get?" Michael said. "It couldn't possibly be as prestigious a showing as the Michael Sanders Gallery, Aubs."

"Only about three million people walk through it a year," Rusty said.

"Exactly, small potatoes," Michael replied in jest.

Best known for his pieces that combined Neo-Dadaist and Pop Art concepts into the more specific theme of love, or sometimes the lack thereof, his name was quickly becoming commonplace in artistic circles.

I first met Rusty at an art convention in Downtown LA where we were two of 231 artists from 73 different galleries nationwide. We were both looking at Willem de Kooning's 1941 painting *Seated Man (Clown)* when he turned to me like we'd been friends for years and said, "Not a good painting, but proof that with time a craft can be perfected. Even still, it should probably be in the back of someone's garage and not on display. What do you think?" I agreed and we spent the next hour ripping it apart like catty teenage girls at the prom. He made you feel like you were important and your opinions mattered, regardless of whether he'd known you for 20 years or five minutes. However, harsh judgment applied to everyone, including me, and he didn't hesitate to tell me I needed to push things further: code for *I don't like it*.

He and I often joked about how each of his pieces was the result of a broken heart, so much so that when I asked him, "How many?" he knew exactly what I referred to.

"Sixteen."

"Sixteen!"

"I had a few repeat offenders," he smiled devilishly.

Rusty was the most emotionally vulnerable guy I knew. One of my favorite pieces of his was a 10x20-foot canvas littered with newspaper headlines about people murdering for love. The words and phrases varied in size from actual nine-point newspaper font to large, 12-inch letters, weaved in an abstract painting of a nude couple making love. Unlike so many of our peers who focused on abstract expressionism and making art weird for the sake of being weird, Rusty sought to create meaning through the conventional form of symbols. *Headlines for Love* was an expression of absurdity in the modern dating world: It touched on obsession, lust, and deadly romance.

Unlike Rusty, whose body of work was driven by emotion, I was hailed as being one of the best technical painters. When I was interviewed by the LA Times, the writer called me a chemist of colors because I had demonstrated how I created "Cadmium Red" by combining cadmium sulphide with selenium, which produced a warm and opaque hue. Knowing I would never again be able to mix my own colors was maddening.

My friends knew me as a bulldog with thick skin. It was they who turned to me when life slapped them in the face with public criticism, unexpected death, betrayal, creative fear, and self-doubt—not the other way around. Convinced that they wouldn't know how to react, I vowed not to tell anyone until I myself was okay with the situation. I planned to deal with it like I did my parents' death, by making it a non-issue.

Mentally exhausted, I was just about to excuse myself when Mr. and Mrs. Gibson approached.

"Frank and Ellen have officially added *Midnight in Paris* to their collection of Aubrey Johnson pieces," Michael informed me.

"Thank you so much for your support. I'm glad you enjoyed the opening." I shook their hands and walked them to the door. "It was so great to see you both again." As they headed out, Mr. Gibson wrapped his arm around his wife's shoulders and kissed her on the forehead, reminding me of my parents who, even after 20 years of marriage, walked like they couldn't get enough of each other.

At 2:15 a.m., after the gallery had emptied out, Michael and I sat down for a breather. Of the 26 canvases on display, 11 sold. Exhausted, but proud, Michael offered a half-dozen times to get me a cab home, but I assured him I was fine to walk. I liked to be alone after my openings, to absorb and reflect on the events of the evening.

Closing up shop wasn't my job; in fact, no other gallery ever allowed it, but Michael and I were friends, which warranted unprecedented access. I liked to spend some time alone with my pieces in the quiet atmosphere of an empty gallery. They were my babies and, like a mother at graduation, I was proud to see them succeed but sad not to have them in the house anymore. I did my customary stroll through the gallery and stopped at the one Jeff had been looking at earlier, *Home*. I had painted it just before moving from Houston to Manhattan, as a kind of cathartic sayonara.

It occurred to me then that Jeff had slipped out at some point without saying goodbye. I hadn't meant to leave him alone for so long. Looking at my phone, I sent him a text: *Sorry I didn't get to say bye. Lunch tomorrow at Urth Cafe sound good?*

Twenty seconds later he replied: *Sure.* I texted back: *12:30. Cool?* His reply: *K.*

I locked up and started the walk toward home. *Disintegration of the retina...* I thought the walk would lessen my anxiety, but it didn't. *Transition programs and support groups available.* How could I hope for things to get better when told with scientific certainty there was nothing they could do? As I wracked my brain for any kind of upside, a horrible stench invaded my senses, making it hard to breathe, let alone concentrate. At the end of the block I found its source: a homeless guy squatting in the shadows with his pants around his ankles. He seemed to be finishing up and used the front lapels of his soiled, button-down shirt to reach under his crotch and wipe up. The pile of human excrement was foul to see and putrid to smell. Yet, it was appropriate, seeing as how the universe seemed to be taking a massive dump all over my life.

CHAPTER TWO

Change

My apartment, a hole in the wall studio that once served as the third bedroom in someone's house, was small but cozy. When I arrived in Los Angeles, I had only one requirement: that I be near the beach. It was an incredibly naive desire considering my entire net worth at the time was equivalent to a beat-up, fifteen-year-old Pontiac Sunfire.

On the upside, coming from a three-bedroom apartment shared among four women in Manhattan, this was an upgrade. Rectangular in shape, my apartment featured a carved out nook for the kitchen to the far right, my living/ sleeping area in the center, and a disproportionately large bathroom on the opposite end. I painted in my apartment, so where someone else might have had a TV console I had a simple wooden easel and stool on top of a large brown tarp. Next to that stood a floor-to-ceiling bookshelf full of color pigments neatly arranged in jars, a row of paintings stacked in the adjacent corner, and a small leather couch. Forty feet from my doorstep, the sand marked the beginning of the beach, and 150 feet beyond that, the Pacific Ocean. Perhaps it was the astrological Pisces in me, but the moment my toes sank into the sand, I knew I was home.

On nights when I was plagued by insomnia, caused either by stress or the terrible choice to drink caffeine before bed, I tossed and turned until the sun peaked above the horizon. Then, throwing on sweats, I'd head to the beach to watch its light slowly illuminate the earth. The morning after my gallery opening was one such day.

Before the tourists could crowd the boardwalk and jam the bike lanes, I grabbed my family photo album off the shelf and headed for the shore.

The sun was already burning through the morning Pacific fog as I sat listening to the sound of waves crashing gently into the sand in front of me. Two playful dolphins surfed the breaking waves near the shore. It was a day just like this one that I got the phone call about my parents' car accident. They'd been hit by a teenager who was texting with her boyfriend instead of paying attention to the red light in front of her. The Jeep Grand Cherokee she was driving went barreling into my parents' Infinity sedan like a monster truck running over a go-kart. Four years had passed and I still missed them all the time.

I opened up my family album to the only photo of my dad and me. I'm seated on his lap with a cup of hot chocolate in my hands, as he tells me a story from the album. The two main characters are he and my mom. After getting married, but before they had me, they traveled around the United

States and to a few foreign countries together and the album was a timeline of their love story.

I turned to a photo of my mom and dad at the top of Half Dome in Yosemite. Standing on the beak, my dad is posed to jump and my mom is standing behind him with both hands on her cheeks and a look of horror in her eyes. The first time I remember him telling me that story, he said my mom was scared but he told her not to worry. My dad apparently knew how to fly. And together they soared down the mountainside gliding over waterfalls and rivers and even saluted a roaring black bear before returning to their campsite.

My dad liked to embellish his stories. Sometimes they'd be regular travel log type stories and other times he'd add in mythical creatures or give himself superpowers. Another story he told involved him having to defend Mom from a hungry tiger. "You can't tell from this picture, but just to the left, only a few feet away was a massive, larger-than-life Tiger. And boy was he hungry. Lucky for me, I had a bologna sandwich in my backpack, and everyone knows that tigers love bologna. I held it out and he delicately stuck it between his teeth before disappearing down the mountain." I could still hear the intonations of his voice as I repeated these stories to myself time after time.

As I got older the stories stopped—I don't remember when or why exactly. But looking back I regret not asking for more. Rich in memories, I valued the real as much as I cherished the fiction. When I felt lonely, the stories connected me to them and I felt their presence like a warm embrace.

I thought about how my parents would react to my news.

My mom would worry—she'd give me a practical list of things I needed to do: learn braille, count steps, organize my apartment, acclimate to using a walking stick, and maybe get a dog. My dad would embrace the positive—he would tell me I'd be like Daredevil with heightened senses of smell, touch, taste, and sound. He'd tell me to pay attention to the small things and see as much of everything as I can. He'd want me to soak it all in so that I could paint it later.

I took a quick look around me, closed my eyes, and breathed in deeply. I could taste the saltiness of the ocean air. I listened to the wind blow around me, kicking up sand. I heard the waves break rhythmically as they crashed upon the shore. I could picture all of it and I smiled. Behind me, a new sound emerged: laughing children. I tried to incorporate them into the image I had built in my head by visualizing what they looked like, but I came up empty. There was no image to remember.

Before I could even attempt to blink them back, tears rolled down my face. A resigned apology from a body that knew it was failing me. I didn't want to feel sorry for myself, but I let the tears fall until my ducts dried and my body could let go of the built-up tension my mind so badly wanted to ignore.

Back at my apartment a couple of hours later, I showered, threw on a long, navy blue cotton dress, my brown wraparound bracelet, and gold feather earrings. I slung my flower print crossover hobo bag across my chest before heading out the door. Having arrived at Urth Cafe early, I ordered my favorite things on the menu: a green tea latte and the chicken curry sandwich.

Venice hipsters gravitated to any outdoor coffee shop that sold organic, fair trade, love-the-earth products and Urth Cafe was no exception. As a result I had to wait twenty minutes for a two-top table. Despite the crowd, I liked the laid back atmosphere, but on this particular day I was nervous. Jeff and I were childhood friends, but we grew apart in college. We drifted, as people tend to, each focused on our own lives at opposite ends of the country. I went off to NYU undergrad to study art and he left for UCLA to study…well, I wasn't sure exactly.

Just a week before my gallery opening we had reconnected at the Department of Motor Vehicles, of all places. I had gotten a ticket for rolling a stop sign and Jeff had gotten one for speeding. He had actually been issued the ticket three months prior and was only there because one more day meant he'd be facing jail time. The Jeff I knew never drove more than five miles above the speed limit. Even at 4 a.m with no car in sight, he would still chose to wait for the green light before entering the intersection.

I hadn't seen him in person since high school, so I barely recognized him behind his scruffy beard. Wearing bootlegged Levi's jeans, a 2006 Rise Against concert T-shirt, and Pumas, he was a typical 27-year-old, 6'2", All-American farm boy. When I entered the traffic school auditorium, I saw him slouched down in his seat toward the back of the small auditorium, eyes glued to the bright images on his phone. I started to walk toward him and just as I was nearly convinced it couldn't be him, he chuckled at something on his phone and his skin creased around his eyes. Like James

Franco, he had three distinct wrinkles that appeared on the sides of his eyes when he smiled.

Sitting down next to him, I said, "I rolled a stop sign, what are you in for?"

Without looking up from his phone, he said, "Speeding."

"Jeff, you've never been above 65," I say, genuinely shocked.

Recognition slowly set in. "*No way.*"

"Yes way. It's been forever, how are you?"

"I'm good, you look great!" he said.

"Thanks," I replied and I instantly regretted not keeping in touch all those years. His light blue, almost gray eyes were piercing, and when he smiled at me my stomach fluttered. I still had a distinct impression of the Jeff who, at the age of five, wrote, "You're the pretiest girl in skool" on my valentine. We dated for a half of recess before I declared holding his hand to be yucky and broke it off. Our kindergarten romance ended and we went back to being sandbox buddies. No relationship after that would ever be as simple.

"Where-- what are you-- *how* are you here?" he stumbled.

I told him I moved to Venice a few years prior and that I was an artist, which was no surprise to him. He was a high school teacher, but didn't offer any more information. Jeff always played his cards close to his chest. In college, our friendship drifted from chatting every other day to sending cards on holidays, but when I saw his mom at my parents' funeral and he wasn't with her, I considered our friendship to be over.

The lecture had just begun when he took one of my info sheets and wrote: *I'm having déjà vu, are we in Driver's Ed again?* I smiled. Taking the paper, I drew eight dashes and the Hangman; category: mascot. Immediately he guessed Bulldogs. I looked at him and he whispered back our high school chant: Go Big Red! I laughed as quietly as I could. The last clue I wrote, I thought was an obvious one: Rendezvous. I put in enough blanks for the word "water tower," the place where we would meet when Jeff needed a break from the arguing in his house.

His parents fought all the time until our sophomore year when they decided to get a divorce. Had I paid attention before, I might have noticed they were never home at the same time.

"They're better off without each other," he had said. For as long as I could remember, Jeff had been this way—always opting for logic over emotion. Their relationship lacked passion and he told me he suspected they had only stayed together for him. So one night when I was over for dinner, his parents started bickering and he flat out said, "You guys should get a divorce. Don't stay together because of me. I'll be fine and I'll live here with mom because she needs me more." I was shocked. What kid says that to his parents?

Between the two of us, I was by far the wild one. I could almost guarantee anytime we got into trouble, the blame could be traced back to me. But Jeff was loyal, always taking equal blame and never once ratting me out to get a lesser punishment. Our kindergarten stint aside, a relationship between us never progressed past anything purely platonic, though now I suddenly wondered about our compatibility as adults.

As class came to an end and he still hadn't guessed the

word, I was disappointed that the memory meant more to me than him, but that went away as soon as he asked when he would see me again. I gave him my phone number and invited him to my opening.

I was still reminiscing about our day at the DMV when Jeff arrived carrying a bouquet of flowers. "For you," he said, kissing me on the cheek. I stood up to hug him and mistakenly reached up around his neck rather than under his arms, which would have been more appropriate given our 14-inch height difference. He lifted me into a bear hug, as he'd done a million times before and we laughed before sitting down.

"Y'all throw quite the party," he said, tugging on the knees of his pants to make himself more comfortable. In rugged jeans, a polo shirt, and aviator sunglasses, Jeff made me nostalgic for Houston, especially when "Howdy" or "Y'all" slipped out of his mouth.

"Don't think I didn't notice you bolting early," I chided as I laid the flowers on the cast iron patio chair beside me. "You didn't even say 'bye.'"

"And risk getting trampled by your adoring fans? No way," he smiled. "Actually, Shawn called. He had a flat tire, needed me to come to the rescue."

Shawn was Jeff's older brother, and, like most siblings, they were polar opposites. Jeff had memorized π to the 200th digit by the time he was 14, while Shawn mastered the art of single-handedly undoing a bra in the backyard shed of his parents' ranch.

"How convenient. Speaking of which, how is Shawn?" I

asked.

"He's great. As of six months ago he's officially licensed as a professional pot grower," Jeff laughed.

"Seriously?"

"He's got this crazy formula that calls for coconut husk instead of soil, can you believe that? Coconut husk," he said, his tone a mixture of disbelief and adoration.

"Are you a pothead?" I asked, wondering if I had mistaken sadness for being high. Never in a million years would I have imagined my nerdy elementary school friend giving me tips and tricks on growing marijuana—medical or otherwise.

"I smoke on occasion, but I wouldn't classify myself as a 'pothead'…" he replied sheepishly.

"Ever been baked while teaching…what is it you teach again?"

"World History and Computer Science, and yes, but only once," he said, looking ashamed and guilty. I laughed.

"I knew it. You're a stoner," I smiled.

"You would know considering you live in the marijuana mecca of the city."

"Touché," I laughed, giving him a two-finger salute. The residents of Venice were not shy about supporting the legalization of marijuana and on 4/20, the smell of ganja in the city was as ubiquitous as barbecue on the Fourth of July. "I'm glad Shawn's doing well," I said.

Shawn Miller was Jeff's half-brother, whom neither of us knew about until our junior year of high school when Shawn showed up at school. Jeff and I had been walking towards the parking lot when we saw a guy standing in front of an illegally parked, cherry red 1992 Dodge Shadow convertible.

He was impossible to miss, especially with his handmade sign that read *"Looking for Jeff Anderson."* Jeff and I looked at each other, confused, and I asked, "Did you win something?"

"I don't think so…" Jeff said.

"Are you Jeff?" Shawn asked, making eye contact.

"Yeah."

"This is probably going to come as a shock to you, as it did me, so I'm just going to come out and say it. I'm your brother. Well, half, anyway. I'm Shawn." He stuck his hand out and they shook, and when he introduced himself to me-- I hate to admit this-- I swooned a little. He had this older, bad-boy confidence I found extremely attractive and later became the type of guy I'd sought out in college. One of my many dating mistakes.

"I'm Aubrey," I said, feeling shy as he shook my hand and smiled with his eyes. He matched Jeff's 6'2" height, but that's where their similarities ended. Shawn had spiked blonde hair, two giant holes in his ears the size of dimes, which I guess classified as piercings, and tattoos peaking out from under the sleeve of his leather jacket.

"Is this a joke?" Jeff asked, looking around. I'd be lying if I didn't say I did a quick 360 scan of the area myself, but Shawn didn't laugh. The look on his face held both compassion and amusement.

In one surreal and long conversation, we learned that they shared the same father, that Mr. Anderson didn't know about Shawn until he was asked to sign a parental release form (which he did), and that Shawn's mother, Celeste Miller, married Shawn's step-dad, Joe Miller, soon after Shawn was born. Two years older than Jeff, Shawn was a wild card. He wasn't a bad person, but he lived with reckless abandon, throwing out-of-control house parties and often being dropped off by the cops for disturbing the peace. After an especially exhausting night, Mr. Miller let it slip that Shawn was not biologically his. Thus began the search for his father.

By the time Shawn showed up in our lives Jeff and I were an inseparable duo. Sometime in the first grade our parents took advantage of our fast friendship by creating Thursday night play dates that turned into Thursday night dinners as we grew older. My first Thursday night dinner with Shawn as the newest member of the family was not as awkward as I expected. He seemed to fit into the dynamic easily.

But as Jeff started to spend more time with Shawn, so began the drifting of my relationship with him. Nothing dramatic or sad about it really, just time for our lives to diverge. We'd spent our entire childhoods together and having accepted admissions at colleges on opposite sides of the country, our friendship was bound to fork regardless of Shawn's emergence.

Outside of an occasional random text, months, sometimes years, apart, we hadn't really been friends for almost nine years.

"So I'm supposed to believe you left my raging party to rescue your brother? That after all these years, you're still a good guy?" I chided, as he looked over Urth Cafe's menu.

"No, you're right, I'm a complete asshole," Jeff said, deadpan. "Can we eat now?" A dry sense of humor accompanied his endearing nerdiness, which I found comforting.

"You were late and I felt weird sitting here without

ordering so I got the curry sandwich and a green tea latte, but I told them to hold off prepping it until you got here."

"Doesn't that defeat the purpose of ordering before me?" he asked as I waved the waiter over.

"What can I get you?" our waiter, a Brad Pitt look-a-like, asked.

"I'll have the chicken sandwich and a large coffee," Jeff replied.

"And two chocolate chip cookies," I added.

"Good choice," the waiter remarked, before taking our menus and walking away.

"You haven't seen me in nearly a decade. What if I've developed an allergy to peanuts? You could kill me," he said.

"Did you?"

"What?"

"Develop an allergy to peanuts."

Jeff didn't say anything; he just looked at me with challenging eyes that told me I missed the point.

"If you don't like it, I'll eat yours," I said, knowing that chocolate chip cookies were his favorite.

Sitting back and folding his hands across his stomach, he made himself comfortable in the stiff chair. "About my tardiness: you're new to LA, so maybe you don't know this, but there's a 15 minute rule. Unless it's a first date."

"First of all, I've been here over four years. And second, I did know the rule, I just don't abide by it. You know why? Because it makes no sense. Friends deserve as much consideration as some random girl you're trying to impress. Period."

Our waiter came by with our sandwiches and drinks.

Popping off the lid, Jeff added creamer and honey to his coffee.

"You put honey in your coffee?" I asked.

"Sounds strange right? It's really good. You should try it."

"You just randomly decided one day that adding honey to your coffee would be a good idea?"

"No, Veronica got me into it and it just stuck I guess."

"Oh, how is she these days?" I asked.

"I don't know," he said and I knew I wouldn't get any more information. "What about you?"

"Single. Have been for a while."

I was trying to come up with something cleaver to say when a pretty blond hopped off her cruiser bike and began locking it up. Jeff glanced at her and started laughing.

"What?" I asked.

"Do you remember that time we thought we could be like Evil Knievel and we built that big bike ramp?"

I laughed. "Yes."

"I still have the scar on my left arm," Jeff said, pointing to a small bump just below his left elbow.

"Well, I cleared it and you still owe me a snow cone," I smiled.

"How about I cover lunch?" he said. "But actually, I kind of have to eat and run."

"Oh," I said, trying to hide my disappointment.

"I'm leaving the country tomorrow."

"Going on the lam?" I asked.

"I'm taking a much needed vacation from my life."

There was something sad about the way he said it, but I looked over at him and said, "That sounds amazing. I'd love to do that."

"Yup. Jordan, India, China, Brazil, and Peru."

"Can I stow away in your suitcase?" I joked.

He was quiet for a moment. "Actually..." he started but didn't finish his sentence.

"Yeah right," I replied to what I thought he was about to suggest.

"Why not?"

"Uh, because I'm an adult and I have responsibilities."

"I'm sorry. I think I must've mistaken you for someone else. The Aubrey I used to know was all for an adventure and wouldn't miss an opportunity to escape for anything."

"You show up after all these years and I'm supposed to just throw caution to the wind and go globe trotting with you?"

"Sure! I don't even know why we stopped talking in the first place," he said.

"Because you weren't at my parents' funeral and I stopped talking to you," I said. I did my best not to sound accusatory but I couldn't help it. A large part of me feared the conversation might lead to an irreparable argument, but I had to get it off my chest.

He bit his lip nervously and said, "I wanted to be there." Then for a long moment he was silent. "Vee's best friend was getting married that same week in Hawaii and for a hundred stupid reasons our relationship was already teetering on the edge. But I wanted to make it work and choosing not to go to the wedding would've meant letting her go. It's not a good excuse, especially given that we're no longer together," he sighed.

"You were my best friend growing up. I *needed* you to be

there." The words came out as more of a necessity than an actual desire for a response. It was a phrase I'd turned over in my head hundreds of times over the years and hearing them only reaffirmed what I already knew. Nothing he could say now would change the resentment I'd harbored all these years.

"I'm sorry," he finally said.

A long silence lingered between us as we ruminated on our feelings. Me, angry with Jeff for abandoning his duties as a lifelong friend, and him...well, I didn't know what he thought, but I hoped he was plagued with guilt. I had aunts and uncles who were supportive, but they lived far away and I hardly ever saw them. Of course Jeff's parents were there, but their apology for Jeff's absence was formal and disconnected, and being around them made the loss of my parents exponentially worse.

"I'm so sorry Aubs. I really am. I know I fucked that one up. But I'm here now. Let me make it up to you."

"You're leaving tomorrow."

"Come with me."

"So you're asking me to come along just as a travel companion?"

"Yeah, we'd be two old friends on a mission to see the world. How great would that be?"

Given my current condition, I wasn't sure that it was a good idea, let alone a great one, so I smiled but said nothing.

That night, I pulled a coffee table book of famous pictures from around the world off my bookshelf. The book covered the Seven Wonders of the Modern World and a few other majestic places. I flipped it open to read a few passages before bed, but found myself engrossed. I stayed up all night shredding its pages into a giant galaxy of photos I glued to the main wall of my studio. I knew tearing out the pages of a perfectly good book was sacrilege, but it was oddly therapeutic.

Starting with China, I created a road using the Great Wall. Along the road came the Taj Mahal, which floated above water I added using images of the Dead Sea. Next came The Treasury, the Temple of Buddha, the Colosseum, then as the wall wound southward I added Chichen Itza, and at the end was Christ the Redeemer. Although it wasn't the entire world, it did feel like a flattened, scaled-down version of it.

Six weeks was a long time to be traveling with someone, and as I lay in bed the next morning I made a list of the pros and cons of traveling with Jeff. The awkwardness of our last conversation aside, he had an annoying habit of making his bed right before going to sleep—not in the morning like a normal person, but literally right before crawling into it and snoring all night. Also, he took showers both in the morning and at night. On the flip side, he was considerate, knew all of my quirks, and to be honest, his cons weren't exactly deal breakers, considering none one of those neuroses negatively affected me. I could sleep through earthquakes. The number one pro on the list was not having to deal with RP alone in my apartment for the next six weeks.

Flipping open my phone I sent Jeff a text: *I'm in.*

His response: Great! I'll e-mail you my itinerary. Meet at my place at 4?

Me: Done.

CHAPTER THREE

Spontaneity

"Art is spontaneous. Brush stokes are not meant to be calculated, but to have free flow." I read that quote in a *Quarterly Arts Magazine* weeks before I even knew I'd be traveling to China and it lingered throughout my visit. What struck me about Cai Guo-Qiang, the man behind the quote, was the subtext of his words. Cai created a literal explosion of art titled *Odyssey*. Using 42 panels, he created a massive, site-specific installation in a warehouse with a large stencil and gunpowder. Once ignited, the gunpowder exploded and left behind a powerful imprint—a dark gray Chinese landscape complete with a waterfall, mountain ranges, a coastline, and a detailed garden full of plants and flowers. By putting down the paintbrush and letting go of his learned discipline he pushed the boundaries of his own work using an unstable element, which created a unique and unexpected image.

The piece represented life's explosive quality: its ability to burst and change.

Anxious and excited about exploring a culture I morally respected and artistically admired, I could hardly believe that in a few hours I'd be on a plane headed for China.

Following the directions on my GPS, I wondered if I had entered the wrong address. All around me were multi-million dollar homes: P-Diddy-style mansions with large pillars, sprawling lawns, and driveways so enormous they had designated "Enter" and "Exit" street markings. *This can't be right*, I thought as I parked my car on the street and walked the 200 yards up the driveway to ring the doorbell. I had an entire speech planned out in my head ("I'm sorry to bother you but my friend Jeff gave me this address..."), but when the door opened, Jeff stood before me.

"Uh, hi," I said.

"Hey," he replied, not at all aware of my confusion. "Come on in. I'm almost ready. Can I get you anything? Water? Soda? Juice?"

"You can give me an explanation," I said, as I followed him through the foyer.

"For what?" he replied casually.

We walked down a couple of steps and into an ultra-modern room with black and steel Barcelona chairs that looked like they belonged in an office building rather than a living room. A huge bar stood to our left, complete with bar taps, top shelf liquor, hanging wine glasses, and LED lighting.

"Wow, all you need are some girls in tight dresses, the guys from Jersey Shore, and a DJ," I said.

"One of the guys from Jersey Shore is a DJ, I think."

"Even better."

"There's a dining room over there and the kitchen, but I'll show you my favorite part," he said. On the far side of the living room stood floor-to-ceiling windows with a shallow pond dug out at the bottom so it was partially inside the house and continued outside. Lightly pushing on one of the glass-paneled doors, it spun open 90 degrees to let us pass through and then made the complete 180-degree turn to close again.

"So when we come back in the door will make a complete 360 degree turn?"

He nodded. "Yup. Both sides of the door are symmetrical so there are actually two locks. One on either side. Double protection." It took me a second to understand that the design was basically a revolving entrance without the typical carousal in the center. Palm trees lined the most brightly lit and colorful walkway I'd ever seen, which led to a huge backyard. Along the right side was a two-foot-wide moat filled with a rainbow array of coral and fish. The best part was that the aquarium followed along the walkway to the pool and then surrounded it, creating the illusion that one was swimming among the fish and coral.

"It's definitely not what I was expecting for a school teacher," I said, looking at him suspiciously.

"Well, let me show you where the magic happens, then you'll really be impressed."

We walked back inside and down a flight of stairs that opened up into a basement living area.

"I didn't think houses in L.A. had basements," I remarked.

"They don't usually, it was an add-on." The basement was minimally furnished with what looked like leftover pieces of mismatched, cheaply made college furniture. On the walls hung 80's movie posters: *Back to the Future*, *Weird Science*, and *The Breakfast Club*. A long, rectangular, foldout table served as a workstation with a large computer tower, some random computer parts, an old PC monitor, a stack of external hard drives on top, and a plastic folding chair pushed in underneath. "What do you think?" he asked.

"So you're renting the basement of someone's house?"

"It's Shawn's place."

"What?" I asked, unbelieving.

"Like I said, he's pretty good at what he does."

"He makes this much money selling weed?"

"Yes—and no. He's a doctor, like a real one, with a M.D. after his name and everything."

"Shawn," I repeated his name. "One-handed bra-popping Shawn who got kicked out of the dorms for building a greenhouse on the roof and selling weed on campus?"

"That's the one."

"Wow. So...why are you living in the basement?" It seemed odd to me that in a house this large he couldn't have a room upstairs. The basement was big, with a living room in the center and three smaller rooms off to the side. Two empty or used for light storage and Jeff's bedroom, which had a master bath and walk-in closet.

"I've only been here for six months," he replied, as if that answered my question. My guess was that the move was temporary.

I looked at the lonely desk in the corner. Wires snaking

everywhere, computer parts broken open with the insides spread across his workstation. "Are you a hoarder?"

"App developer."

"I thought you were a teacher."

"They're all free apps. Just a side hobby for fun," he said. "They're all knock-off apps."

"What do you mean?"

"I take a concept that already exists, like Angry Birds for example, I copy the code, change the graphics a bit, so instead of pigs I'll use women's high heels or something, and voila, I've got 'Burn 'em heels.' Or take a game like Bubble Burst, change the Bubbles to a cartoon image of my ex-fiance's head and poof we've got--"

"Are all of your games misogynistic?" I interrupted.

"Actually, I have a really cool Facebook app called "Top This" that generates fake status updates like, 'I just landed my dream job!' or 'Check out my new puppy!'" with a picture of a super-cute dog, or 'I'm having lunch with Obama! So excited.' Stupid shit," he smiled, clearly proud of his invention. "It's my most popular app. Twenty thousand downloads and counting. In fact, I'm pretty sure Veronica even used it after we broke up to make me jealous."

"And did it work?"

He looked down sheepishly, "Maybe."

"Awesome," I said, handing him my phone. "Download it for the trip. We'll make her jealous."

Jeff laughed and started downloading. "Just out of curiosity, do you still do that awful grinding thing in your sleep?" he asked.

I made a face. "It's not like you can hear it over your

snoring. Besides, I have a super awesome $600 night guard and references from four ex-boyfriends."

"I'll be sure to call all of them," he said.

After he finished packing his toiletries, we headed to the airport, crossed through security, waited for two hours in the terminal, and at 6:20 p.m. we finally boarded the plane.

I spent the first few hours of the flight reading travel books I had downloaded onto my Kindle. I learned about the Forbidden City, studied a map of Beijing—a place full of roads laid out in loops, not unlike Houston—and stared in awe at satellite photos of the Great Wall. Sometime after reading about William Edgar Geil, the first foreigner who explored the whole length of the Wall in 1908, I fell asleep.

Awaking to a chime and the sprightly captain's voice over the intercom, I turned to Jeff who was just waking up as well and I was horrified to see that I had drooled on his arm.

"Morning sunshine," I said, glancing at the puddle. But then I couldn't contain myself and suddenly burst into apologetic laughter. "I'm so sorry!"

He looked down at it and grimaced.

Still laughing, I handed him and a napkin. "It must be the airplane or something. You know, being so high up and the gravity…" He surprised me by using the napkin to wipe the drool off my face before cleaning his shirt.

"You might want to stick in that night guard thingy when you take naps too. I kept trying to move my hand away 'cause I thought you were going to grind my fingers off in that machine you call a mouth."

"Now how is it possible for me to be grinding and drooling at the same time?" I protested. I laughed it off, but I was thoroughly embarrassed.

If walking through the terminal of Beijing Capitol International Airport was any indication of China's size, I was in for a rude awakening. I lived in a big city, but standing in the airport's enormous glass tunnel, my own physical being never felt more insignificant. A high ceiling made of metal buttresses combined with a long central nave gave the airport an aura of cathedral importance in a modern day setting. Sleek, barely there, tandem sling seats were neatly arranged around equally modern reception desks. Brightly lit duty-free shops boasted upscale brands like Chanel, Louis Vuitton, and Yves Saint Laurent for wealthy travelers. Flight numbers, times, and gates flickered across large LCD screens floating on crystal center islands. I watched the information switch between familiar roman characters and intricate Chinese symbols that looked more like art than words. Some of the destinations were familiar but others were totally foreign and suddenly the world became exponentially larger. *Where was Xingtai, Jixi, or Nanyang? What were they like?* I wondered.

Once we picked up our bags, we were funneled into customs—a huge room divided into two categories: citizens and non-citizens. Airport security was abundant and I saw signs everywhere prohibiting the use of cell phones. Even though I obviously wasn't smuggling anything illegal into the country, I was apprehensive about talking to the stern-looking customs officer, and became even more nervous when I discovered Jeff and I had to speak to them separately.

"Are you here for business or vacation?" my customs

officer asked.

"Vacation," I replied.

"How long are you staying?"

"Four days."

"Where are you staying?"

I had no idea, so I gave him my best "I'm innocent" half-smile and light shrug and said, "I'm not sure, my friend Jeff booked the hotel." I gestured to Jeff, who stood about ten feet away talking to another officer.

He yelled something to Jeff's officer, who curtly said something back. The other officer did not nod or give any form of approval, so he very well could have been saying either "Yes, this man booked a hotel" or "Detain them both!" My fears were assuaged only when my officer stamped my passport and said, "Okay," gesturing for me to pass through.

Finally outside, a wave of heat poured over us as we hailed a cab and Jeff gave the driver directions to our hotel. We sat in the back with our small daypacks between us expecting an easy ride into the city, but we ended up on the edge of our seats the entire time. New York City had nothing on Beijing: cars were bumper to bumper with only inches of space between vehicles.

Once on the crowded highway, another cab lightly rear-ended us. Our driver got out, yelled at him for 30 seconds, hopped back in the cab, shook his head in irritation, and continued driving. No swapping of insurance or pulling over to assess damage—the verbal lashing was the end of it. The lack of consequence made me so certain we were going to be hit a few more times before reaching the hotel that I kept my eyes on the road, unable to fully focus on the bustling city we were passing.

The Beijing Inn Hotel (either a bad translation or tourist trap) was the Chinese equivalent of a Best Western. By the time we finally arrived, it was 7:00 p.m. local time and my body was wide-awake.

"We made it!" I said, plopping down on the bed. "So, whatcha wanna do?"

After we each showered, we changed, grabbed our packs and headed out.

The second we stepped foot outside our hotel lobby, we were thrust into a mosh pit. Pedestrians, bikers, motorcycles, and cars moving in every direction dodged each other like they were in a game of *Frogger* on speed. Utilizing every inch of space, the city was like San Francisco without the hills. Buildings were erected only inches apart from one another (if not actually touching), streets were exactly wide enough for two small Toyota Corollas to pass each other, and it wasn't uncommon to look up and only see a fraction of the sky for entire blocks because of signage hung vertically from upper level awnings or poles and advertisements strung on wires stretching from one building to another. The air trapped between buildings was thick from lack of circulation, making it difficult to breathe. The oppressive heat made my clothes stick to my skin and I was glad I decided to change out of my jeans and into shorts.

"Let's go this way," Jeff said, taking initiative.

"After you," I replied. As I followed him, we passed by a squatting, middle-aged woman rotating skewers of meat over a barbecue that barely emitted any smoke at all. The round grill was maybe 14 inches in diameter, and next to the cooking meat she flipped pieces of sesame flatbread using a pair of bamboo tongs. She used swift and mechanical movements, and I noticed that the flick of her wrist was similar to mine when trying to create texture in my paintings.

"Do I need to hold your hand?" Jeff asked, looking at me. "I almost lost you." Without realizing it, I had stopped.

"Sorry," I said, breaking my gaze and continuing to walk with him.

"What were you looking at?" Jeff asked as we reached the sidewalk surrounding Beihai Park.

"Nothing," I said. The significance of watching the flick of someone's wrist was personal. Pocketing the image in my memory, I continued on.

In the center of the park stood a large white pagoda surrounded by lush green clusters of trees, and encircling the island was a lake. I came across a large golden plaque with a photo of Beihai Lake. The plaque described the white pagoda as a reliquary containing Buddhist scriptures, monk's mantles, alms bowls, and bones of monks. I learned that Pagodas were a common part of Chinese architecture, but this was the first time I'd ever seen one and it made me wonder how many other things I would never see after going blind.

I closed my eyes and tried to recall the image I had just seen.

"Am I boring you?" Jeff interrupted.

"No," I laughed. "I'm really glad I decided to come. Thank you."

"You're a pretty good travel companion so far," he smiled.

"Were you supposed to come here with Veronica?"

"No," he said, surprised. "I booked this trip after we broke up."

"Why did you break up?"

"I asked her to marry me, and she decided we weren't right for each other. Then a couple weeks later she was dating someone else."

I turned to look at him, wanting to comfort him with a hug like I used to do when we were kids, but we weren't that familiar anymore.

"What?" he asked, catching my stare.

"Nothing. I was just thinking you haven't changed much since we were kids."

"You either. In fact, I was thinking I'm probably still faster than you and I bet I can beat you to the next Pagoda," he said.

"Oh yeah?"

"Yeah."

"One, two—go!" I shouted already running toward the building.

"Cheater!" he yelled sprinting after me.

I smiled to myself as I reached the Pagoda. Victory.

CHAPTER FOUR

Grit

If I had to describe the Great Wall in one word it would be 'grit.' Stone by stone, the Great Wall was built on a determination so fierce that well over two thousand years later, after the advent of the light bulb, the car, and a walk on the moon, it is still considered one of the Seven Wonders of the Modern World. At the base of the Great Wall, I looked up and thought about how naive I had been to think the three hundred-plus steps to the fourth, and highest, tower along the Badaling section of the Great Wall would be easy.

Most people came see the Wall, walk a few hundred yards of it, and then turn around. Not me. I wanted to walk until I couldn't walk any longer. If I thought it possible, I would've tried to walk from one end to the other, but apparently it was the equivalent of walking from New York to Los Angeles. *Don't attempt it, because you will die* was the impression I got while doing my initial research. After climbing about 20 steps, it was definitive.

I was unprepared to climb the jagged and uneven steps. If my first step was four inches, my next was fourteen. Forget about mechanical movements. I had to watch every step I took, and at some sections, the wall became so steep I had to crawl. It was impossible to navigate with any sort of grace. We stopped when we reached a plateau near the peak of the mountain and perhaps it was delirium, but I think I saw God for the first time. He was sitting in the sky, legs crossed and looking down on me with pity. The image lasted only a second and then it was gone.

"How is it possible that I'm this winded? I run two miles a day," Jeff said, as we collapsed on the ground, each draining an entire bottle of water.

"The locals seem to be struggling too, it's not just us," I said, panting. I watched as several Chinese people passed us before I realized the ones who were struggling were older, and by older, I mean senior citizens. One lady was so tiny, I was certain she didn't clear four feet, but she briskly passed us, moving slow and steady. If I weren't so tired I might have been embarrassed.

"Wow," we said in unison, watching the lady ascend.

As I continued up with my attention fully focused on clearing one step at a time, I barely noticed the view beyond the wall. But once at the top, I turned to look over the edge and found a landscape that opened up like a lush pop-up book of green sprawling mountains. Treetops of an endless variety, from deciduous pines to smaller shrubbery, all blended together in shades of green as endless as the ocean and disappeared into the horizon in much the same way.

After a while I said, "Jeff, I know this is going to sound weird, but could you leave me alone for a few minutes?"

"No worries, you were cramping my style anyway. I'll do a little roaming," Jeff said, walking back down the steps.

I pulled out my iPod nano and turned it to my painting playlist. The list was full of soft, melancholy melodies that helped me focus. At random, Tan Dun's "For the World" from the *Hero* soundtrack began to play. Talk about serendipity. The long, drawn-out violin notes were as epic as the view in front of me, but embodied an undertone similar to my internal feelings of fear and sadness. Fierce, yet humble, the notes came at me strong but never sought to overwhelm me.

As the drums were introduced, signaling the beginning of battle, I walked up a few more flights of stairs to a second plateau. Slowly gliding my hand along the wall I caressed the rough and, bumpy stone with my fingertips. Each stone was individually placed by the hands of men, and though their time had come and gone, a legacy remained in this wall that emanated warmth absorbed from the sun. I stopped to look out at the landscape. Then, stretching my fingertips as far as they could reach on either side of me, I leaned forward so my entire torso lay on top of the Wall. Relaxing my neck, I closed my eyes. There was a rolling breeze that I could hear before I felt, and it comforted me the same way the ocean did, by being constant. The sounds of waves crashing and winds blowing were rhythmic, repeated beats, like breathing.

The song finished, and I was no closer to finding an answer—or even the right question for that matter—but for the first time since I learned I was going blind, I felt calm. I had read that in Thailand, monks walked barefoot for 25 days in meditation over scalding hot roads and rocky surfaces in an effort to purify the land. They were so focused on their task that they ignored their own physical pain and limitations. On a much smaller scale, I noticed that my personal focus on the goal of reaching of top was how I overcame the challenge of climbing hundreds of steps, and for a split second I felt a glimmer of hope that I would be able to work through the challenge of losing my eyesight.

I lifted myself from the Wall, opened my eyes, and came face to face with Jeff. Leaning easily against the wall with his backpack slung lazily over one shoulder and his Nikon camera strap looped around his neck, he stood watching me.

He cleared his throat. "Are you one with the wall now?" Jeff asked.

I smiled. "Did you get any good photos?"

"I want to show you something," he said. We walked up and into one of the towers, and Jeff poked his head out of a window and pointed off in the distance. "What do you see?"

"Umm, the Great Wall?"

"Remember our green and black snakes?" he said.

I looked at him and smiled. "Yes," I said. At the rodeo one year Jeff and I got two toy snakes made out of plastic pieces clipped together so that the body of the snake wiggled about. Returning my gaze to the Great Wall I saw that it snaked through the mountainside with a similar mechanical roughness. On the car ride home that day Jeff kept trying to get his to bite mine and ended up breaking my snake in half. When I cried about it, he gave me his. I had it in my backpack for a week before taking it out to play at the park and forgetting it in the sand.

"Are you seriously still mad I left it at the park?" I asked.

"You always were careless with my feelings," he said, flippantly.

"What's that supposed to mean?"

"I'm kidding," he smiled. "C'mon, let's go."

Turning away from the window I rammed my shoulder into the cement, "Ow!" I yelped.

"Are you okay?"

"Yeah," I mumbled, rubbing my shoulder.

"How did you miss the giant stone wall?" he laughed.

I looked back at the huge wall in front of me and thought, *How did I miss that giant wall?*

"Hey, everything alright?" Jeff asked.

"Yeah, I'm fine. But I am getting kind of hungry. Do you remember seeing any places around here?"

"I know the perfect place," he said with a mischievous smile.

Two hours later we stood in a Beijing night market. All kinds of animals hung from canopies, on display for eager patrons: fried soft shell crab (not bad), frog legs ready to be fried on kabob sticks (gross), snake, also on a kabob stick (really gross), and live tarantula, again to be deep-fried (absolutely disgusting).

"That is not exactly what I had in mind," I said.

"Oh come on, it'll be fun. You have to eat whatever I pick and I have to eat whatever you pick."

"Okay," I said. "Whoever pukes first buys drinks."

"Deal. And to be a gentlemen I'll even go first," Jeff says, untying the bandana from his neck and wrapping it around his eyes.

"What are you doing?" I asked.

"Just because I have to eat it doesn't mean I need to see it."

"You are a sick human being, Jeff." This adventurous side of him was new to me, and I found myself amused.

Handing me his Nikon, he said, "Make sure you get all of this…for my app."

"No one wants to see you puking up spiders," I laughed.

"They're gonna love it. Take the photos."

I led him through the market as the local vendors laughed and pointed at us. Red and white striped awnings lined the street, lit by dangling, bare light bulbs attached to the tent tops. Raw poultry hung from hooks while fried and candied insects stuck out like lollipops at Disneyland. I looked up and down the rows trying to find the perfect snack.

My eyes lit up when I saw them: fried scorpions on skewers. I gestured to the vendor, grabbing a skewer and handing him a bill.

"Open up, here it comes," I said, sticking the scorpions into Jeff's mouth as I snapped a picture. He chewed like a champion as I cringed.

"Not bad. Crunchy."

"Do you want to know what it is?"

"Let's see, too big to be grasshopper or roach. Crab?" he guessed.

"You wish. Scorpion," I laughed.

"Let's go two for two. I'm feeling good about this."

"Done," I said. Drinks seemed a small price to pay to not

have to endure this awful eating extravaganza.

I took his arm and walked a little further along until I spotted my next victim: boiled worm.

Jeff held his mouth open patiently as I dangled the worm above his lips. I had to retake the photos several times because I was laughing so hard the images came out blurry. He looked like a bird waiting for dinner. I dropped the worm into his open mouth, and his facial expression said it all.

"Uck, I wasn't expecting an explosion of poop to ooze out of it," he said, still trying to choke it down. "And the outside is chewy in the worst possible way. This has to be the snake we saw earlier."

"Nope."

"Worm?"

"Yeah. Juicy, boiled worm," I taunted.

"Do we have water or something? God, the aftertaste is…I can't even describe it, it's so bad. Awful to the tenth degree," he said, pulling the bandana off his face and reaching for his bottle of water. "Your turn."

"Do I really have to wear this thing?" I asked. "Can't I just close my eyes?"

"Yeah right. You'll take one peak and the jig will be up," he said, reaching over my head to secure the fabric. As soon as it was on, I froze; blinking my eyes open, I still couldn't see anything.

"You ready?" Jeff asked.

"K," I said, afraid my voice might crack if I dared utter a longer syllable.

He took my hand to guide me and I begged it not to shake. As we moved along the street a rush of sounds came at me: voices, the clamoring of metal, the repetition of a singular bang of a hammer and toss of something—shells maybe—into a pile, firecracker pops, bells, horns, engines, and too many others to identify. My nostrils filled with the scents of: rosemary, mint, lemon, and a very light odor reminiscent of the inside of a shoe, which I assumed was the raw meat.

We stopped and I waited for Jeff to order and pay for whatever I was about to ingest. I heard him say, "Thank you," as he let go of my hand. "Ow, it's hot," he said, blowing into what sounded like a container. "Hang on a sec," he said. I heard a light tapping and crack, more blowing, and then the feel of something slimy at my lips. "Open up wide," he said. I opened my mouth halfway and heard the shutter of his camera open and close several times before I felt the spoon slide into my mouth. The consistency was similar to chicken. Still, I cautiously chewed, tasting the salt, lemon, and pepper seasonings. Honestly, it wasn't all that bad, until I bit into something hard and heard a crack.

"Ohh!" Jeff said.

"What was that?" I asked, mouth still half full and ready to spit.

"Swallow," Jeff warned.

Reluctantly, I ground the meat up a little more before swallowing hard. "Done," I said. "Now what was it?"

"Duck fetus," he laughed.

I gagged. Gross. "That bone—"

"The beak."

I was instantly sorry I'd asked.

He led me a little further and then, without notice, I felt

something slimy and bumpy part my lips, which instinctively snapped shut. I reluctantly opened them again. The texture was thick, rubbery, and…wait a minute… was I imagining things or was it still moving?

"Uck, nope. I can't do it," I said, spitting out what was left and pulling off the blindfold. Jeff laughed hysterically and took photos as I turned to see what it was I'd had in my mouth: live octopus.

"I think I'm gonna be sick," I grumbled.

"That was fantastic, but nowhere near as disgusting as the worm, which by the way was the most foul thing I've ever tasted. I win."

"Remind me to get you a trophy when we get home," I said. "Drinks?"

"Drinks."

There wasn't much in the way of hard liquor near us so I bought us each two Tsingtao beer bottles, which were popped open and served warm. When I asked for ice I received a curt "No," in response. Warm beer wasn't at the top of my list of favorite things, but the taste of octopus still lingered in my mouth and I was desperate to dispel it.

We took a seat at one of the many brightly colored foldout tables surrounded by mismatched plastic stools.

"Cheers," I said.

"Cheers," he replied, clanking my bottle. He took a long swig and I waited for the verdict. "It's surprisingly smooth."

I, too, was startled at how light and smooth it tasted. There was no bitter aftertaste I'd come to expect from beer. "I'm surprised you like it," I said. "Weren't you always a Guinness guy?"

He laughed. "I don't know if stealing a couple of Guinnesses from my dad constitutes being a 'Guinness guy'. But you're right, I do like darker beers."

"Honestly, I can't even remember the last time I had a beer. I drink cosmos," I said, hanging my head in shame.

Jeff laughed. "Well if it's any consolation. I'm pretty ashamed to admit that I get the reference."

"Jeff Anderson, you watch Sex and the City?" I gasped.

"Watch-ed, past-tense, and not by choice."

"Aha! Amazing. What other dirty little secrets are you hiding?" I asked and waited. As Jeff thought for a second, I blurted, "Why are you really on this trip?"

"Why does anybody travel? To see the world," he said matter-of-factly.

"Alone?"

"Why not?"

"In my experience, people who up and travel the world are usually running from something."

"Only women think that," he said.

I smiled. "You mean, only women are willing to admit that."

Jeff took a long swig of his beer and said, "I'm not running, I'm re-evaluating."

"Was it that bad? Your break-up?"

"I mean, it wasn't fun."

"No, I guess not," I smiled.

"What about you?" he asked. "What are you running from?"

"Who says I'm running from anything?"

"Correct me if I'm wrong, but you bought a ticket to

China with less than 24 hours notice, which by your own calculations makes you the Usain Bolt."

Jeff always was good with the logic games, but I wasn't ready to talk about RP, so I said, "Same reasons."

As we walked though the rest of the market, watching others nervously order something new and mysterious and then take a bite of it, Jeff became uncharacteristically quiet.

"Whatcha thinking?" I asked.

"Huh?" he said, looking down at me. He shrugged a little. "Nothing. Should we head back to the hotel?"

I could have pressed it, but I instead I said, "Sure."

Back at the hotel, we got ready for bed in relative silence. In the bathroom I brushed my teeth and changed into my oversized T-shirt and gym shorts. I caught a glimpse of myself in the mirror and instantly wished I'd brought cuter pajamas. As I opened the door, Jeff was getting into bed, bare-chested, wearing a pair of boxers. He looked at my ensemble and said, "Nice jammies."

"Wait, aren't you going to remake the bed?" I asked.

"I don't do that anymore," he replied.

"Oh. Why?"

"Veronica hated it."

"Gotcha," I said, wondering what else I didn't know about this new Jeff.

"Night Aubs, don't forget about your night guard," he said turning out the light.

"Night."

After a quick continental breakfast at the hotel, we walked

for miles and miles all around the city, going from neighborhoods with narrow alleyways to wide streets full of shops. Beijing was so dense and vast that in the two days we spent wandering we only covered a small part of the city.

The sun had already begun to set as we walked home, but the streets were busy as ever. Vendors selling food, glow-in-the-dark toys, T-shirts, magnets, and other theme-park-type souvenirs lined the street before a set of huge, cast iron gates that led into a giant garden. Once inside, there were only a few carts selling candles and giant paper lanterns; the rest of the area was full of people taking photos of the colorful lotus flowers permeating the scenery. The lotus was everywhere: in the hands of kids as a glowing lotus wand; as a giant, ceramic art piece in the center of the garden; carved into the wooden railings of the 30-foot bridge crossing from one side of the small lake to the other; and even clipped onto women's ponytails and buns. A British lady next to us explained that this was the end of a week-long festival celebrating the return of the lotus. She told us the Chinese had a high regard for the lotus because it grew from mud to become a pure, beautiful flower, and poets often used the lotus as an analogy to inspire people to push through difficulties. They believed the bendable nature of the stalk represented love, because although you can bend it, it is very difficult to break. "In eastern religions as a whole, it represents purity, divine wisdom, and the individual's progress from the lowest to the highest state of consciousness," she said.

Was this the universe talking to me?

The woman was a writer for BBC, there to cover a story. I

wanted to talk to her more but she got a call on her cellphone and had to leave. I will be forever grateful for the last piece of advice she tossed our way as she left: "Make sure you stay until the end, even if you've got a flight at 3:00 a.m. It is absolutely worth it." Then she was gone.

We shuffled through the crowd, taking photos of the different lotus flowers. All the various colors—red, pink, white, and pale yellow—were on display and in mixed stages of bloom. Then, in the dark of night, a single, shining lantern floated upward followed by three more, then ten more, and before we knew it the entire sky was filled with them. For a moment, everyone was silent as they gazed at the lanterns. It was the most beautiful thing I'd ever seen.

As the lanterns rose higher and higher into the sky, they shrank in size. Joining the ranks of the stars above them, the floating lights fused with the night sky as man's addition to the universe—at least for the moment.

"Have you ever seen anything like this?" I asked.

When Jeff didn't answer I looked around for him. Surrounded by strangers all speaking a language I didn't understand, I started to panic.

"Jeff?" I called. "Jeff?" I began to walk around when he tapped me on the shoulder. "What? I'm right here," he said. In his hand was a flattened paper lantern. "Here, hold this," he said as he pulled the paper lantern from its flat two dimensions into its full three-dimensional form. The two of us held it up as he lit the fuel cell at the bottom and we waited as it filled with hot air. As it slowly rose to the height of the others, we watched until we could no longer tell which one was ours.

"Can I borrow your camera," I asked?

"Sure," he said, handing it to me.

Lifting it to my eye I pointed the camera at the lanterns and took a photo. When the image reappeared on screen the picture was far away and distorted. The photo looked nothing like what I saw.

"You have to turn off the flash and use the manual focus. Try to get the closest lamp in focus," Jeff said, adjusting his camera and handing it back to me.

I set the frame, retook the photo, and saw that the image was clearer, but still only an abstract image of what I was actually seeing.

"Thanks," I said.

I started clicking back through the photos, smiling at how well they turned out, but Jeff stopped me. "I think it's time to put down the camera and just enjoy the moment."

Turning my head, I saw that he was looking at me intently. Our eyes locked and he took a step toward me—I could tell he wanted to kiss me, but I wasn't ready for that and all it entailed.

"I can't," I said, stepping away from him. "I'm sorry, but I came on this trip to kind of sort out some personal things and I don't want to make things complicated."

"Yeah. No, of course. Me too," Jeff said.

Quickly lifting the camera to my eye I took a photo of him, and then said, "I really want a photo on the bridge. Will you take one for me?"

I saw his face fall, but he said "Sure" and followed me to the bridge. I could hardly breathe as I walked, trying to imagine what he must have been thinking. I wanted to kiss him but I had so many questions. If Jeff knew I was going blind, would he still want to go there? When I reached the bridge and turned to face him, he already had the camera up to his face, "Ready? One, two, three." Snap.

The next morning, still quite early, I quietly grabbed my brushes, mixing plate, dry color pigments, a bottle of distilled water, and a pre-primed canvas, before slipping outside to the balcony of our hotel room to paint. Using a metal fold-out frame, I stretched the canvas and clipped it tightly into place. I grabbed a sheet of paper from inside and began to fold it into the shape of a crane. Creasing the paper with the lines I would need to later bend it into the shape I wanted was a ritual I'd practiced since my dad taught me origami as a kid. My fingers moved automatically and when I was done, I set the crane down on the table next to me. Time to work. Pouring a tablespoon of magenta pigment onto the mixing plate, I mechanically stirred the mixture while I focused on the blank canvas.

I painted a lone lotus bud floating in the Mekong River with glowing lanterns littering the night sky behind it. Next, I set the river in the middle of Downtown Beijing. Ancient Chinese art used the same techniques as calligraphy, so I used long, thin brush stokes, but still painted the modern society as a city sprawling along the famous river. At first it didn't sit well with me, and I thought I might have to scrap it, but the painting transformed the longer I sat with it. Turmoil had created ripples in the strokes. It was an emotional juxtaposition of my life, captured in a flower. Neglected and forgotten by modern society, the scene begged the question of whether or not the bud could come to term and bloom in unfamiliar conditions. At the bottom of the painting, strategically placed just outside of a downtown skyscraper, was my signature—a red fire hydrant.

CHAPTER FIVE

App World

I was a graduate student at Columbia when I wrote a paper on the third dimension of paintings. My argument was that the layers of a painting, although microbial in volume, had depth. A face on a canvas did not exist, for example, without several layers of paint. Starting with the primal base, nude shades were layered in, darkened by shadows, and topped off with specks of red beneath a final sheen that made up the color of human flesh. To push my idea further still, I also argued that a painting without a viewer ceased to exist. By considering the viewer as part of the equation, I argued that denying the three-dimensionality of a painting would be to deny that we ourselves lacked a third dimension. I got a "C +" on the paper.

My teacher thought I was mocking the assignment, which to be honest begged to be mocked. She wanted us to come up with a unique theory on art and map out an argument; if she was swayed by my argument, I got an "A", if not I got a "C." I think she gave me the "+" because although she thought I was full of shit, she also thought it was funny. The only problem was that I wasn't trying to be funny.

Of course I knew my paper wasn't going to change history. The complexity of dimensions was far beyond my scope as an artist, but I truly believed two-dimensional paintings had three-dimensional value. I firmly believed emotion, though not measurable in the spectrum of art, mattered.

When I proposed this same argument to my good friend Charles, who after getting his PhD from Colombia was offered a job doing research at the UCLA School of Physics and Astronomy, he said, "Unless you add a physical object to your artwork, your argument doesn't hold water. It doesn't matter how many layers of paint you add to your canvas—at the end of the day, when that paint dries, it becomes one unified mixture of paint."

"But we conceptualize and create our work in three dimensions. You draw the outline, lay the foundation, and layer in dimensions with tone, texture, and color," I argued.

"Yeah?"

"So, paintings are three-dimensional!" I exclaimed. "The definition of being three-dimensional is that an object has volume, right? If you look at the painting as layer upon layer of paint and texture, then just because it's paper-thin doesn't mean it lacks the third dimension."

"Yes it does," he answered. "When, and only when, you can pluck a mug out of the painting and drink from it, will I consider your theory."

He went on to describe the Standard Model of physics and how I should read some article he published about exotic models that combined hypothetical particles and something about extra dimensions. To be honest, most of what he said flew right over my head, but the one thing he made very clear was that I fully deserved my C+. If anything, it seemed like he thought my teacher was being generous.

Still, I was obsessed with the idea of layering, certain that without it, a painting was little more than a photograph. And although I appreciated the art of photography, I hated it as a medium. Photos, the really good ones, were the culmination of skill and luck; knowing how to take a really great photograph and being able to find the right subject. In my opinion there were too many variables, whereas with a painting every inch of the canvas was controlled. And control was something I was much more comfortable with.

Jeff and I were en route to Delhi from Beijing. Only one country in and we were already past the point of needing to sustain idle conversation. I glanced over at his laptop as he punched in lines of code—ellipses, dollar signs, quotation marks, and semi-colons interspersed with words that meant nothing to me—without distraction. I admired his work ethic. Picking up his camera, I looked through his photos from the past couple days.

They were incredible. I had never known Jeff to be a photographer, but his shots had great depth of field and followed the Rule of Thirds. The one he took of me splayed out across the Great Wall captured my vulnerability in a way that made my cheeks grow flush. Had I not been the subject of this photo I would've told him how beautiful I thought it was, but complimenting him on a photo of myself seemed narcissistic.

When we emerged from the airport, all at once my ears were filled with noise. Bollywood music, exhaust pipes, honking from every direction, bicycle bells, hawkers selling their wares, cussing, yelling, the screech of bad brakes, and the squeals of children chasing each other around street vendor stalls. I could smell chai spices mixed with incense, exhaust, and urine. There was so much activity going on around me that I didn't know where to look.

My friend Rati, who I knew from college, met us at the airport in Delhi, where a driver was waiting to take us back to her home. She had an oval-shaped face with thin lips, big eyes, and dark wavy hair, and at 5'3" she was petite. Wearing skinny jeans, sandals, and a short-sleeved cotton blouse in a deep shade of purple, she looked like she hadn't aged a bit. Rati was born and raised in India but spoke amazing English because she was educated at an English-medium school. The first time I met her at school I thought she was British because of her posh accent, but she quickly corrected me.

"This is Jeff," I said to Rati after giving her a hug.

"Howdy," Jeff said, extending his hand.

"A cowboy…nice," she remarked as they shook hands. Then she turned to me with a raised, questioning eyebrow and gestured toward Jeff.

I shook my head at her as we hopped in the car.

As we drove off, I noticed that the chaos in the street was similar to China, but Delhi was different still. The poverty was evident. So rampant in fact that people lived stacked on top of each other and every nook and crevice seemed to be occupied. Crumbling cinder blocks and gaping holes in the walls of buildings would have left these structures abandoned in the United States, and yet here they seemed very much lived in. Walls and columns stained and damaged by rainwater covered almost every building, and clothing was hung out to dry on every porch and balcony. Storefronts were littered with tattered and torn advertisements for everything from old movies and concert events to Red & White brand cigarettes and Cadbury milk chocolate. Kids with palm-sized tears in their shirts and bare feet begged for money at the car window whenever we stopped in traffic.

"Poverty is a business," Rati said, warning me not to give them any money.

"One in desperate need of support, don't you think?" I asked.

Handing me a large bag full of small bags crackers, she said, "You never know where the money will end up but they could probably use some food." I took the bag from her and quickly distributed the small bags into the tiny hands peaking through the crack in my window. "Tell me, how was your trip? Where have you been? I can't believe you're in India! What made you decide to come?"

"I'm actually piggybacking on a trip Jeff planned to go on alone. We're traveling on a one-way ticket around the world," I replied. "We started in China, came here, then we're off to Jordan, Italy, Peru, and Brazil."

After my parents' death, Rati became like a sister to me, checking in on me every day, bringing me food and movies to numb the pain, and occasionally forcing me out into the sunlight.

I was in my first year at Columbia having coffee with Rati on the Upper East Side of Manhattan and discussing how my boyfriend had ambushed me into letting him move in when I got the call from my parents' attorney and family friend, Eli Bader, telling me about their accident. Without hesitation, Rati flew with me to Houston and got me though the funeral before finally heading back to school at my insistence. She had missed an entire week of classes and had to reschedule a ton of interviews but never once complained about it. I wondered how she would handle my diagnosis.

I shifted my gaze out the window and watched as a cow pulled a barrel filled with wheat. Something in the way this cow's legs moved, slow and with heavy, thudding steps, made the whole scene feel unnatural—like the owner meant to use a horse but blindly saddled a cow, and the cow knew it.

I pointed out the window. "I thought cows were sacred?"

"Just because they're sacred doesn't mean they can't be used for practical purposes," she said, almost as an aside. "Have you traveled much before?" Rati said, turning to Jeff.

"I've been to a few places," Jeff replied. " Amsterdam and Paris, and Athens and Mexico when I was a kid with my parents."

"I take it Paris and Amsterdam were with an ex?" she asked.

"Rati has a slew of theories regarding love and relationships," I injected before Jeff could answer.

"Just so we're clear, the PhD at the end of my name kind of makes me an expert on these matters," Rati smiled, mocking herself.

"She's a blogger," I explained. "Actually, you two kind of have that in common. Jeff's a programmer."

"What was your dissertation on?" Jeff asked.

"The new balancing act modern Indian women have adopted in a need to protect the self while still being able to forge deep and meaningful relationships with others," she replied. "Over the last six years I've interviewed over 2,000 women in India, from mothers to CEOs."

"My favorite parts of her research are the discussions on sex. How women evolved past the fairy tales of love and moved towards the male perspective of sex being an act of pure lust," I said.

"They actually talk to you about their sex lives?" Jeff asked.

"Yes," Rati said. "But you have to consider that over the course of years, I've built quite a rapport with these women and I am as open with them as they are with me."

Rati was a few years older than I. We met in a coffee shop when I was still an undergrad at NYU and I'd accidentally taken her drink thinking it was mine. She laughed it off and asked me if I wanted to share a table. Rati divulged that she had crush on the barista, who, coincidentally, I'd dreamt about as well—and the floodgates were open. Our hour-long conversation covered everything from worst kisses to optimal sexual positions. Never before had I laughed so much with someone I'd just met.

"I'm pretty sure the sex talk was how we became friends," I said. "You told me you'd had dreams about you and the barista…on the counter…after hours…"

"That I did," Rati reminisced. "But didn't he ask you out at a party once?"

"Yeah, but I was dating Calvin remember? We had a whole discussion about fantasy hook-ups and whether it was wrong or not to cheat if it was purely physical."

"Right," she said. I looked at Jeff whose eyes were wide with interest, but he didn't say anything.

"One of my many regrets from college, considering what a dick Calvin turned out to be."

As the gate to her home opened and we pulled into the driveway, I felt like we were stepping into an oasis. The semi-circular cobblestone driveway was surrounded by deciduous trees with small white flowers in bloom. There was an array of botanical flowers, organized into groupings by type, which decorated the trunks of the trees below. When our driver pulled directly into the carport I realized he wasn't just a driver, he was Rati's *personal* driver. After finishing her PhD at NYU, she moved back to Delhi and was living with her parents, so technically it was their home, but regardless, it was beautiful. Just inside the front door, the house opened up into a large living room with floor-to-ceiling glass windows that looked out onto a garden. There was a set of staircases flanking the entrance that led to our three adjacent rooms upstairs. Starting in the far right was a large study with two office desks and an impressive library; Rati's, mine, and Jeff's rooms were all in a row. There was a bathroom next to a set of double doors leading to the master bedroom. Downstairs, the kitchen, servants' quarters, and dining room were on one side, the living room was in the middle, and on the other side was an indoor jacuzzi and gym.

There couldn't have been a starker contrast to the world outside. Modern in structure, the house was accented in antiquity. A wooden bookshelf with hand-carved latticework on the sides and an equally ornate front was only one of many intricate pieces of furniture. On the back wall was a huge Rauschenberg piece and opposite that were three numbered Warhol prints. In addition to those extraordinary pieces, they also had a painting by Tagore, a famous 19th century poet who developed the Bengal School of Art and subsequent style. They had a cook, two maids, and a round-the-clock driver.

For all these amenities, certain conveniences were noticeably missing; dishes were still done by hand, even though the kitchen was as modern as the rest of the house, and I was mortified to find that my clothes would be washed by a servant and then hung to dry.

"Wait, you mean my underwear is going to be washed by a stranger and then hung outside for everyone to see?" I asked.

Rati waved me off, saying, "Whatever, you'll get used to it. Besides, sun-dried clothing actually smells better."

"How come no dryer?" I asked.

"They're not common here. Electricity is not reliable, and neither is water for that matter," she said.

The bathrooms were small, with the shower, toilet, and sink all pressed together in a confined space so that when the shower was on, everything became wet. Minimalist, some might call it, but luxurious in a country where most people still used a bucket and pail. Feeling sticky from the flight, I washed quickly before we reconvened in the dining area for a home-cooked Indian lunch. The aroma of curry and spice filled my nostrils, and I found myself salivating. There was nothing more appealing to me than an authentic home-cooked meal, and the unfamiliar spices added a whole new hue to the color wheel of my tasting palette.

"I hope you're hungry," Rati said, as we sat on three sides of a rectangular, clear glass dining table, which rested on what looked like a hand-carved wooden base. "Dhairya always cooks too much when we have guests." Taking a piece of naan, she dipped it into the orange curry. Following her lead, we ate with our hands—no utensils were required. It brought meaning to the phrase "licking the plate clean" because when we were done, the dishes looked like they could be wiped down and put back in the cupboard.

"So what else is new with you? Last time we talked was what? Three months ago? And I think you were prepping for a show," Rati said, walking us through the foyer and into the living room, where a pot of hot tea sat waiting for us. She poured us each a cup as we eased onto the couches.

"Yup. The show was last week. It went well as far as I can tell. I sold eleven pieces," I smiled.

"That's great! I have that Brooklyn Bridge piece you gave me in my room," she said. "It's right above my bed and I never tire of looking at it."

"I didn't know you did landscapes," Jeff said.

"She hates them," Rati answered. "They were the pieces she'd pawn off to tourists just to make a few bucks, but I always thought they were beautiful."

"Thanks," I smiled.

"Are you dating anyone?" Rati asked, moving the conversation swiftly into the topic I was sure she'd been waiting for all night.

"Where are your parents?" I asked, not wanting to risk them overhearing a possibly unsavory conversation.

"They're out of town on business."

Slouching into a more comfortable position, I shrugged. "I have more important things to worry about than finding a boyfriend."

"Like what?" Rati asked.

"Like my career. Love requires consideration of another person and at the moment I can only really concentrate on me," I replied in earnest.

"And you, Jeff?" Rati inquired.

"Oh no," he said. "I don't need to be a part of girl chat. In fact, I think I'll leave you two to catch up."

Jeff said goodnight and headed upstairs.

"What does he do?" Rati asked.

"He teaches and develops apps." I told her about his automatic status update app, as well as the ex-girlfriend head bursting and shoe burning game apps.

Scooting closer to me, Rati crossed her legs comfortably and said, "Go on, I want to hear everything and I mean *everything*." She rolled her eyes upward with the tilt of her head to indicate I wasn't to leave Jeff out.

"There's nothing happening there," I smiled.

"Right."

"Do you remember my friend Jeff from high school?"

"Your first kiss Jeff? The one whose brother you accidentally kissed at a New Year's Eve party?"

"That's the one," I said.

"Does he know?"

"About the kiss or the crush?"

"Both."

"I doubt he knew about the crush. As for the kiss, all these years I thought he did, but now I'm not so sure. We almost had a moment in China."

"You almost had a moment? Could you be anymore vague? Details, Aubs."

"You sound like Dr. Drew," I laughed. Rati and I used to stay up late to listen to *Loveline*. "He leaned in to kiss me and I dodged it."

"Why?"

"Well, for starters he just broke up with his fiancé like six months ago so he's basically on the rebound."

"So what?" she said.

"So I'm pretty sure that's a recipe for disaster."

"I'm pretty sure that's never stopped you before," Rati argued.

"Yeah, and look where that's gotten me," I countered.

"Speaking of Dr. Drew, I had a *Loveline* moment the other day," Rati smiled. "This woman in her early forties e-mailed to ask if the burning sensation she felt when she peed was a UTI and if the UTI itself meant her husband was cheating on her." I laughed.

"I can almost hear Dr. Drew's annoyed response to go see a doctor," I said.

"That's basically what I told her, with a disclaimer that I wasn't a medical doctor. If you had told me a year ago that I'd be the Dr. Drew of India I would've laughed at you, but here I am."

Her blog, Sex with Rati, was huge in India, raking in

about 300,000 views a day with over 3 million subscribers via newsletters and Twitter followers, making her an actual quasi-celebrity.

"But seriously, whatever your reservations, I think you're doing yourself a disservice by not exploring the possibility," she said, going back to the topic of Jeff.

Sitting across from Rati made me nostalgic for all the times we had stayed up late together drinking chocolate milk and smoking cigarettes on the balcony of our 3rd North dorm at NYU. India might have been unfamiliar, but Rati was more than familiar—she was family, and sitting cross-legged in front of her made me want to divulge everything.

"I'm not in a place right now for that type of complication," I said.

"What do you mean?"

"I'm going b-lind," I replied, stumbling over the word, and realizing as the words came out that it was the first time I'd said it aloud.

"What?" Rati said, a little too loudly.

"Shh. Jeff doesn't know," I whispered.

"What? How? When?" Rati whispered with desperation.

"It's called Retinitis Pigmentosa," I swallowed. "And it's pretty much as bad as it sounds." My voice began to tremble. "There's no cure. The doctor said I have about eight weeks."

"Are you sure? There must be something you can do," Rati said with sincere concern.

Before I could control it, my eyes started to tear up and she uncrossed her legs and leaned in to envelop me in a hug as I sobbed uncontrollably into her shoulder. I cried and cried for what seemed like a long time, and when I was finally able to catch my breath I looked over at her and smiled, before saying, "So that's my news. What's new with you?" We both laughed nervously.

"Do you have support? Do you need me to come stay with you?" she asked.

"I'm not really ready for that step, or any step for that matter, but when I am you'll be the first person I call," I said. I smiled again, a nervous response to a feeling I hadn't felt in a long time—loss. A stubborn tear slid down my cheek and I quickly wiped it away with a tissue Rati handed me.

"This is probably not what you want to hear, but...I still think you should tap that up there," Rati smiled. I shook my head at her and laughed.

Later that evening, Rati left to meet with a few women who were the subject of her next article, and Jeff and I sat on the balcony catching up on all of our social networks. With my feet propped up on a coffee table, I used my iPad to send a long e-mail to all of my close friends about the trip so far, and I attached a photo of me standing in front of the Great Wall. Then I updated my Facebook status with that same photo and 26 others from the trip that I had idly taken along the way.

Among my favorites were a couple of panoramas and several candid photos that Jeff had e-mailed of me lurking around China as a tourist. I stopped again at the one of me leaning over the Great Wall with my arms spread across the top. Looking at the image as though it were of someone else, I found that I was moved by how peaceful yet exposed she was. He had captured all of my feelings in that moment—

the fear and the calm—without knowing any of it. The image was remarkable and I knew photos like this didn't surface often, so I cropped it, threw on a hipster filter, and posted it to all of my social media outlets.

"Dude, check it out—that photo you took of me yesterday has 628 likes on my Instagram. Isn't that awesome?" I said. Jeff was sitting at a nearby table furiously typing on his PC laptop.

"Seriously? Do you even have 628 followers?" he asked.

"I have over 30,000."

"And yet you claim to not be a social media enthusiast," he smirked.

"How many followers do you have?" I asked.

"Across all social media? Just over 50,000," he replied.

"Wow! How does someone who never posts to Facebook have so many followers?" I asked.

"How does someone who claims to be technically inept have 30,000?" he countered.

"Touché," I laughed. "What are you working on?"

"Nothing, I'm just catching up on geek news."

"Geek news? Like who the next Batman is going to be?" I quipped. Standing up, I walked over to where he was sitting and leaned over his screen. The headline read: *CEO of Juice joins forces with Yahoo!*

"Yahoo! is merging with a juice company?" I asked.

"No. Juice is a tech venture fund based out of Silicon Valley. The company basically looks for new ideas and then finds money in its rolodex of angel investors to launch an app," he said.

"I'm sorry, I fell asleep after the word tech," I joked.

"Does this mean you're looking for financiers or something?"

"I don't know. Maybe. It's crazy though, these guys are our age and they're all multi-millionaires."

"When you're successful that young, I think it has more to do with creating something you love than hoping to make a million dollars," I said.

Jeff shrugged noncommittally, looking at his screen again.

"Well, what's the app you're working on now?" I asked.

"Nothing new—just maintaining the *Top This* app. It's gone up by 250 users since we left, by the way."

"I hope you don't take this the wrong way, but I think the difference between your 20,000 app downloads and Instagram's 100 million is the continual use on a daily basis for entertainment."

"How is mine not continual? It literally uploads something awesome for you every day," he argued.

"It's a very cool idea and I can see how it would attract a lot of downloads, but if I were using your app and people kept asking me how my fake trip was, I'd eventually have to tell the truth. In the long run it'd be depressing."

"I disagree. It's a conversation starter," he said.

"Right, it's a cool idea. And I think it'll keep growing, but if you want something on par with Twitter then you should consider what everyone is looking for," I replied.

He looked at me blankly. "What is everyone looking for?"

"*Happiness.* Something that makes them happy and you money."

"You think it's pathetic that I live with my brother, don't you?" he asked.

"That's not what I meant. But now that you mention it,

don't you want to live in your own?"

To my surprise, he laughed. "Jeez Aubs, don't hold back."

"I'm sorry," I said.

"Don't be," he replied, turning back to his coding.

One of my favorite things about Jeff was he never got defensive or malicious like some of the guys I had dated. One guy actually slashed through a painting I was working on with an X-Acto knife to illustrate how deep my words had cut him. It was so dramatic I started laughing, which was not the brightest idea considering he was still holding the knife. Luckily, destruction of property was about as far as his temper went—at least with me—and he stormed out of my apartment never to be seen again.

I started sketching images of objects or designs I had found at the Taj Mahal. Ideas for what I thought my next painting might be. Looking up from my sketch I saw that Jeff was typing obsessively, his face lit up by the screen. He wasn't smiling, but he looked to be enjoying the work. "What's so interesting about coding?" I asked.

"What's so interesting about being a painter?"

"It's a conversation starter," I smiled, mocking him. But then I started to think about the question. Jeff folded his arms and waited. "It's a form of expression unlike anything else. It's personal and, if done right, universal at the same time. I like to watch people connect to something I created."

"Well, coding, if it's done right, as you say, can connect millions of people to one application. So if you think about it in terms of connection, social media is kind of an art form," Jeff said.

I hadn't thought of it that way, but I couldn't deny that it had become the new way people expressed themselves—though I couldn't imagine connecting to mundane status updates and cat pictures the way I would to the Mona Lisa.

"When I look at your screen almost none of what I see makes sense to me. So how do you conceptualize your ideas without being able to see the big picture?" I asked.

"I guess it would be like breaking apart all your different brush strokes. You have an image in your head and when you start painting on an empty canvas, your seemingly random brushstrokes don't make sense to me either. Alone and separated, the brushstrokes are like incoherent puzzle pieces, but after you place and layer them we see the picture."

I laughed.

"What?" Jeff asked, confused.

"When I was selling paintings on the street, I had this guy walk past me and shout, 'Get a real job, hobo!'"

"No…"

"Yes. A New Yorker of course. I could tell by the way he walked: elbows out, face forward, and fast." Jeff laughed. "It made me so mad," I continued, "because he acted like painting was this whimsical thing I chose to do. That it didn't require any technical skill or practice. Anyway, I was thinking your comparison of coding to brushstrokes would've been a nice comeback."

Jeff laughed harder, "No, it wouldn't have. He was probably an investment banker who knows even less about computer software than he does about painting. But I like that you're still so upset about it all these years later."

"I know it sounds crazy, especially because New Yorkers are notorious for being outspoken and uncensored, but that comment really did bother me," I said, feeling my blood curdle.

"Well, not many people can say they've followed through on their dreams. So you've one-upped that guy in my book."

Actually, I'm going blind, so technically he wins, I thought. But there was a somber tone in Jeff's voice that trumped my personal concerns for the moment. I wondered if he was talking about himself. "Do you think that you've settled by becoming a teacher?" I asked.

"I'm not dead yet," he smiled.

When we were young Jeff used to make fun of how seriously I took my art. How I would think for hours on a blank canvas and how I refused to let anyone be in the room while I worked. As teenagers, I think that was his way of trying to connect with something he had a hard time understanding, but I heard him scold one of his buddies once for calling me weird. *Aubs is gonna be famous one day and you're all gonna eat your words,* he'd said. Even when he didn't know I was in the room, Jeff was always my biggest cheerleader. The memory made me smile.

"Why are you smiling?" Jeff asked, leaning forward past his computer to see if I was looking at something he couldn't see.

"No reason," I said.

CHAPTER SIX

Love

I read in a guidebook that the Taj Mahal was something I had to see in person. Photographs not just wouldn't, but *couldn't*, do it justice. The internet begged to differ though. I discovered a website that had detailed panoramic views and 3-D virtual tours. As the viewer, I could walk through the Mausoleum and double-click anywhere in the room to zoom in on details. So I found it hard to believe that seeing the actual structure could be *that* much better than the virtual tour.

As our cab pulled up to the entrance gate, I was on the edge of my seat. A large crowd had already formed and the throngs of people suggested that perhaps the book was right.

"Are you excited?" I asked, looking over at Jeff, who was also hunched forward.

"If you're asking if I'm excited about the architectural design, which utilizes the interlocking arabesque concept in which each element stands on its own and perfectly integrates with the main structure, then yes, I'm excited to see it." Call me crazy but I think I even saw his eyes sparkle for just a fraction of a second.

Rati, who was sitting in the front seat next to the driver, laughed. "Most people come for the love story."

"Yeah..." Jeff said, as though whatever was to follow would be in disagreement. He left it at that.

Few people talk about the entrance to the Taj Mahal, probably because once you see the monument, everything else pales in comparison. But for me, the execution and mastery of it could not be overlooked. It was the *amuse bouche* before the main course. Made of sandstone and marble, the building was a symmetrical structure consisting of four double-stacked arches flanking a main arch, which recessed deep into the structure where six additional arches broke up the interior. Designed perhaps to guide one's eyes through the central tunnel, the dark reddish-brown color of sandstone complemented the neutral off-white marble accents and acted as a tent shielding us from the bright sunlight so that we could focus on what lay ahead.

Crossing through the threshold of the main gate, I could see the grand complex in the distance. It looked just as I thought it would from photographs. Sparkling in the sunlight, its unique, floating illusion was stunning, but I had expected that. I was looking for something deeper to connect to, something more than superficial beauty.

We walked along a pathway on the right, flanked by a large pool of water on one side and lush green gardens on the other. I noticed a few cracks on the side of the pool and rust on the fixtures inside it. The flaws, I felt, gave the grounds an aura of authenticity. For a structure that was built in 1632, I expected quite a few more imperfections and was looking forward to discovery. Flaws humanized the art.

"What do you think?" Rati asked us.

"This is a goldmine for my app," Jeff replied. Feverishly snapping photos, he looked like a crazed paparazzo trying to get that one unexpected million-dollar shot.

"People will do crazy things for love. Can you imagine spending 21 years building a mausoleum? To work on something that is a constant reminder of a lost love? It sounds unbearable," I ruminated.

"It's a symbol of idealized love, not real love," Jeff said.

"That's a pretty cynical view. Why do you question the sincerity of his gesture?" Rati asked.

"He probably believed her to be this saint who loved him, but in reality she just didn't live long enough to break him."

"Project much?" I asked.

"All I'm saying is she died young so their relationship probably didn't have to endure any of the nitty gritty, therefore it is unrealistic to look at this as any kind of testament to true love. Look around you: it's a fairytale, it's not real," he said, surprising me. In all the years I'd known Jeff, he'd never even come close to opening up as much as he just did.

"No, you're right. You should just give up and continue making mean apps for bitter exes," Rati argued. "Check back in with me in a couple of years, I'd like to see how that works out for you."

"Forty-two thousand downloads and counting. I'm clearly not the only person who thinks love sucks," Jeff replied, as if the volume of downloads mitigated its malicious inception.

"You're full of shit. You're just mad because you got dumped," I said. "Had it worked out with you and Veronica you'd be singing a different tune right now."

Just then Rati's phone rang. "Sorry I have to take this, I'll be right back," Rati said, walking away.

"It would have ended sooner or later," Jeff said. "And I'm glad it did because otherwise I wouldn't be here with you. Smile!" I posed for a photo with a big bright smile and Jeff snapped a picture of me. "I was thinking of going over to take some photos of the reflection pool, wanna come?"

"Nah, I'm gonna take a stroll and do my thing," I said.

With both of them gone, I pulled my iPod out of my hobo bag, I popped in my earbuds and scrolled to an Indian song I had recently found called "Shiva Panchakshara Stotram" by Uma Mohan. The harp at the beginning was what really drew me in initially; it felt soothing and the lyrics resembled that of a southern gospel song infused with the sounds of India. I gave myself a moment to clear any lingering thoughts. Then, feeling serene despite the fact that I was surrounded by hundreds of spectators, I walked up the steps to the mausoleum. As I drew closer, the first thing I noticed was how small I felt next to the massive building, and the second thing was the Arabic calligraphy outlining the door frame.

"Ey! Ey!" a man yelled. I pulled out my earphones,

annoyed by the disruption. "No shoes," he said pointing towards my feet. "No, shoes."

"Oh, sorry." I said, feeling like an idiot. I looked around and sure enough, no one had shoes on. A few people were hopping around on the hot marble, waiting for these funny bag-like covers to be handed to them. I waited until the gentleman handing out the covers reached me before taking off my shoes because, although the Taj Mahal was beautiful, I was not about to sacrifice the bottom layer of my feet to it.

The exterior was covered in floral designs etched into the marble as a mosaic. No wonder it took twenty-one years to build. The detail was extraordinary and overwhelming, with lattice windows that had been sculpted in floral and geometric shapes. Every inch of the Taj Mahal had something to offer.

Blocked from view of the guards by hordes of onlookers, I reached out to touch the walls. Slight bumps underneath my fingertips confirmed what I saw. Things like leaves, stems, and petals, weren't carved out from the marble itself but were inlaid individually. The single flower that my pinky grazed over must have taken hours to complete. I took notice of the drooping flowers above the arches of the multiple entrances—purposefully designed that way as a sign of eternal mourning for the beloved Empress.

Scanning the room for other things I'd read about, I was certain I'd find a flaw or two in the structure—cracks, barely-visible holes, a wrongly-proportioned design, mismatched pillars...anything. There were none. Shah Jahan didn't mess around. Based on the astute labor and abnormal level of perfection, my guess was he threatened to behead anyone who left sloppy work on his wife's final resting place.

What did Mumtaz Mahal have that the rest of us were lacking? It had to be more than beauty that kept the Mughal Emperor Shah Jahan so enraptured. I was enormously curious, but hundreds of years had passed and the story of their love had been told, retold, and distorted a hundred times over, so I suspected the answer was lost forever.

One version of their love story recounted an intense, polyamorous relationship. Shah Jahan had two other wives with whom he bore one child each, but it was said that he chose to be with Mumtaz exclusively. I thought about what Jeff said regarding how we idealize love and that it isn't real because eventually it dissipates. The Taj Mahal was supposed to represent everlasting love, but all I could think about was how it eventually all comes to an end one way or another. My parents were gone and the thing I loved most in the world, my art, was also going away. And maybe my art would connect with people like the Taj Mahal, or maybe it wasn't meant to last forever.

Standing over Mumtaz Mahal's burial chamber, I felt conflicted about what her mausoleum represented. A surge of loneliness rushed through me. It was the same empty feeling I had the morning after my parents' funeral—I was alone in our house and everything felt cold. Standing in a monument dedicated to symbolizing love's ability to stand the test of time, I couldn't help but question whether or not it was all just make-believe.

"You know it's a fake, right?" Jeff said, cutting into my thoughts. He walked towards me from across the room with Rati following. "Yeah, I just overheard a tour guide back there say she isn't buried here."

"What do you mean?" I asked.

"This is just a decoy, the real one is hidden deep beneath the surface, never to be disturbed," Rati answered.

"Huh," I mused, taking it in and detaching myself from my previous thoughts.

"Have you noticed how much color is in here?" Rati added. "Everyone always talks about the white, but my favorite parts are the colorful details."

"What's even more impressive is the angle of the four pillars outside. They tilt outward slightly. It's an illusion to make them appear straight. Isn't that odd that we have to trick our eyes into seeing correctly?" Jeff remarked.

"I can't tell if that's a sarcastic comment or an astute observation from someone who admires the architecture," I said.

"The latter," Jeff said. "Contrary to popular belief, I have a great appreciation for solid craftsmanship."

"There's the sarcasm," I replied as he winked at me.

By the time we were ready to leave, the sun had nearly set and the outside looked like a completely different building than the one we had entered earlier. Light reflecting off the marble gave the building a golden glow. Leave it to the royals to build a monument representative of purity and still have it emanate gold. I looked back one last time before following Jeff and Rati out the same entryway we came in.

"What's next?" Jeff asked.

Rati laughed. "How about an outdoor market? They have some things that are definitely unique to India."

"I'm all about different," I said.

"Yeah, I'm cool with that," Jeff said.

The drive back from Agra to Deli took a few hours and I napped most of the way until the driver dropped us off at an outdoor market. We stopped at a color stall full of both organic and inorganic pigments. A painter's paradise. I walked into the sectioned-off tent feeling like a kid jumping into the ball pit at a McDonald's playground. I was drowning in color and loving every minute of it. I filled bag after bag with colors I would be hard-pressed to find in the United States: Quinacridone Magenta, Transparent Pyrrole Orange, Dairylide Yellow, and Dioxazine Purple, to name a few.

"I'm in heaven," I said.

"We can tell," Rati replied as she and Jeff stood at the edge of the tent.

"Isn't this the same stuff you have in your apartment?" Jeff asked, squinting to read a label off one of the pans. "Is Anthra-qui-none blue really *that* different from cobalt blue?"

"Anthraquinone," I corrected. "And yes, it is." I feigned insult before turning my back on them with a smile and going back to scooping mounds of color into twist-tie bags.

Color pigments were worth more to me than gold. Running my fingers along the edges of the shallow wooden containers where bits of pigment had fallen, I felt the different colors between my fingertips. The organic pigments were rich and smooth, a nice departure from what I was used to.

Excited at the prospect of working with new colors, I tried hard to keep thoughts of going blind at bay. Forcing myself to stay in the moment and focus on what I'd create when we got back to Rati's house, I did my best to keep up with Rati and Jeff, but I was already hardly paying attention to where we were going when I spotted a couple of kids jumping on what used to be a mini trampoline. I stopped to watch.

The springy surface material had been ripped and shredded, leaving only the metal ring and a few dangling pieces of green fabric. A group of seven or eight children were playing some sort of game that looked like a combination of Hop Scotch and Jacks with dice. Whoever's turn it was would throw the pair of dice and then jump into the center while balancing on one foot. The number on the dice would dictate the number of times the kid had to spin around inside the trampoline before picking up as many pebbles as he could in one hand and then hopping out. If they lost balance and fell they were out. It wasn't a complicated game but they seemed to be into it.

Careful to keep Rati in the corner of my eye, I continued after her and Jeff haphazardly as I watched the kids play.

When I was nine years old, my dad installed a trampoline in the backyard and I used to jump up and down on it for hours on end. I loved the euphoric feeling it gave me. To be up in the air, detached from the earth, was the greatest feeling. I became so good at flipping around on it that numerous family friends suggested my parents sign me up for gymnastics. But the two activities couldn't have been more different. I didn't like the rigidity of form and posture in gymnastics and those stupid poses they made me strike so as to "stick" the landing. All I wanted was to be free, which didn't require any kind of training, focus, or ridiculously tight leotard. To master the trampoline, I needed the exact opposite of calculated flips: I had to learn to let go of my inhibitions and trust that I when I flipped, I would land somewhere on the large, springy surface.

The very first time I made the flip was truly an exercise in conquering fear. I stood at the edge of the mat with adrenaline pumping through my body as my heart beat a mile a minute. My dad looked up at me from the edge of the trampoline and said, "All you need to do is lean in at the crest, and the laws of motion will take care of the rest. I promise you."

"Stop, dad," I said, concentrating. He laughed and waited patiently for me to jump.

I knew I had to trick myself into believing it was easy at the exact time I needed to hurl my body forward. So for 15 minutes I bounced up and down, waiting for the right moment, and then in a split-second decision mid-air, I did it. I landed on shaking knees but I had completed the flip unharmed. The fear of becoming a paraplegic was gone and then I did it again, landing a little more gracefully; then again, and again, until an hour had gone by and the fear was a distant memory. That kid who was always saying, "It's easy, just go like this," before effortlessly doing what everyone else was afraid of—that was me. Fearless.

That momentary decision, made in a microsecond, to trust myself—and the makers of my trampoline—was so powerful that I tapped into it a second time, and after some false attempts, I learned to do the flip with my eyes closed.

When I was nine, the darkness was freeing. I'd close my eyes, and the world held endless possibilities. Now, nearly two decades later, darkness had become my greatest fear.

When I pulled out of my daze I was walking on autopilot

behind Jeff and Rati, who seemed deep in their own conversation.

I thought about picking up my pace and rejoining the conversation, but I chose instead to keep to myself and focus on the city all around me. Delhi was captivating and I stopped often to photograph the details. On the sidewalk in front of a newly renovated store, I found leftover drippings and splatter of blue-green paint. Most people probably saw it as messy or a mistake, but it made me think of Jackson Pollack. The guy somehow figured out how to convey movement and action on a canvas that looked like five and six-year-olds were given dripping paintbrushes and told to run around. *That is what I should aspire to*, I thought. Changing the way people see art. As we continued walking, I moved at a leisurely pace. I looked for other images to inspire me and stopped to take a photo of the only fire hydrant I remember passing in Delhi. It was yellow.

When I looked up, I saw Rati turn a corner and I ran to catch up. "Hey! Wait up!" I shouted, but as the girl turned to face me I realized she wasn't Rati. "Oh, I'm sorry. I thought you were someone else," I said. Panicked, I spun around, heading back in the direction I had come.

SCREEEEEEEECH! HOOOOONK! A car barreled toward me out of nowhere to make a right turn. Instinctively, I jumped back, tripping over the curb behind me.

"Hey!" Jeff yelled after the driver, who was long gone. "Are you okay?" he asked, helping me up off the ground. The smell of burnt rubber lingered in the air.

"Yeah. I'm okay. I just didn't see the car coming," I said, catching a look of concern from Rati.

"This is my fault. We shouldn't have been walking so far ahead of you," Rati said. "This kind of thing happens all the time in India."

"No, no. Trust me, it was my fault," I said, trying my best to sound nonchalant.

Physically, I was completely fine. What jolted me was a realization: How many times had a driver turned in front of me only to apologize halfway through the intersection for not seeing me? This was the first time I realized there was a danger to going blind.

"You scared me half to death," Jeff said, giving me a squeeze and smile. *I scared* myself *half to death*, I thought.

"It's not a big deal," I said, trying to hide the fact that my legs were shaking.

The distance from the market to Rati's house was just over a mile, so we were right around the corner when I had nearly been run over. When we entered the house, the aroma of spices filled my nostrils. My stomach grumbled.

Dhairya made us basmati rice, kebabs, kofta, and paneer cooked in spinach. He also toasted naan for us to eat with the dishes. We ate in silence mostly, the events of the day finally settling in.

Afterward, we moved upstairs to the balcony where Rati and Jeff roasted marshmallows over a propane stove, and I thumbed through a set of postcards I'd picked up at the Taj Mahal gift shop. I wanted to find an angle I could reference as I painted. My inspiration for the painting was the abundance of color in Delhi. I started with a sketch of the Taj Mahal and added hundreds of locals, all to be covered in my newly acquired pigments. We had missed the famous festival of color, Holi, which happened a few months before, but standing among the throngs of pigments at the color stall made me wonder what it would be like to watch a celebration of color splashed across the white landscape of the Taj Mahal.

"So you've known Aubrey since kindergarten," Rati said. "That's a long time."

"You've known Aubs since college, right? So that's what, four or five years?" Jeff asked.

"Holy crap. Has it really been five years? Wow, yeah I guess it has," Rati ruminated. "But I knew we were going to be friends the second I met her. I mean, look at her. Most people backpack around the world in hiking shoes, cargo pants, and tank tops. She looks like she belongs in a French cafe with a cigarette in one hand and an espresso in the other."

I laughed. The implication was that all artists dressed like bohemians, and though I wasn't by any means shopping on Rodeo drive, I liked to think that I made good fashion choices with the little money I had.

"Aubs is definitely one-of-a-kind," Jeff smiled.

"Speaking of which, I hear you were her first kiss," Rati asked.

"What?" Jeff asked, confused.

I could tell where this was headed and did my best to catch Rati's eye and get her to stop, but she kept her face glued to Jeff's.

"Weren't you?" Rati asked.

"You count Spin the Bottle as your first kiss?" Jeff said,

looking at me.

"I mean, it kind of was, wasn't it?" I replied.

"No. Yeah, I mean it was the first time I'd kissed anyone, but it's not like we were girlfriend and boyfriend or anything."

"Well whatever, it was awkward anyway, right?" I said.

"You thought it was awkward?" Jeff asked.

"You don't even count it as your first kiss," I argued. "It obviously wasn't that good."

Jeff didn't say anything, which I took to mean that he agreed.

I set down the stack of postcards before adding a few more details to my sketch.

"Do you still do that thing where you collect postcards? Like used ones, with messages written on them to other people?" Rati asked.

"You still did that in college?" Jeff asked me.

I shrugged, "Old habits die hard."

"You mean she did it in high school?" Rati interjected.

"I was there when it *started*. We were 14, I think? On our walk home from school we passed by a yard sale where she bought her first one. From then on, it was every estate sale in the Houston area," Jeff boasted.

"Postcards are meant to read by others. Why else would they not have envelopes?" I said. "I like reading the messages and making up stories about the people who send them. Kind of like my dad used to do with his photos."

"It's a little weird, Aubs," Rati said.

I sighed. "Alright, y'all need to stop distracting me. I have to concentrate." They laughed.

"I'm going to get some more tea. Anyone want anything?" Rati asked.

"I'll come with you," Jeff said as they both stood up.

"I'm okay, thank you," I said.

After they left I leaned back, examining my sketch one last time before mixing the color pigments onto a plate Rati let me borrow. The bags of color were vibrant compared to my usual tones, and the more I looked at the sketch the more I felt like it was a more accurate reflection of myself. I liked juxtaposing images, but I also viewed the world as a colorful and fun place, even if I didn't paint it that way all the time. Lifting my brush to the canvas, I took a deep breath to calm my nerves. Even after so many years as a painter, I still got the jitters right before adding the first layers of paint.

CHAPTER SEVEN

Luminosity

"Oh my god!" I yelped. Jerking upright, I knew my eyes were open but everything was black. I quickly touched my face, and then breathed a sigh of relief as I felt the face mask I wore to block out the brightness of a streetlamp outside. Ripping it off, I jumped out of bed, tossed my hair into a bun, brushed my teeth and washed my face—the bare minimum of personal hygiene—and quickly threw my things into my suitcases.

"Are we late?" I asked, opening my door for the first time. It seemed far too bright out, and I had forgotten when our flight took off. I thought it was pretty early.

"We've got three hours. I'm sure if we get there in two we'll have plenty of time to check in," Jeff shouted from his room.

"Oh," I said, taking a deep breath.

"Do you need help with anything?" Rati asked, appearing

at my door.

"I don't think so," I smiled. "Thank you so much for having us. It's been really fun."

"Are you kidding? I'm so happy that I got to see you. Are you sure you're going to be okay?" she asked.

"Yes. I'll be fine," I assured her.

"Will you let me know if there is anything I can do? I know I live literally halfway around the world, but you shouldn't be alone during this transition. You say the word and I can be in LA in less than twenty-four hours," she said, and I could tell she meant it.

"Thank you, but I have some time to process it all and I really think I'm going to be okay," I smiled, with more confidence than I felt.

"We really need to stay in better touch. I'm gonna have Dhairya pack you guys some food to take on the plane," Rati said.

"Oh, you don't need to do that," I said, but she waved me off and disappeared.

The ride to the airport seemed shorter than the ride from it before. Her driver stopped and helped us with our suitcases as we said goodbye to Rati: Jeff first, giving her a hug and kiss on the cheek. Then I gave her a hug and asked, "When do you think you'll come back for a visit?" I asked, squeezing her tight.

"I don't have any plans as of right now, but it's been awhile so I'm definitely due for a trip. Soon I hope."

"Good," I said. "I've missed having you around."

She smiled and gave me another hug before I headed for the security checkpoint.

Exhausted after a late night of chatting with Rati, Jeff and I didn't say much the entire way to Jordan. Even after I woke from a short nap to find my feet wedged underneath him, I smiled at him but didn't engage in conversation. Deep in thought, Jeff didn't seem to mind.

"Wow," I said, breaking the silence as we entered the Queen Alia International Airport in Jordan. Jeff nodded.

Sleek and modern, it had pod-shaped roofing, beautiful lush green grass outside, open-space architecture, and simple, uniform seating at the gates. The airport was brand new—posh and rich with pride. After stopping in the post office to ship my two completed paintings home, we made our way through customs and baggage claim, then hailed a cab. For miles and miles along the road, there seemed to be nothing but desert and other passing vehicles. But before long, we made a right turn down a beautifully paved road and pulled onto a wide and extended driveway lined with palm trees and lit by recessed floor lights.

A modular building made up of three symmetrical rhombus-shaped sections, the Kempinski Hotel had two square archways linking the structures together and a roof that was flat like the top of a graduation cap. The entire facade, including the walkway, was made of white stone and marble, and the giant rotating glass door opened up into a long regal hallway, at the back of which stood the reception desk. Walking through in a long maxi dress, sandals and my hobo bag, I felt underdressed against a backdrop of beautiful women wearing long chiffon cover-ups over bikinis designed for maximum sex appeal rather than swimming. Men wore long robes with either board shorts or Speedos.

"This place looks pretty pricey," I said.

"This one's on me," Jeff said.

"What? No."

"It's not a big deal Aubs, they were having a deal online so I bought it. You can buy me a drink or something later," Jeff said.

"Do you remember what happened the last time you tried to buy me ice cream?" I warned in jest. My dad had taken us to the Kemah Boardwalk during the summer after eighth grade for some roller coaster rides and carnival fun, and he'd given me some money to go buy ice cream at a nearby stand while he rested on a bench. But when we got to the window, Jeff took out his own money and paid. Instead of being grateful though, I put my hands on my hips and accused him of being sexist. He protested as the lady handed us our cones, saying that he was just being nice. But I rolled my eyes, asking, "Why don't you buy ice cream for every guy in line then?" That shut him up. My dad, hearing the entire exchange, came over and scolded me for not being gracious and then forced me to apologize to Jeff. I attempted to argue because I could tell my dad was amused and not really mad at me, but his stern look put me in my place and I apologized through gritted teeth.

"People don't easily forget being chastised in public," he replied.

I smiled. "You're not paying for this."

"You're welcome," he said with finality. We had just about reached the front desk as Jeff leaned toward me and whispered, "Just one more thing: in order to get the deal I had to tell them you were my wife, because they frown upon non-married couples sharing a room. So just go with it."

Before I could say anything we were greeted by the receptionist—an older, matronly woman who said, "Welcome, Mr. and Mrs. Anderson."

I tried unsuccessfully to suppress my smile. Jeff put his arm around me and I squeezed his hand a little too tightly.

"You're all checked in. Here are your keys. Enjoy your honeymoon," she said. I looked at Jeff and it was all I could do to keep from bursting into laughter.

A huge smile spread across the receptionist's face. "You two definitely have that newlywed glow. You must be so happy."

I couldn't help myself. Returning her smile, I said, "So far, it's not bad!"

As we made our way up to our room, it dawned on me that everyone we came across spoke English.

"What's the national language in Jordan?" I asked Jeff.

"Arabic, but the language of commerce and banking is English, which is why most everyone speaks it. I thought it was odd too when I called to check on prices for hotels and most of them said 'Hello?'"

I laughed. "Hold the elevator," a voice called, as a slender hand sliced down in-between the closing doors. A beautiful, exotic, woman stepped into the elevator mouthing, "Thanks," as she finished up a phone call: "Yes. Okay. I've only seen one or two," she said, looking Jeff up and down with a smile. "Meet me there at 8. Bye," she finished, hanging up and turning around to face us. "Did you guys just arrive?"

"Yup," Jeff said. "Any tips for the newcomers?"

"Scrub yourself with the salt of the Dead Sea," she replied, tossing her long brown hair back with a smile. "Your skin will thank you for you it."

The elevator doors opened and she got off, but not before looking directly at Jeff and saying, "Come join my friends and me at the bar later if you're not doing anything. Both of you." She looked at me and smiled.

"What's your name?" Jeff called.

"Bridgette," she replied as the doors closed.

Our room wasn't huge, but it came with a king-size bed. Exactly what two romantic newlyweds would want. I turned around and gave Jeff the eyebrow raise.

"What?! We're newlyweds, remember?!" he exclaimed.

"Not to be a prude or anything, but I'd rather not have to sleep with you getting it on next to me with your elevator floozie, so…"

"She seemed nice," he said.

"What kind of bourge-y name is Bridgette, anyway?"

"Aubs, are you jealous?"

"Just put a sock on the door if you need me to stay away," I replied, making him laugh.

Plopping down on the incredibly fluffy pillow top mattress, I sunk in way further than I expected and burst out laughing. Watching me bounce up and down with amusement at first and then curiosity, Jeff hopped onto the bed as well. Flipping on a TV for the first time since leaving home, I was shocked to find a rerun of *Saved by the Bell* dubbed into Arabic. In the episode, Zack and Jessie have to kiss for a high school play and end up questioning their feelings for each other.

"Do you wanna watch a movie?" Jeff asked.

"Sure," I said.

Jeff flipped through the channels and found the XXX section, "Oooh, there we go," he laughed.

Beneath the mounted television was a mirror that ran the length of the wall. I smiled at the image of us watching TV just as we had as kids in Jeff's bedroom. His childhood room had the same set-up, with his bed on one side and a TV atop a large dresser in the corner. Jeff liked to sit straight up on the right side of the bed, and I liked to lie flat with two pillows propping up my head. Time, it seemed, hadn't changed everything.

"Well look at that…it's us circa 1993," Jeff said.

"All you need is a *Jurassic Park* comforter, Snoop Dogg's *Doggy Style* in the CD player, and porn under the mattress!"

"I did not hide porn under the mattress!" he said. Then, smiling mischievously, he declared, "It was in my ski boot, behind a bunch of junk." He was so proud, grinning from ear to ear, that I didn't want to tell him I already knew. Especially given the fact that his mom was the one who told me.

Jeff's mom, Cherri, and I routinely watched romantic comedies when the boys bailed on our regular Thursday night dinners at the Andersons'. One night as we were watching *Shallow Hal*, she turned to me and said, "I really hope Jeff doesn't turn out like Hal, with all the porn he's got stuck in his ski boot."

I look at her, amused. "Ski boot, eh? That's creative." We both burst out laughing.

With only boys in the house, I think sometimes she secretly hoped they wouldn't make it for dinner just so she and I could watch the latest Hugh Grant or Matthew McConaughey movie. The tradition began in the eighth grade, when I was too young to realize that the movies were completely unrealistic and delusional, and it remained a tradition until I left for college. She was always so excited about our 'girls' nights' that I couldn't bring myself to tell her I had outgrown them.

"Next time you write home, tell your mom I said 'Hi', okay?" I said.

"Mm," he replied. Jeff's eyes were closed and he was already drifting off. Jet lag had really begun to take its toll on him. From New Delhi to Jordan, we gained three-and-a-half hours, so the sun was just about to set.

Slipping off the bed, I gently slid the door of our balcony open and stood at the edge of the railing looking down at a bright, aquamarine pool filled with couples chatting, laughing, and cuddling in the comfort of one another. Beyond the lip of the pool, the Dead Sea shimmered with the last rays of sunlight and within minutes disappeared into the dark.

The weather was almost uncomfortably warm for nighttime and the black abyss of still water in the distance was like something out of an existential movie about the nothingness that awaits us after death. My eyes were open, but they may as well have been closed, and for a moment going blind wasn't all that scary. In fact, it was peaceful—like being in a constant state of meditation. I hadn't stopped wishing for the diagnosis to be wrong, but in this moment, I not only acknowledged that RP was real, I believed it. The disease was no longer something that was going to happen, it was here.

A high-pitched yelp followed by a flirtatious laugh cut through my thoughts. I shifted my gaze from the darkness to the well-lit area beneath me. Two drunken lovers on a lounge chair had forgotten they were in public and the man had stripped the woman of her already barely-there top, causing the shriek I'd just heard. I knew my glance had turned into a stare, but I couldn't peel my eyes away. The serenity of darkness I'd felt just moments before was replaced by fear and jealousy. I wondered if this was what I had to look forward to: me staring into the dark as the world moved on without me.

"I had the most bizarre dream last night," I said, speaking for the first time the next morning. Jeff was sitting at his computer, a position he had been in since I woke up, took a shower, got dressed, made coffee, and started planning out the day.

"About what?"

"I was on a bench next to this guy, Tim, who I don't even really know that well. He was a friend of this guy I dated for a few months back in college, so we naturally lost touch after Tony and I broke up."

"Uh-huh," Jeff said, his attention elsewhere.

"Well we were sitting there talking and I remember pretending to be happier than I was. In the dream I was blind and kind of in a desperate place. But I was acting as if it was the greatest thing that ever happened to me."

"You were blind? That sounds scary," he said, still not looking at me.

"I wasn't scared about it, but for some reason every time I tried to pick up my paintbrush it felt like I was trying to dead-lift 500 pounds."

"Sorry, Aubs," Jeff interrupted. "I've got another half-hour or so of programming. Can we talk about this more while we float in the Dead Sea?" he asked.

"Forget it," I said. "It was just a stupid dream."

I grabbed my blue and white candy-striped bikini and went into the bathroom to change. After brushing my teeth, I started packing a bag full of beach essentials as Jeff got ready. Grabbing my sunblock from the desk I noticed that Jeff had been looking at Facebook. There were a couple of programmer screens covering the page itself, but there was no mistaking the tab that had been left open to Veronica's page. He almost never posted anything, despite being the developer of the automatic status update generator, so I wondered what he was looking at or if he'd sent her a message. Coming out from the bathroom, Jeff caught my eye and closed the computer. I considered pressing him on the issue, but I didn't feel like discussing the woman who'd kept him from my parents' funeral. It bothered me that he still pined after her—a person who, to me, had no soul. I wanted her to be the enemy, the common denominator of hate that brought us closer together, or for her to simply cease existing.

She mattered to him though. I knew because he had a pained look on his face any time he was forced to mention her name, and because in all the idle time we spent traveling together he hadn't brought her up. It was almost as if he went out of his way *not* to mention anything that had to do with her.

On our way down to the beach, Jeff stopped to buy two Frisbees from a local market. The store was only four aisles wide and a mixture between a hardware store and grocery store. A typical dollar store in the United States would be the closest comparison.

"Did you play Ultimate in college?" I asked.

"What?"

"Frisbee. Ultimate Frisbee. It's one of those intramural sports they have for the athletic non-athletes."

"Is that what those guys were doing on the field?" he wondered aloud. He didn't bother answering my underlying question, which was why was he buying Frisbees at all, but my excitement trumped my need to know as the beach came into view. I took in a deep breath of fresh air as we reached the water and quickly undressed.

Years of studying art had turned me into a connoisseur of misplaced details and errors in paintings as well as in my natural surroundings, but at the Dead Sea my skills were null. There were none. In fact, what I noticed was a lack of visual noise. The shoreline was the color of salt, the water crisp and clear with no aquatic life lurking below. Above us, a few clouds lingered in the powder blue sky; directly in front of us on the horizon was the Israeli coastline, which, from our vantage point, was nothing more than a crust of sandy-colored earth; and below the horizon was the vast expanse of Dead Sea water. The topography was simple, natural, and seemingly pure. Of course, industry and commerce pulled from the wealth of natural minerals—packaging expensive, highly-sought-after beauty and health remedies for sale—but the landscape, as far as I could tell, remained untouched.

"Are you ready to experience magic?" Jeff asked.

"I am so ready, though, I still fully expect to sink," I said.

He laughed. "The water is 33.7% sodium chloride. Scientifically speaking we're guaranteed to float."

The second my toes hit the water I noticed they were buoyant. Scooping up a handful of water, I peered at its cloud-like color and made a mental note of its density. Releasing the salt water back into the sea, I cautiously sat down, trusting Mother Nature to cradle me, and actually found myself not only floating, but feeling like I was being pushed up and out of the water. With the two Frisbees in his hand, Jeff started doggy paddling into the water and probably ended up drinking enough sodium chloride to cause a severe spike in his blood pressure. I watched as he got out, ran to our bags to gulp down about half the jug of water we brought, then dry heave as his body tried to remedy the situation. His taste buds would never be the same.

"Are you okay?" I asked. He nodded yes and gave me a thumbs up. When the two Frisbees he'd abandoned reached me I shouted, "What are these things for?" He tried to reply, but his throat was so dry that nothing came out and he ended up dismissing me with a wave of his arm. The water wasn't moving much, so I left them to drift nearby as I took in the sights.

From where I lay bobbing in the water, shapes and color in the distance lacked any real definition, so I tried to focus on an object. The blue sky turned gray at the horizon, which then melted into the brown of the earth. Muted tones were ubiquitous, with only a small patch of green way off in the distance. A spaghetti-thin black line dangled in the center of my vision breaking the singular scene into two continuous images, but if I squinted I could almost make it go away.

I hadn't seen any sprawling lawns since arriving in Jordan, so I wasn't sure what the thin, narrow patch of green was, but it looked like a single blade of grass. I began to think about the uncommon singular identity of grass and found that even the singular word—grass—described the multiplicity of it. I pictured its life cycle in my head: it grew, was stomped on, survived, and then died. And wasn't that simply the cycle of all life? I grew, struggled to become a painter, found a niche, and was about to lose my ability to see. Luckily—or perhaps unluckily—Retinitis Pigmentosa was not fatal, which left me to ponder how it might be survived.

Drifting on the surface of the water, I noticed the dark spots lining my peripheral again. The contrast of dark black against the bright blue sky accentuated its effects.

"I'm going blind," I said, in a low mumble to myself.

"What?" Jeff asked. He had just managed to float toward me with two books in hand—mine and his—which he placed on the floating Frisbees. They were meant to be floating tables.

"Ahh," I said, purposefully ignoring his question. "Very cool."

Giving my Frisbee a light push towards me, he closed his eyes and asked, "What were you talking about this morning? You had a weird dream?"

"I can't remember anymore," I lied. "It wasn't important."

Jeff was silent for a while and then he said, "I quit my job."

"*What?*"

"Yeah…" he said.

"When? And more importantly, why?"

"I'd been planning on it since before we left, but today I officially did it," he said.

"Why? What changed?" I asked, wondering if it had anything to do with Veronica.

"Around this time they usually send out classroom assignments and when I was checking my e-mail this morning I realized I didn't want to be getting one." He opened his eyes, letting them adjust to the bright sunlight.

"Do you feel good about it?" I asked.

"I think so. I'm on this new app that I think is going to be huge."

"A different one?"

"Yeah."

"Cool, what's it called?"

"I Travel Better Than You," Jeff said.

I was silent for a few seconds as I tried to figure out how to delicately ask him whether it was another hate app. "What does it do? Is it like a comparison of people's travel experiences? Like Yelp?"

"It's so much better than that," he said, excitedly. "I'll show you when I get a little further on it. It's still in the initial stages so I think it would be hard for you to conceptualize how it might work," he said.

"Deal," I said, backing off. "I can't wait to see it."

"Thanks," he said, sincerely. I could tell he meant it.

"How are you feeling about it? Nervous?"

"Not really. I think it's just kind of sinking in at the

moment," he said.

"Michael, who you would have met at my gallery opening had you not snuck out early," I said, unable to resist the jab, "he would always tell me to sit with my fears. He'd say that fear is a powerful friend. Being afraid of something means that there is something to lose, and the greater the endeavor the more fear you have to overcome."

"I agree," he said.

"Did you tell your brother?"

"I sent him an e-mail, but I'm not worried about him. He'd just say, 'It'll come to you when it comes to you, bro'. He never thought teaching was a good career for me anyway."

I nodded. "Maybe it'd do me some good to become a stoner."

"It helps," Jeff smiled.

After an early dinner of yellow and white rice, falafel, and hummus, Jeff wanted to go back and work on his app, so I went down to the pool, ordered a glass of pinot noir, and watched the sunset—or "magic hour", as my friend Carolanne called it. "Everything is prettier at dusk, even though the colors aren't as vibrant. And there's less contrast because the light has to travel through more atmosphere," I remembered her saying as she snapped pictures of a sunset to go with a magazine article someone had written about Venice Beach.

Refraction of light created rainbows; without light there would be no red, orange, yellow, green, or blue at all. What if tomorrow the sun came up blue and the sky was yellow? What difference would it make to me? Just the other day in

Delhi, I was swimming in a sea of magenta, Indian yellow, cyan, tangerine, hot pink, olive green, and endless other variations of the spectrum. Four or five weeks from now, color would be relegated to a simplified word, cyan would be nothing more than light blue. Creating different shades and hues of colors had always brought me joy, and RP was stripping me of all of it.

On my way back up to the room, I passed by the lobby bar, stopping for a second when I saw Jeff sitting on a stool next to Bridgette. She was sitting so close to him she might as well have been sitting on his lap, and he, well… he looked to be having a pretty good time. He laughed at something she said and even from a distance I could see the smile-wrinkles at the corner of his eyes. Quickly turning away, I headed upstairs to get ready for bed.

CHAPTER EIGHT

Story

"You took a gun to one the Seven Wonders of the World and shot it?" I asked Atef, who drove as Jeff and I sat in the back of his boxy green Jeep. On either side of the road, large rock mountains made up the vast majority of Jordan's topography.

"Yes," he replied with a proud smile. He was telling us about the bullet-ridden urn at the top of the Treasury when I interrupted him. As far as tour guides went, Atef was a beautiful, godlike specimen of a man—a Jordanian Jesus. In his mid-thirties, he was dressed in brown cargo pants, a gray pullover sweater under a black leather jacket, and covering his head was a red and white checkered turban. Lean, with naturally muscular arms derived from manual labor rather than steroid-driven gym sessions (my college boyfriend was built the same way), Atef had a ruggedness that merged with the landscape harmoniously.

The vast expanse of golden-red desert was covered in a

haze of dust, just as I imagined it looked in biblical times. We had been driving for over two hours on bumpy dirt roads peppered with checkpoints and tanks, making the Middle Eastern conflicts hard to ignore, but I never felt the need to lock the door or thought the country any less beautiful.

For most of the morning, we listened to Atef tell us the history of Petra, the Lost City. Hidden deep in the deserts of Jordan, Petra was accessible by only one entrance, known as the Siq. Thought to have been part of Egypt's eighteenth dynasty, it was a city of great proportions. Spanning more than sixty square kilometers through canyons, up mountains, and along riverbeds, the city was thought to have had a sizable population. From the rock, they carved huge monuments like the Treasury and Monastery, but all along the main avenues of the city were rock cut-outs where people lived, worshiped, and were buried.

The Treasury, so named because people thought it held hidden vaults full of gold, jewels, and other precious metals, was the most famous structure in Petra. Carved purely from the rock, the structure was forty meters high, broken up into two tiers, and fit for giants, according to Atef. At the top was an urn, which many people believed to be the key to unlocking the Treasury.

For centuries, Petra was kept hidden because the Bedouin people were afraid western magicians might unlock the secrets of the storehouse and steal the wealth that belonged to the locals. Hundreds of years later, a treasure had yet to be discovered.

Jeff noticed me staring at Atef in the mirror and whispered, "Jesus, Aubs, you're drooling."

"Oh please," I hissed. "I saw you at the bar last night."

"What are we in high school again?" Jeff said, looking confused.

"What's that supposed to mean?" I asked. Jeff said nothing.

"I have been a tour guide for ten years, how can I tell you for certain that no treasure exists if I have not attempted to claim it myself?" Atef continued, seemingly unaware of our backseat conversation.

Bold *and* candid. I was in heaven.

It was mid-afternoon by the time we reached our destination. "This is perfect time to arrive in Petra. It's not as hot and we'll be able to catch a beautiful sunset," Atef said as he pulled into the parking lot. Getting out of the car with our small daypacks, we walked right past the ticket booth and straight to the entrance, which was a few hundred yards ahead.

As we passed by, I watched a French couple arguing heatedly with the ticket counter lady over the French woman's immodest outfit: her strappy summer dress and sandals were a definite no-no. Jeff and I were both dressed conservatively: me in jeans and three-quarter sleeve crew neck t-shirt, and Jeff in a light gray, fitted t-shirt and drawstring pants. Atef had informed us of this dress code when we called to book the tour: no shoulders showing and long pants.

Shaking his head, Atef said, "That is embarrassing."

"No kidding," I added. "Who's her tour guide?"

"By the way she is yelling, I would say it is her boyfriend," he laughed.

Our tickets were waiting with a friend of Atef's who had come early and stood in line so that we didn't have to. This was a perk of having Atef that even Jeff could appreciate.

Once through the entrance, we followed Atef across the vast span of desert toward the facade of pink sandstone mountain ranges. There wasn't much of anything in any direction; just endless mounds of red rock and flat desert. Then, as we got closer, I started to see it: a crack in the seemingly never-ending span of reddish rock.

It was as if a violent burst of lightning had struck the rock, leaving a crooked, narrow path through the mountain. This was known as the Siq and, much to my surprise, the walkway would continue for quite a while (1.2 kilometers). Jeff's claustrophobia made this a little unsettling for him, but I was actually surprised at how open it felt for being such a narrow crevice. The tops of the rock opened up to a bright and cloudless blue sky, giving the space an aura of endless expansion. No wonder it was kept hidden for so long. Blink and I would have missed the opening.

Above us, Atef pointed at what looked like primitive gutters carved into the wall and explained that they were used to irrigate water from Wadi Musa to the city. I had no idea how far Wadi Musa was from Petra, but the system stretched farther than I could see. While the surface of it appeared primitive, I thought it looked efficient and aesthetically pleasing. Set well above eye level, the people would've had the ambient sound of flowing water as they traveled though the Siq.

Call it my imagination, or maybe my other senses rising in

sensitivity, but I heard the water—I felt it, moving with a natural ebb and flow. Only, there wasn't any water gesticulating. The only real evidence I had to go by was Atef's description.

I pulled my digital camera out of my backpack to take a photo for color reference later. I snapped a couple of shots and then, for whatever reason, I closed my eyes and took another shot, and then another, and seventeen more after that. With the sun as bright as it was, the insides of my eyelids had a reddish hue to them, and as I moved my left hand along the wall, my right clicked away at images I couldn't see. I brought my face closer to the wall and away from it, watching as the light darkened and brightened behind my still-closed eyelids.

"What are you doing?" Atef asked, causing my eyes to pop open in embarrassment.

"Oh! Uh, just taking some photos for my friend," I replied.

"Do you know how to use your camera?" he asked, taking the camera from me. "You hold it up like this," he instructed, putting the camera closer to my face so I could see the LCD screen. "And then you push this to make the photo."

I laughed. "I know, I was just trying something different."

"Oh. Yes, of course," he said, looking slightly embarrassed as handed the camera back to me. "Do you know the story of Moses?" he asked.

"Vaguely."

"As Moses led his followers through the desert, they became sick with thirst, and it was to our east, at Wadi Musa, that Moses' cane struck the wall and released cool water for his people," Atef said. He then went on to talk about how the pipeline promoted open channel flow and particle settling basins were designed to produce potable water supplies.

"I bet bottled water would've blown their minds," I joked. Atef laughed deeply, which made me smile.

"I think there are more miraculous things than bottled water," Jeff said. I looked over at him expecting to see a sarcastic smirk across his face, but he had already turned away. His lack of eye contact made his comment seem passive-aggressive. Maybe his claustrophobia was getting to him.

I waited a few minutes to give him space before saying, "I wonder if we'll be able to find a 'Moses was here' etching somewhere on the wall," and when he still didn't say anything I wondered if he might be in the midst of a panic attack.

"Jeff, are you okay?" He nodded yes. "Are you sure? We can stop if you need to."

"*No,*" he responded tensely. "Just need to get to the end."

I patted him on the back and squeezed his arm, "Don't worry. In 2,000 years it hasn't collapsed. Maybe it will someday, but trust me when I say today is not that day." He kept walking and I was about to say something else when the crevice opened up.

Before us was a 40-meter-high, hand-carved edifice on the red rock mountainside. Six enormous round pillars held up the two-tiered facade, which was so smooth it was a juxtaposition with the very rock from which it was carved. Centuries of erosion had stripped the facade of many of its original details. The large figures of Castor and Pollux, the sons of Zeus, had been carved between the lower pillars and, though preserved, they were difficult to discern without Atef's help. Yet, there was no question the craftsmanship poured into the Treasury was extremely sophisticated given the rudimentary tools available at the time.

At the very top, underneath the flat fascia were the markings of bullet holes, as well as vague remnants of what used to be an urn. Unfortunate as it was for the urn to have been nearly destroyed in visitors' quests for treasure, the destruction became a trademark symbol for one of the most fascinating stories in history.

"Which one is yours?" I asked Atef, pointing to the bullet holes.

He smiled wickedly, moved closer to me, put his hand on the small of my back, and pointed at the center of the urn. "It's that one, in the middle, I hit it dead on and still nothing." There was absolutely nothing flirtatious about his response and yet I felt myself blushing.

"I bet all the tour guides claim that bullet hole is theirs," Jeff said. Atef seemed unfazed as he smiled and continued walking.

"What's with the attitude?" I asked Jeff once Atef was out of earshot.

"He shot it dead in the middle? Yeah right."

"He's telling us stories. Who cares if he fibs where his bullet hit?"

"He's just trying to impress you."

"So?"

"Okay then," Jeff shrugged. He walked off towards the

Treasury leaving me wondering what the heck had just transpired. I looked after him for a few minutes, expecting him to come back and apologize for his rude behavior, or at the very least come back with an argument, but he just kept on walking.

Giving Jeff space, I kept my distance and took photos of the unfinished Greco-Roman Treasury, which appeared like a stamp on the side of an enormous mountain. I say unfinished because the area surrounding it looked as natural as it probably had back when the facade was being carved. Rough and jagged spaces between smooth, finished ones meant the city had plans for expansion. Built to withstand the test of time, the carvings and pillars, though damaged, were still sharp at the edges and evenly rounded at the curves.

When I finally caught up to them, Atef continued his tour, saying, "This structure was carved starting at the top and working their way down. On the sides you can see the markings for the scaffolding still in place. It was designed to protect the bottom sections from being damaged while they hammered and chiseled into the mountain. You will see, all around Petra there are Greek, Roman and Egyptian statues. Here, these columns are Roman; up top, the carved goddesses were derived from Greek mythology; and on the sides, the winged eagles were Egyptian-influenced. Inside, you will see carved-out spaces where statues of the gods resided. Also, you will see seats carved out on the opposite side for visitors. Take a look around for a bit, walk inside and then we'll visit to one other place before heading back to the campsite for dinner."

"I'm gonna take a walk," I said, looking at Jeff for some kind of clue about what he was feeling.

All I got in return was a confusing "Yeah." I stuffed my earbuds in and walked away.

The interior of the Treasury was so small that normal chatter echoed against its walls, creating a reverberating noise. I quickly powered up my iPod and used the song as white noise while I ruminated in mental solitude. I thought about giving myself the space to experiment and create some sort of art after I was blind, but I wasn't keen on the idea of releasing that work. How could I trust my hand to paint my memories in an accurate way, and with meaning, if I couldn't see what I was painting? How could I connect fully to the piece if I couldn't skillfully control the images? And if I couldn't completely connect with my work then how could I expect anyone else to? The thought of having to start over and redefine my artistic voice was overwhelming. And even more horrifying was the thought of whether or not my new work would be accepted by the art community.

With all of the other tourists around, it was difficult to sit with my thoughts, let alone get a sense of the space. Along the left wall, I found the seats Atef mentioned carved out of the rock surface. I sat, turned my head to the far right, then did a slow sweep of the room, mentally taking a panoramic photo. When I was done, I closed my eyes and sketched in my mind's eye its dimensions, without the distracting people who obstructed my view.

I tried to stay focused on the art and history before me, but all I could concentrate on was the darkness. Two months didn't seem like nearly enough time to transition from seeing to not seeing. It wasn't even a full season. Every time I thought about being blind I wanted to kick and scream and cry, but I wasn't a kid and my parents were no longer around to listen. The best I could do was to push it out of my mind. Unlike my parents, who disliked seeing me in pain, life could not be persuaded to change its mind. I thought about all the shallow things I'd wished for before: fame, fortune, and the perfect husband.

Opening my eyes, I saw Atef looking at me from the entrance and smiled. He waved. I waved back, trying to hide my embarrassment, and moved to another part of the cave.

Earlier when he had adjusted his turban, Atef's dark hair fell across his face and beads of sweat dropped off his sideburns, and I had to stop myself from reaching up and touching his face. As he carefully guided us around rocky terrain, offering his hand to help me when needed, I could tell he was the kind of guy who took care of his loved ones, and in this moment I wanted that to be me.

Forcing myself away from thoughts of self-pity, I lifted my fingers to caress the organic patterns on the wall. Reminiscent of a striped picnic blanket rippling through the air just before being set down on the ground, the hues of red (ranging from a pale salmon to a deep crimson) made me think of Rusty. He raved about a Brazilian artist, Henrique Oliveira, whose paintings mimicked the movement in rock formations. Oliveira's famous technique was to use a non-blending viscous paint mixed with pigments that he stirred in to create his palette. His work was also the inspiration for one of Rusty's most famous paintings, *Seasons*. Cubist in design, the piece broke apart the human body and reconstructed it to show different angles at different times. *Seasons* was a metaphor for the stages of our lives and how time plays an important role in our connections with one another.

Transfixed by the colors in the rock, I did my best to capture their natural tone in the photographs I took. I hoped these hues might lend themselves to an idea I had been turning over in my head since we arrived in Petra. I didn't know what the central image would be yet, but I did know that whatever landscape I painted in Jordan needed to consist of these same raw shades.

"Hey," Jeff said, coming up from behind me. "Are you ready? It's time to go."

"Hey, are we okay?" I asked him.

"Yeah, why wouldn't we be?"

"No reason," I replied, not quite believing him, but also not wanting to pick a fight where there wasn't one.

That night, we grabbed our overnight bags from the trunk of the car and followed Atef to our campsite. Part of Atef's two-day tour was a night's stay in a tent city. Small flickerings of tea lights tucked into the rock lined our walkway, and at the entrance a huge sign read "King Aretas Camp." Just beyond where we stood were white, cloth-covered wigwams, lined up into organized blocks. The isolated area looked like a forgotten Bedouin civilization.

With Atef still in the lead, we were greeted by our enthusiastic host, Enmar. He was a short but stout man in his early fifties, dressed in a bright blue and green button-down shirt, and light, beige drawstring pants. As he led the way to our tent, we passed by a large area with ornate coffee tables, fluffy sitting pillows, and shaggy rugs begging to be sprawled out upon. I made a mental note to return to this spot later.

Our personal tent was simply furnished with two twin beds, a nightstand, coat hanger, and a large mirror in one corner. I couldn't wait to plop down and relax, but before I could even sit, we were ushered out for a white tablecloth dinner buffet. The cooks served up an international cuisine of fried rice, broccoli stir-fry, spaghetti, lamb curry, flash fried fish, humus, baba ghanoush, olives, pickles, and the national dish of Jordan: Mansaf, a staple food made of lamb cooked in fermented, dried yogurt and served over a bed of rice. The feast was far more elaborate than I expected for camping and gave new meaning to the term "luxury camping." Or perhaps was the definition of it.

After a hot shower in simple stone stalls equipped with organic soaps, Jeff grabbed his laptop as I grabbed my sketchbook and we headed for the cozy communal area under the stars.

"Come, join us!" Atef said, beckoning us towards him and Enmar.

"You like him don't you?" Jeff asked.

"Atef? What's not to like? He's attractive and he lives here, where I don't have to ever see him again."

"How convenient, I never pegged you for a one-night-stand-type of girl," Jeff said.

"You're one to talk," I said, but before Jeff could answer Atef called to us again.

"Come over! My friend here was just about to tell me stories," Atef said.

I hadn't realized it before, but the centerpieces, which I assumed were coffee tables, were actually small pits filled with burning coal—innovative!

"I guess camping anywhere in the world is pretty much the same then," Jeff said.

"In America, you do this too?" Atef asked.

"Absolutely, when we go camping it's very similar to this with the fire in the center and one person telling stories. But it's not quite this fancy," I told Enmar.

"Thank you," Enmar smiled.

As the night progressed, we sipped single malt whiskey while Enmar told us about the "real" history of Petra: secret maps leading to buried treasure; a golden phoenix; strange sightings in the night sky; and most recently, a larger-than-life ten-foot-tall male skeleton. Our host told these stories with such passion and avidity that I found myself buying into the possibility of a great treasure in Petra. He made me think that maybe the guy who wrote Indiana Jones wasn't just making it all up. By the time he was done, I was certain that Petra was full of riches, but I believed it to be in spirituality rather than in gold.

The few times Atef and I caught each other's gaze, I was certain there was something there. He had such dark, intense features that it was hard to tell what he was thinking, and for a while I felt very self-conscious about the way I was sitting, what I was saying, and my overall appearance. To help myself unwind, I drank my first cup of whiskey in one gulp, and Enmar poured me another.

They asked us where we were from and what we did. Jeff told them he was happily unemployed but working on a new project. I told them I was an artist and they immediately handed me a pencil and paper so I could draw their portraits. They told me they would proudly boast about having an original Aubrey Johnson because they met me on my journey and one spontaneous night I "created a masterpiece" of them. How could I say no?

"You are the most beautiful painter...I have ever met," Enmar slurred.

I blushed. "Not a fan of Hani Alqam?"

"You have heard of Alqam?" Enmar asked. He seemed shocked.

"I wrote a paper on one of his paintings. It was a black and white painting of the backside of a girl bent over while undressing. Such a vulnerable moment to be captured rather grotesquely, I thought. Her flesh was made of thick clumps of acrylic paint so her body appeared inverted, her insides being the components of her exterior. By positioning her in a vulnerable pose of undressing and further exposing her unsavory insides, Alqam forced the viewer to address the frailty and complexity of the human psyche, by stripping away all layers of deflection. I think I was drawn to him because I was fascinated by how much a work of art could disturb me," I smiled.

"Forgive my honest speak, but I have always wanted to know: why do you paint? What is the reason inside?" Atef asked.

"I do it because there is something I want to say," I said.

"Why not just write it?" he asked.

In a long and sobering moment, I thought about how to respond. "Everything in life—our thoughts, our emotions—

are always fragmented. For me, art brings it all back together. With any kind of art, you can feel something and empathize with it on a very deep level without having to put restrictive words to it," I said. "Music is the same way. Take Beethoven for example, his combination of notes and spacing evoke emotion without the use of any words."

One of the most powerful experiences with music I had ever had was listening to Beethoven's Appassionata in a college lecture hall. The song opened quiet and ominous and ended in complete tragedy. He wrote that song a few years after coming to terms with his progressively declining hearing, but to describe it as tragic would have been to diminish the experience. Beethoven's single and double notes were my absolute and appositive brush strokes. In the same way his notes, when strung together, created a complex symphony, my brush strokes, when laid out in calculated and meticulous designs, made up a work of art layered with meaning. That he and I now shared a common tragedy was purely coincidence.

"That is God damn poetic," Jeff slurred.

"Beethoven is a genius and you are a genius. Please, make me look handsome," Atef said.

I couldn't make you look ugly if I tried, I wanted to say. Instead I shrugged and acted coy. "I promise nothing."

The compliments and blandishments were showered onto me as I continued to drunkenly sketch their portraits. They stopped only after I sternly asked them to so I could stop laughing and steady my hand. When I was done, I handed each drawing to its respective owner.

"Amazing photos of an amazing artist," Jeff said, not

making much sense. I smiled and laughed, noticing that his arm rested on my thigh and stayed there long after he'd set his portrait off to the side.

Leaning back to relax against a large sitting pillow, I thought to myself, *This is a night I'm going to remember.* I didn't know if it was because traveling drew people together or because I was in such a vulnerable place that others were drawn to me, but by the end of the night, Enmar and Atef felt like family.

Before going to bed, Enmar handed us a bag of juice, which he made us promise to finish before falling asleep. A hangover-preventer of sorts that burned through the system —some kind of ginger, lemon, and spice combination that I was certain would give both Jeff and me the runs. But being the drunks that we were, we drank with enthusiasm.

Instead of being a cynic, I should've gotten the recipe. On our second day in Petra, I felt better than I had in awhile. I was alert, light on my feet, and maybe I was being overly optimistic, but even my vision seemed clearer. At the very least, it wasn't worse.

Day two was to be traveled on camelback. It was the same pathway we had taken the day before, but we were traveling a longer distance to the Monastery. Having never been much of any kind of rider, I wasn't entirely comfortable with the idea. I told Atef I was fine walking, but he said, "Aubrey, trust me, this is part of the experience. Camels are a part of this world and have been since the ancient times. Please, you will enjoy it." So I hopped on and begged the animal to forgive me for my weight.

Even though these camels made the same trek every day, I didn't trust them not to spook and throw me fifty yards across the desert. Did camels spook? Or was that just a horse thing? No matter, I was holding on for dear life and the experience was far from relaxing.

I sat atop the slow but steady animal for an hour before arriving at the base of a mountain where we traded our camels for surefooted donkeys. The astute name did nothing to ease my angst as my wobbling legs moved from one to the other. Only then did we climb the 800 steep steps to the famous monastery. Safe as the donkeys were, I would have felt much better with my own feet planted on the ground, and it took all of the strength of my muscles combined with fierce willpower to steady my shaking legs once we reached the top. If any ride on an animal could have conjured up a fear of heights, this would've been it.

Carved out of pure rock was an enormous, trophy-like structure situated at the top of the Monastery. Like a banister typically found at the top of a wooden staircase, the structure had several geometric shapes stacked on top of one another with the bottom cone tapering out into a large disc at the bottom. Walking along the slanted surface was scary only because of the close proximity to an edge. With great effort and concentration, I crawled out onto the platform for a panoramic view of Petra.

Being on my hands and knees while small Arab children walked around with ease made me feel ridiculous, but my legs had only just begun to stop shaking and I wasn't willing to trade my life for my pride. I stopped close to the center where I thought I had the best vantage, and also where I could plant my feet securely. Jeff, who the day before was struggling with the confined spaces of the Siq, had no problem with heights, so even with unguarded ledges he wandered about unconcerned.

I felt a tightness in my chest and tried desperately to take in air, but I couldn't. When I finally did, I let out multiple gasping sounds that sent both Jeff and Atef to my side instantly.

"Are you okay?" Jeff asked.

"Go get her a water bottle from the donkey, please," Atef ordered Jeff.

Jeff hesitated, but took off running.

Atef took my left hand in his and stroked my back with this right hand like a parent trying to calm a hysterical child. "Be calm," he said. "Try to take deep breaths."

"I can't," I stammered.

"You can," he said, helping me off my hands and knees and into a sitting position. Still holding my hand, he said, "You are on vacation, yes?"

"Yes," I breathed.

"Where have you been so far?" he asked warmly.

"China and India," I stammered.

"Oh wow! Then we are in tough competition. And you are traveling more still?"

"Italy, then Peru, and Brazil."

"You are...what do they call it? Running around the world?" he asked, smiling.

"Yes," I said, feeling myself begin to calm.

"Why do you to travel?" he asked.

"I'm going blind," I replied, feeling my chest close again. I gasped for air.

"It is okay. You are okay," he repeated calmly. "You breathe with me okay?" I nodded. "Okay, one, two, three breathe up." He took a deep breath in and I followed. "One, two, three, breathe down." He let his breath out and I repeated.

After a few minutes of breathing exercises I was able to take in longer, more steady breaths. "Thanks," I said, feeling embarrassed. "Please don't say anything to Jeff. He doesn't know."

"You have not talked to anyone about this?" he asked.

"Just my friend Rati," I said, willing my heart to stay calm.

"Not Jeff?" he asked. I shook my head. "Well, maybe you need to speak it out," Atef smiled with compassion.

"Maybe," I said.

"I meet a lot of people in this business, you know...people who travel both a lot and a little, but none who are really seeing the world. Not like you."

I smiled, then returned my focus to breathing.

"I have a drawing worth a million dollars in my pack," he said warmly. I blushed. "I had a blind man once, as my guest," Atef continued. "I asked him why he bothered to travel if he could see nothing. Do you know what he said? He said, 'Just because you can't see the stage, doesn't mean you can't dance on it.' I think he was a very wise man, this guy..."

"Was he an artist?" I asked.

He laughed. "I don't think so, but he did take a lot of photos."

"How does a blind guy take photos?" I asked.

Atef thought about it for a long moment before he responded. "I don't know. He just did I guess. I think maybe he didn't worry about how to frame the photo but just to take a picture for his friends."

I liked the guy's metaphor about being blind, but I felt like more than just somebody who wanted to dance. I felt like a ballerina who worked tirelessly to get into Juilliard only to have her legs amputated. I was losing more than my eyesight —I was losing my career, my dream, and the very thing that defined who I was.

"Do you believe in destiny? That everything in the world happens for a reason?" I asked him.

"No," he said simply.

Looking out over the monastery for the first time, I saw that I had a grand view of a serene expanse of land, and as such, it was a good place for a spiritual revelation, but I didn't have one. Religious people turned to God when things in their life went wrong; all I had was myself.

"I'm afraid I don't either," I said, with a gentle smile. "But I envy people who have faith," I said. "For the rest of us, the burden and disappointment of life sometimes feels unbearable."

"Not if we share the burden with others," Atef said, gesturing to Jeff who was running toward us.

"There wasn't any water in any of the donkey saddles so I had to run down to a vendor," Jeff panted. "Are you okay?"

"Yeah. I think so," I said, feeling both touched and embarrassed at the horrified and scared look on his face. "Thanks Jeff."

That night, back at the Kempinski Hotel, I created my first surrealist painting. Using the rose-red colors of Petra mixed with the colors of my natural skin tone, I painted a Picasso-esque self-portrait of a naked girl, hugging her right knee. Etched into the rock, she was one with the earth. It evoked a sense of loneliness through hard, broken lines and lack of substance—there was only the girl and the earth. There was no sense of a higher being. She existed on her own, completely isolated.

"That looks nothing like anything I've seen of yours," Jeff said, coming up behind me.

I didn't say anything.

"It seems...sad?" he questioned.

"Maybe."

CHAPTER NINE

Detour

People describe being blind as living in darkness. I thought about this as I stood on my balcony looking at the sleeping city cloaked in shadows. Sharp corners appeared rounded and isolated buildings now all blended together in the low light, but even in darkness I could still make out a path to the sea. When the sun left us, the moon took its place and our eyes adjusted to the change in light. I felt queasy as I thought about trying to find my way in a world of total darkness.

I sat there for hours, unmoving. Watching the slow shift between moon and sun was like being in a place without ecstatic happiness or devastating sorrow—a purgatory of sorts. For a small fragment of time, nothing moved forward or backward. I wasn't going blind, nor was I *not* going blind. Then a car passed, breaking the invisible bubble I had manifested as a means of stopping the clock. Slowly more cars emerged, then a bicyclist, pedestrian, and a truck. The first signs of sunlight appeared in the east, and the city began to awaken.

Grabbing Jeff's camera, I carefully placed it on the balcony facing my canvas and set the timer to take a photo every five minutes. Taking a charcoal pencil from my box of supplies and holding it between my teeth, I pulled the belt from my robe and blindfolded myself.

Mentally exhausted but physically alert, I sat as still as possible and tried to decipher the sounds around me: the squeak of rusted breaks, the low rumble of an engine, bicycle wheels running over potholes, chatter in a language I didn't understand, and water running down a drain. With my fingers I traced the size of the canvas until I found what I guessed to be the center, took the pencil from my mouth, and started to draw. I sketched fast, not worrying about placement or perfection. If my pencil went off the canvas, I let the image fall off as well. The warmth on my back grew with intensity as the sun rose and the heat became my marker of time. I drew roads, bicycles, and people walking, but stopped when a shift in the atmosphere made me jerk my head up. I reached for the blindfold.

"Don't stop on my account," Jeff said, placing a hand over mine.

"Morning," I said, embarrassed. "I was just doodling."

"With a blindfold on? That seems counterintuitive," he said. Unable to see, I was keenly aware of his hand holding mine. Warm and soft, it sent a tingling sensation through my spine. He had a firm grip. In all the years I'd known Jeff, the insides of our palms had only made contact a few times, and I had the urge to return the grip, to fold my hand into the safety of his, but I didn't.

"I can't," I said, peeling the blindfold off and wincing at the chicken-scratch drawing before me. "I lost my concentration," I lied. The truth was, it made me self-conscious to have someone watch me create something that I myself couldn't see.

"I don't quite understand the exercise," he said. "Is this supposed to help you create free flow or something?"

The image was pretty horrid. My hand-to-canvas coordination was terrible. What were supposed to be bicycles had wheels that were overlapping or abnormally far apart. What I intended to be a circle looked more like a slinky, my river was mid-canvas instead of near the bottom, and the sun fell off the top. Nothing was as I imagined it.

"Atef mentioned yesterday that he gave a tour to a blind guy once, and the guy was something of a photographer. I thought the concept was interesting," I said. "It's pretty terrible huh?"

"I'm not an artist, but generally when trying something new the first few are throwaways anyway, right?"

"Is that your way of telling me it sucks?" I was disappointed that he didn't tell me he thought it was decent for my first try, or that it was actually pretty good for someone who couldn't see. But no, Jeff didn't say any of that.

"I think all of your paintings are equally odd, but you know, being older and wiser now…I can say with some truth that they're starting to grow on me," he said. I laughed.

He looked at me and smiled with a genuine kindness that made me want to cry. He had no idea what was happening to me, yet he somehow came up with the right words to comfort me.

"Right. Well, I have a feeling my patrons would agree with you on this one."

He walked over to my camera, which was presumably still taking photos. "Uh, am I going to have to delete a camera full of Aubrey selfies?"

"They're not selfies. They're purely for educational purposes," I said. "I wanted to see what I couldn't see."

"What does that mean?"

"I wanted to be able to see the progression of images as I created them."

"Well, for something educational they're actually pretty cool," he said.

"Huh?" I was genuinely surprised. I got up and went to stand beside him.

"See that?" he said, quickly scrolling through the photos on the camera. "As the light changes, so does your canvas."

The photos were interesting, but also disappointing. He seemed more impressed by the time-lapse shifting of the light than my drawing.

On our flight to Rome, Jeff and I had the row to ourselves, so I sat by the window with my feet stretched across the center seat and tucked under his thigh. He sat upright, typing away on his laptop and stretching his legs into the aisle when necessary. The sun was shining directly in through our window. Most of the other passengers had pulled their shades down, but I kept mine open. I lifted my hand to the glass, felt the heat of the sun beneath my fingertips, and did my best to ignore the RP line that split my hand in two.

"Blue light is hotter is than red, right?" I asked Jeff.

"What?"

"Do you remember the Bunsen burners in Schultz's class? How a blue flame was a higher temperature than the red flame?" I repeated.

"Yeah. What about it?"

"Maybe this is crazy, but I was thinking that maybe I could create an art installation about light and the way we interact with it. How cool would it be if I could get iconic paintings and display them with colors of light that are designed to make you feel a certain way. Don't you think that'd be cool?"

"You want the honest truth?" he asked. "It feels a little gimmicky."

"I think manipulation of light would be pretty innovative and cool," I argued. "What if we took Picasso's Blue Period and cast the work in a gentle gray light?"

"What if you did?"

"It would change the way people felt about the paintings! Give old works new meaning."

"So fifty years from now, you want somebody else taking your paintings and giving them new meaning?" he countered.

Jeff was right, I wanted to find something that worked within the confines of everything I already knew, but maybe that was the wrong approach.

"When do you think I'll be able to see your app in action?" I asked, looking at his screen.

"Wanna see what I have now?"

"Sure."

Unbuckling his seatbelt, Jeff scooted into the middle seat

and I pulled my legs up to my chest. He closed a bunch of windows on his computer and opened a program called Beta.

"So basically this is a combination of Yelp, Instagram Video, and Foursquare for travelers. Everyone has a profile, and you can upload videos up to five seconds long. They're sorted by location using the GPS on your phone, then your friends and random strangers vote on the videos and the one with the most likes gets to be the Mayor of that location. So let's say I travel to China and I post this," Jeff said, as he played a five-second clip of the Great Wall. "I've got videos at every place we've been, even restaurants, and as soon as I get access to Wifi I'll upload them all. I'm creating filters too, so people can make black and white 1920s-style stuff or 90s VHS video."

"Wow," I said, looking at a page more akin to Craigslist (with a huge list of countries) than the cool location-based apps I had on my iPhone. "That sounds really awesome," I added with forced enthusiasm.

"You don't think it's cool?" He knew me too well.

"I think the concept is amazing, but the layout and graphics need a little work?"

He laughed, "Yeah. They need *a lot* of work."

Breathing a sigh of relief, I asked, "How long before you release it?"

"A while. Ideally, what I'd like to have it do is use the GPS on your phone to track you as you move, but that's tricky because right now not everyone who travels gets an international data plan." He clicked on Beijing, and another smaller list of locations popped up in alphabetical order.

They were all places we'd been and he had added videos. "But don't you see how this could revolutionize traveling for people? You'd land anywhere in the world and instantly be able to spot the ten coolest things within 100 yards."

"No, yeah. I mean, it's a super-cool idea, and I don't know anything about this so I will completely not be offended if you think my ideas are dumb, but can you afford a graphic artist? Actually, you'd need like ten of them, right? Google offers the most comprehensive map in the world and even they don't cover everywhere right?"

"Yea, all of that stuff is expensive and not exactly in my ex-teacher budget," he said, with faded enthusiasm.

"But don't these other apps operate like companies?" I asked. I hadn't meant to discourage him. "Couldn't you apply for financial backing? I just think if you're going to do this, you should go full throttle, get some graphic artists on board, and make it as intuitive as the other apps that are out there," I said. Jeff nodded, looking down at the computer screen again and internalizing my suggestion. "Go big or go home, right?" I added.

"Right." He moved back to his aisle seat as I stretched my legs out again and wedged my toes into their usual position under his legs. He didn't say anything at first but then after a few moments, he looked down at my feet and said, "You know, you could just wrap a sweater around your feet."

"Not the same," I replied.

He opened his mouth to say something, but the intercom beeped and the pilot made an announcement.

"Good afternoon ladies and gentlemen and welcome aboard United Airlines. I wanted to take this moment to welcome you all aboard flight 773 to Rome. Your flight attendants should be coming down the aisles with your complementary beverages, and in just a few minutes here we're going to fly over the Pyramids of Egypt, so be on the lookout for that. On behalf of everyone here at United, we hope you enjoy your flight."

Passengers around us started opening their window shades and craning their necks to see. I kept hearing "Can you see them?", "Is that them?", and "Have we passed it?" until the captain, like a magician perfectly timing his reveal, dipped us below the clouds and right over the Pyramids.

"Jeff, come see it," I said, my eyes glued to the window.

He carefully lifted his tray so his computer wouldn't slide off and scooted next to me again. My face was pressed so close that I could see my breath on the window, and at first the three pyramids didn't seem all that impressive. But as we got closer, their massive sizes came into perspective. Just as the California coastline was prominently divided between land and sea, here it was desert and industry (and agriculture). The three enormous tombs were islands in a sea of sand that washed up against the city like waves on a beach. Beyond the 'shore', geometrically laid out blocks of housing and infrastructure displayed a gentrified culture. From above, the towns appeared static, like a photograph, until I noticed a tiny black speck moving along a paved road: a car. It was about as big as the period at the end of a sentence—the pyramids were enormous.

"It's crazy, isn't it? What man can do?" I asked.

"Yeah," Jeff replied as he leaned over behind me and looked out. I could feel his steady breath along the back of my neck.

Once they were out of our vantage point, we both leaned back. "Do you remember that Egyptian-themed party Mrs. Dawson threw for us in the sixth grade?" I asked.

"As a fifth grader, I was called upon to serve the sixth graders, so yeah I remember that party especially well. I thought her reveal of the camels on the menu at the end was the best," he laughed.

"That's right!" I remembered. "They were chocolate cookies in the shape of camels."

"For that alone, she was my favorite elementary school teacher," Jeff said.

"That's interesting because that toga party was the first time I remember considering a career in art. I wore all this plastic jewelry, had my eyes painted dark black, and had on a white tank top with a tablecloth wrapped around my waist. And I remember looking at everyone and thinking, the only reason they even know what I'm supposed to look like is because of some ancient paintings someone found on a wall hundreds of years later. All of this is because of those paintings. It really kind of affected me," I said.

"I didn't know that. That's pretty cool, Aubs."

"As far as we know, they were one of the first to use pictures to tell a story. And that story became part of a legacy they left, which provided us with historical context."

"But your paintings look nothing like the hieroglyphics."

"The influence is there, it's just subtle."

"That's art lingo for 'You're too stupid to recognize my genius,' isn't it?"

"Something like that," I grinned.

I grabbed my 7x9-inch piece of cotton that airlines liked to call a pillow and stuck it on Jeff's shoulder to take a nap. I kept my eyes closed for ten minutes, hoping that sleep would carry me away, but it didn't. Frustrated, I sat up.

Jeff, who had been looking at his passport, snapped it shut. "Have you traveled a lot?" I asked, realizing I didn't know.

"Some."

"Can I see it?"

He handed me his passport and I flipped through the pages. Mexico, Greece, Germany, and France came before the stamps we now shared from China, India, and Jordan. The stamps for Greece, Germany, and France were all made within a three-week span of each other.

"Did you backpack through Europe after college?"

"I did."

"With Veronica?"

"Yes."

"What's your story with her?"

"What do you mean? Like how we met?"

"Yeah."

"We met in college," he replied.

"Could you be any more vague?"

He laughed. "She was friends with my next door neighbor my junior year and she'd always come over to use our apartment laundry because she said hers sucked."

"You fell in love while folding your underwear together?" I smiled.

"It was a little more nuanced than that, but yes."

"Why did you think she was the one?"

He shrugged, "We had been together for a long time and

things were good. At least, I thought they were."

"So why did you guys break it off?"

"From the moment we started planning the wedding things went downhill. We couldn't decide on a date, we started fighting, stopped having sex, and then eventually she moved out."

"What if she changes her mind?"

"She's not going to change her mind," he said, definitively.

"Her loss," I smiled. "Do you remember telling me that after Freddy Ehrmann broke up with me in the tenth grade?" I asked.

Jeff smiled, "How could I forget Freddy the Magnificent?"

I let out a deep laugh. I had forgotten Freddy went on to become a magician. No joke—he was inaugurated into the society of magicians at the Magic Castle in Hollywood when I was a junior in college.

"You told me that if Freddy didn't see how amazing I was, he didn't deserve me. Not bad advice for a sixteen-year-old," I nudged.

"So what about you?" Jeff asked. "Any near misses?"

"No. I never got to that stage. Apparently, I am too independent," I smiled.

The overhead speakers turned on and static noise filled the cabin before the pilot announced our descent into Rome.

Whispers turned into regular chatter and the other passengers began packing up their things in preparation for landing. Stretching, I pulled my feet out from under Jeff and slid them back into my strappy sandals.

"Is it bad that I just want to go straight to our hotel and take a super-long nap?" I asked.

"No, but there's this gift shop on the other side of the airport that's supposed to be world-renowned, and I really wanted to check it out first."

"What's this place called?" I asked.

"Trust me, you are not going to be disappointed."

I eyed him suspiciously. "Why are you being so secretive?"

"I'm not. I know you're tired—let's just stop by. It'll be quick."

Once in the terminal, I followed Jeff back and forth between the airport stores and kiosks looking for this "amazing gift shop." Forty minutes later, he stopped in front of Gate 63.

"You know what? You're going to kill me, but I just realized it's not in this airport." He paused for a moment, looking distressed. "It's in the one in Paris." Just then, an announcement for the last boarding call to Paris came over the intercom. I looked at him confused.

"What?"

Still playing it cool, he said, "Yeah, stupid me, it's this cute little boutique in Paris. You heard the lady, last call for boarding, wanna go?"

Maybe it was lack of sleep, but it took me a minute to realize that this mystery store was all part of a scheme to surprise me. I started jumping up and down.

"Yes! Yes! Absolutely yes!" I shrieked.

As we took our seats on the flight, my knees began bobbing excitedly. I had always wanted to visit Paris and I couldn't believe that in two hours I would be in the most romantic city in the world.

"Listen," Jeff started in an uncharacteristically serious

tone, "I know I can't take back missing your parents' funeral, but I know how much Paris meant to them and to you. So I guess what I'm trying to say is, I'm sorry."

"Is that why you booked this little detour? Because you were feeling guilty?" I felt genuinely touched that he had gone to such lengths to apologize.

"Sort of," he said. "Back in China, I was thinking about your gallery opening and I remembered seeing that painting —"

"*Midnight in Paris,*" I cut in.

"Right, and I guess I thought coming here might help you get closure if you still needed it."

"Thanks, Jeff," I said, pulling him into an awkward sideways hug as he smiled sheepishly. When I realized how difficult it must have been for him to book a trip for me that would be a constant reminder of what he no longer had, I was even more humbled. And I think it was right then that I understood how much Veronica meant to him and why he would've done anything to try and salvage their relationship; including missing my parents' funeral.

With only three weeks' notice, the only hotel with a reasonable price was in Montmartre, just north of the city center near the red-light district of Paris. Jeff thought it might feel too seedy, but I reminded him that Venice was no Beverly Hills.

The location was nice and the concierge friendly, but good lord the place was small. When the elevator opened, Jeff and I stepped inside and it was at capacity. Forced to squeeze into one corner with our two carry-on-sized suitcases pressed up against the elevator door, Jeff's face was pale and stoic for the entire thirty-second ride. The stairs, we later discovered, were no better. Designed to maximize space, the narrow stairwell was an enclosed spiral, which meant that only half the step was functional. In an attempt to ease his nerves, I pointed at a sign above his head that read, "Maximum occupancy 4" and told him I badly wanted to add the word "children" at the end. If he thought it was funny, he didn't laugh—not that I blamed him.

When Jeff opened the door to our room, I gave him a sideways glance as we both stood in front of the single queen size bed in the middle of a petite room.

"Again? I know it's been a while since you've gotten any, but seriously?" I quipped.

"Oh shut up, I'll sleep on the floor if you want, but it was all they had."

"Doesn't look like there's much room on the floor either," I said. There was a two-foot perimeter around the bed for access and that was it.

Jeff also took note of this, smirked, and said, "Agreed. I guess we're sharing." He dropped our bags and plopped down on the bed. I followed suit, surprised at how aware I had become of his close proximity to me. Feeling oddly uncomfortable, I slid off the bed and went over to the window, which was low to the ground, and pushed it open to find a small platform. Taking a huge step up onto the ledge and then another small step out onto an iron balcony not much larger than a park bench, I leaned over the railing to look out.

Across from us were the backsides of brick industrial office buildings broken up by an occasional mom-and-pop shop or convenience store. Dim street lamps and neon signs lit the sidewalks.

I turned and faced Jeff, who was still on the bed. "I love the architecture of Paris. Where else would a large window open up to a balcony. It's so... *cozy*." Jeff nodded. "Everything is connected. Your window is your balcony..."

Peeling himself off the bed, Jeff joined me. "You call it efficient, I call it a death trap."

I smiled at his joke and wondered if he felt it too—that special something in the air.

CHAPTER TEN

Midnight in Paris

Of all the bedtime stories my dad told me as a kid, Paris was the only one he retold with consistency. Repeated like the pages of a book permanently imprinted in his mind, the story always made my dad the most animated. I think he believed their love story to be greater than Romeo and Juliet's.

Blasting the air conditioning to a cool sixty-five degrees, my dad would light up the gas fireplace and toss in a couple of cinnamon logs. The spicy aroma quickly filled the room as I nestled myself into his lap with a blanket and waited for him to hand me my hot chocolate. "For the young..." he'd say, handing me my cup, "and for the old," he'd finish, taking the other for himself. "On a bright summer day in Houston, your mom and I cozied up on an airplane headed for Paris." He held the album out in front of us as he read from nonexistent text. "This was our two-year anniversary and your mom had been talking about this trip since the day we graduated from college. Now, being the romantic that I was, I had lots of surprises in store for my pretty lady, and the first one was a single red rose for the airplane, which was carefully hidden in the inside pocket of my jacket. But as I reached for the flower, I was extremely disappointed to discover that most of the petals had fallen off! *What happened?* I wondered to myself, before remembering the scuffle I'd had with our paunchy suitcases and the overhead bin. Looking down the aisle behind us, sure enough, there was a scattering of red rose petals on the floor. I turned to Marie, my head hung low in shame with the sad-looking stem in my hand, and to my surprise she burst into joyous laughter. 'Oh sweetie, that was so thoughtful.'" My dad mimicked my mom's voice terribly, but he loved to do it anyway.

"And you know what she did?" he asked, rhetorically. "She hopped out of her seat, collected the petals, and suggested that we leave one everywhere we go as a memento of us being there."

Pictures of my mom or dad holding a rose petal in various places accompanied the story. In one, my mom posed in front of the window on the flight from Houston to Paris. Another captured both of my parents in their small hotel room, a pile of petals left on the nightstand. My favorite was the photo of my mom sitting on the metro train with a map of Paris behind her head—a petal taped to the center. The silly ones like my dad biting into a croissant outside of *Le Croissant* with the petal in the foreground always made me laugh.

"Your mom and I walked all around the city, from the Arc

de Triomphe to the Avenue des Champs-Élysées, then hopped on a train to see the Notre Dame Cathedral, and when day became night we made our way to the Eiffel Tower. We stood in a long line of tourists all wanting to get to the top, and when we finally reached the window, I went to pay and found that my wallet was not there! Quickly retracing my steps, the only plausible explanation was that I'd been pickpocketed on the metro. I turned my pockets inside out and some petals fell to the ground. *Gosh darn it!* I yelled to myself, embarrassed to have to ask Marie for money. 'I didn't bring a wallet, remember?' she replied, reminding me that I had told her not to bring anything with her for the exact reason that I was wallet-less at the moment—thieves."

"This is the good part," I squealed.

He smiled before clearing his throat and getting serious again. "So there I was, standing at the bottom of the Eiffel Tower, with the most beautiful woman in the world, and I couldn't take her up. Your mom could read the disappointment on my face and said, 'It's okay honey, the view from down here is just as good. Plus, we can come back tomorrow!' And when I still didn't say anything—my anger festering and boiling inside—she pulled me out of the line and said, 'Come, let's dance.' Reluctantly, I followed her over to where a street violinist was playing and even though I hated to dance, especially in public, I obliged." My dad's uncanny ability to make a romantic gesture seem incredibly macho was one of his many charming qualities.

After giving me a tight hug and a kiss on the cheek, causing me to laugh, he continued. "So there we are dancing, with me stiff as ever and raging mad at a thief I know I'll never find, when your mom looks up at me and says, 'Ray, I've had the most wonderful time in Paris. Thank you, honey.' Still stewing in my own thoughts, I only really heard the words 'thank you' and was flabbergasted. The whole time I'd been feeling like I ruined Paris for her and was kicking myself for it. The music stopped, I leaned down to kiss her, and the two of us went on to live happily ever after."

"Did you know then that you were going to marry Mom?"

"Yes," he would smile.

A photo of my mom kissing a petal at the top of the Eiffel Tower was on the last page of the Paris section, but my dad ended the story with them dancing every time. I loved that story.

I stared at it for a long moment, perplexed. "Humm."

"What?" Jeff asked, not even looking at the Eiffel Tower.

"I've always imagined what it would be like to stand here and I can't believe that I'm actually here."

At the ticket line to the Eiffel Tower, a sea of loving gestures surrounded us: a gentle squeeze of the shoulders, swinging entwined hands, laughter followed by a tiptoed kiss, arms wrapped around each other's waists. Jeff was staring at the tiptoe kissing couple next to us. "What did Veronica think of the Eiffel Tower?" I asked.

"She thought it was ugly. To be honest, our trip was kind of annoying. She spent most of the time shopping, which made no sense to me 'cause every store she went into was a chain that we had in L.A.: Gucci, Prada, Chanel. Are they really that different in another country?"

I caught a touch of sadness in his voice and asked, "But she must've loved being at the top?"

He shrugged, "We didn't go up."

"You came all the way to Paris and didn't go up the Eiffel Tower?"

"Nope."

"Well, do you want to?"

"I wouldn't have brought you here if I didn't," he smiled, handing the cashier €28 in exchange for our lift tickets.

I looked up at the massive steel plates and bolts that made up an intricate, interlocking weave of parts that held the Tower together. Its lack of color made it hard to describe as 'pretty' but there was no denying the innovative structural design and engineering.

The initial ascent reminded me of the glass elevator in Charlie and the Chocolate Factory, which moved not only up and down but sideways as well. We were moving at a diagonal, which was just like going up an escalator, but for some reason I kept expecting us all to tilt sideways into each other. The elevator was packed to the max with people, and when I looked down I noticed that Jeff was shifting on his feet and tapping them nervously.

I slipped my hand into his, squeezing it tight. He looked down at me and laughed, realizing how transparent his discomfort was. Then, he lifted his head and sighed deeply as the elevator doors finally opened.

A chilly breeze greeted us as we emerged onto a small platform at the top of the Tower. Jeff released my hand, and I curled it into a fist before quickly stuffing it into my pocket.

I was so distracted by the hauntingly beautiful view that I

failed to notice the goosebumps that had formed on my arms. Standing up there was like being on a Ferris wheel at the pivotal point of descent, and perpetually waiting to exhale. I watched as the city, shrunken down to the size of Monopoly pieces, ran on autopilot.

"Doin' alright down there?" Jeff joked behind me. Squeezed in-between other tourists who all wanted to stand at the edge, I stood shoulder to shoulder with strangers.

"I do kind of wish I was your height right now," I said.

"I could lift you up on my shoulders."

"That would be awesome," I replied, jokingly. He started to kneel down. "Oh my gosh! I was kidding! Get up. Don't be crazy."

"Suit yourself," he said as he straightened back up.

A decent-sized space opened up to my left and Jeff slid into it. The light had begun to change and we stood with a direct view of the reddish-pink sky reflected onto the Arc de Triomphe in the distance and the Seine River directly below. Like an intricately spun web, the French gate stood at the center of the city with its streets dispersing outward equidistant from each other.

"I love it," Jeff said, gazing out at the vast and sprawling city.

"What?"

"The perspective. Up here, nothing down there seems as important," he said.

"Yeah, but knowing that the world down there is the one we live in is kind of depressing, right? I mean, look at the people. They all want to matter, but from our perspective..." I trailed off. There were thousands of people moving about below, all planting seeds and hoping to sprout some kind of flower, when the reality of it was most of us would amount to little more than blades of grass in an enormous lawn.

"You don't actually believe that," he replied.

I looked up at him with a half-broken smile. "Yeah, I kinda do." The occasional gust of wind made the cold hard to ignore as I hugged my body for warmth.

"Do you want to head back down?" he asked.

"In a bit," I replied, my lips quivering. Cold as I was, I wanted—and perhaps needed—the moment to linger. Without saying a word, Jeff moved behind me and wrapped his arms around me as if it were the most natural thing in the world. I could feel his every movement, right down to the muscles in his arms tensing and relaxing as his lungs took deep breaths. Shifting only slightly, I cupped my hands over his wrists and pressed them to my chest to reciprocate the gesture.

"Have you been up to the Griffith Observatory?" I asked. "My friend Rusty took me there the day I arrived in Venice. He brought a jug of wine that he poured into red plastic cups and we made a toast to my arrival."

"Of course, yeah, I've been there," Jeff said, his warm breath grazing the top of my head.

I smiled. "Sometimes I'd drive up there by myself just to look down at the city. I'd look at the hundreds of thousands of people moving around below and remind myself that we all have big dreams. Every single person down there wants the same thing I do. Well, maybe not the *exact* same thing, but we all want to be successful and not just in a monetary sense. We want recognition. We want the world to remember us."

Jeff said nothing.

"But I guess we can't all be Picassos or Rembrandts."

"Why not?"

"I'm just saying, maybe I need to be a little more realistic about my expectations."

"People who are realistic about their expectations never aspire to be greater than what they are."

I scrunched my face, perplexed at his insight. "Okay Socrates, where did that come from?"

"From my last fortune cookie." I laughed.

I wanted to believe him—that everything happened for a reason and people ended up where they were supposed to. But I'd run into one too many colleagues who had shifted away from art and settled into other careers to hold on to the notion that hard work eventually led to success.

"We should head down," Jeff said, gently sliding his wrists out from under my hands and stepping away from me.

"Yeah," I relented with disappointment.

With Jeff's arms around me, my world was only as large as the two of us and I found that comforting. But within seconds of us moving, a group of teens crowded into the space and that cocoon of safety evaporated.

We took the elevator down in silence. Outside, shades of pink, orange, and red had been replaced by dark blues, blacks, and scatterings of yellow cast up from the city lights.

Back on the ground again, we walked for about two blocks when all of a sudden a flash of brightness lit up everything around us and we turned around to see the Eiffel Tower lit from bottom to top in yellow lights. Blinking on and off in scattered patterns and then jetting from the base to the top and back down again, the tower transformed into a show host saying, *Welcome to the city of love, now come dance with me.* It illuminated the area with a glow that commanded all attention, like exploding fireworks without the boom.

"Wow," I said as we headed back over to it.

"Yeah, I'm really glad I got to see it this time," he smiled.

A scattering of merchants flooded the already crowded area selling all kinds of glow-in-the-dark tchotchkes, souvenirs, and various paintings of the Paris cityscape. To our left, a violinist played a hauntingly beautiful melody. A significant crowd quickly formed and the streets became congested with traffic. I smiled, feeling as if I had walked into my own painting. Jeff's eyes were on me, waiting for me to say something, and I let him wait. I was standing on the edge of my parents' memory—I couldn't chance missing it.

As the lights danced up and down the tower I let myself imagine my mom and dad moving about this space we now shared. I pictured them standing in line, taking photos with the petals, and dancing to the music. Then it dawned on me that this was their story, not mine. In another life, the three of us might have danced in a circle to the sounds of Paris, but this wasn't another life.

"Dance with me," Jeff said.

"Thanks, but I'm okay," I replied, lowering my gaze.

"It wasn't a question—now hurry up before I change my mind," he said as he placed his hands gently on my waist and started to guide me back and forth.

I wasn't in the mood to dance, but I liked being in his arms. Pulling myself closer to him, I rested my cheek against his chest, and together we danced to the melancholy violin.

We moved in unison through two songs as other couples and a small audience formed to watch and join in. I didn't want the music to stop. But like all good things, it eventually came to an end, and when it did, I looked up at Jeff. We stood there for a moment suspended in time before I reached up, pulled his face to mine, and kissed him. His lips were cold but soft.

I pulled away, holding his gaze for a moment then looking down at my feet in embarrassment. "Thanks for an unforgettable trip."

Tilting my chin up with his finger, he smiled and said, "You're welcome."

His eyes held mine for another moment. But the intensity was too much and I had to look away. "Are you hungry?" I asked, breaking the silence.

"Starved."

"Want to go get food?"

"I made a reservation at this place called Opaque," he replied, looking at his watch.

"Is it cloudy there or something?"

"Not exactly. It's trendy."

"Oh, my favorite," I replied, smiling only half-flirtatiously. It was awkward to try and turn on the charm with someone I'd known for over twenty years.

We walked just a few yards before I shouted, "Wait! Hold on a second." I rushed over to buy a rose from a street peddler walking by. "Will you pose for me?" I asked him.

"You're buying me a flower?" he asked quizzically. I started plucking the petals off the stem. I dropped a handful of them on the ground beside him, stuffed a few into his pocket, and then added a single one to the palm of his hand. "Now, I need you to pretend—"

"I know what I'm supposed to do," he said, cutting me off. I had forgotten that Jeff was sometimes privy to storytime as well. I walked back to position myself for the photo.

I paused for a moment before taking the picture. A couple behind Jeff stood in a kissing pose while a stranger took their photo, and for the first time in years I considered the moment to be sweet. I smiled to myself.

Like most restaurants, Opaque was located on a busy street surrounded by shops and other brightly-lit restaurants. The exterior, however, was nothing more than a wall of black with a small, dim placard that read: Opaque Dining Door Handle, with an arrow pointing to a camouflaged, black steel handle. As Jeff pulled open the door, I noticed braille letters at the bottom of the nameplate.

"Are you sure this is a restaurant and not a strip-club-slash-whorehouse, slash-front-for-drug-deals?" I joked.

"I'm positive," he replied simply. Once inside, we stood in a small, dimly lit room roughly the size of a freight elevator.

A hostess wearing dark sunglasses greeted us at the entrance saying, "Bienvenue a Opaque."

"Bonjour, uh, J'ai une reservation a Anderson."

"Ah, yes. Welcome to Opaque Mr. Anderson," she replied in startlingly good English, obviously aware that Jeff's accent and fumbled sentence meant he was American. "Have you dined with us before?"

"First-timers."

"Well, we're delighted to have you as our guests. As you probably read, our restaurant is served by a staff that is blind. Our philosophy is that without being able to see the food, your sense of taste is heightened and the meal becomes a whole different experience."

As I listened to hostess explain, I turned to Jeff in a sort of panic and asked, "How did you know? Did Rati tell you?"

"About this restaurant? No. A friend told me about it a while ago, but I didn't actually think of it until I saw you painting on the balcony with a blindfold," Jeff said. "Why, you think it's lame?"

He obviously didn't know.

"No," I said. *Just highly coincidental,* I thought.

The hostess asked us to hold each other's hand and follow her as she guided us to our seats. Taking my hand, Jeff squeezed it and whispered, "Don't worry, I checked the menu in advance, there's nothing weird or gross."

I laughed, "I'm sure we'll be okay." What wasn't okay was the tingling sensation I felt, yet again, in the hand that he took hold of with such ease.

Once we were seated, our waiter immediately began an introduction to our place settings. We fumbled around a bit, slowly feeling for the surface of our plate, the location of our silverware, and the stem of our wine glasses. In case we knocked anything over, they had staff standing by to clear away any hazardous messes. The menu (spoken to us) was small, offering only four different main courses: chicken, steak, fish, or vegetarian. We both chose steak.

"For wine, we have a Sauvignon Blanc, Pinot Noir, Pinot Grigio, and Merlot—all local French wineries. To accompany the steak dish, our chef recommends the Pinot Noir: It's a 2009 medium-bodied, fruitful red wine. Is that okay with you? Or if you would prefer another bottle, we're happy to switch," the waiter said.

"Pinot Noir is my favorite," I said.

"I'm good with that," Jeff added.

"Great, you won't be disappointed," the waiter replied. I listened as the squeaky spin of a metal wine opener met the bottle's rubbery cork. After a slow pull and faint pop, I heard the sound of liquid fill our glasses. "Enjoy," he said before walking away.

"Hold on," Jeff said as I cautiously felt around for my wine glass. "Reach forward with your left hand until you find mine." Slowly, I slid my hand across the table until the tips of my fingers met with his and he gently took my hand in his. "Now, if we slide our glasses over toward where our hands meet, we'll have a reference point to toast." Lifting my glass with my right hand, I slowly extended it toward Jeff until they met in an awkward clank.

"Not bad," I laughed.

"Pretty cool though, right?" he asked.

"It's sweeter than I thought it would be. The wine, I mean," I fumbled. *Sweeter than I thought it would be?* What was I saying? I was trying to sound cool and cultured, only I was really coming off as a bumbling idiot. And with Jeff of all people, who I was sure could see right through it. "The streets are super-cute here and the people are fabulously sexy," I added with a cringe. Thank God he couldn't see my face.

"You think Parisians are sexy?" he laughed. "Please

enlighten me on how a sexy nation looks."

About the same way your voice sounds, I thought. "There's something about the way they walk. It's more of a sashay. They're thin with defined stomachs and hips that swing from side to side with purpose."

"Um, you should paint a picture of that," he mused.

I slid my hand from his to slap him, but he caught it and held it firm, almost daring me to pull away again.

Was this really happening? And what was 'this,' exactly? A date? For a brief moment being in the dark was comforting. The unlit space provided a kind of shield between me and everyone else. To be honest, I'm not sure how I got all the way through half a glass of wine before I understood the gravity of my situation. I could hear the sounds of mixed chatter and the clinks of silverware meeting with people's plates, but spatially all I knew was what I could touch. Void of pretty purses, patterned clothing, fancy hairdos, chiseled faces, or expressions of any kind, everything was dark.

"The house soup for today is a creamy French onion soup, made from the finest local provolone and Swiss cheese in France. Your spoon will be located at the top of your plate and crackers are in the center of the table. Bon appétit," the waiter said, breaking into my thoughts. I was so ensconced in my own problems that I barely registered Jeff's hand break from mine. All of a sudden this whole world, which I had been traveling across, shrunk down to a small space. Confined solely to the elements within my reach, I had no context for anything other than what was near me. Did the restaurant seat forty people or four hundred? I had no idea. Were we underdressed? Should any of this even matter to me?

I moved my fingers along the outer edge of the plate in front of me until I found my spoon. Doing my best to steady my now shaking hand I lifted the spoon to my mouth surprised at how easily I found my lips.

"I think it's the best soup I've ever had. I wonder if it looks as good as it tastes," he laughed.

I forced a laugh and said, "I can't imagine anything looking better than this tastes right now."

"I'm really glad you decided to come on this trip with me, Aubs," Jeff said. I wanted the lights to turn on right then so that I see the expression of warmth I knew was on his face.

With suspiciously perfect timing, the waiter came by just as I'd finished my soup. "I'll take that," he said from somewhere behind me. The plate in front of me was taken as another landed heavily onto the table. "Alright, we have two medium rare filet mignons with a side of grilled asparagus and garlic mashed potatoes. To your left is a warm towel and then using your knife and fork you can feel around your plate for where things are. I personally find it easier to use my fingers. Some people find it distasteful, so I'll leave it up to you. Do not, however, try and use your finger as your fork when cutting, it's dangerous," he said wryly. "Enjoy."

"I honestly don't know how blind people do this," Jeff said. "Every little thing requires so much attention."

"They say our greatest quality as humans is our ability to adapt," I said, unsure if I was trying to convince Jeff or myself of its truth.

Almost immediately after I made my sweeping comment about adapting, I was challenged with the simple task of feeding myself. Using my index finger, I slowly poked around my plate until I memorized the orientation of my food: steak to the left, grilled asparagus up top, and potatoes to my right. The thought of having to orient myself every time I sat down with a plate of food was enough to make me want to only eat finger foods for the rest of my life. Scooping potatoes was the easiest because when I stuck my fork in I knew something would stick. The veggies were far more difficult to discern and after the first few futile attempts I decided to just use my fingers. To cut the steak I brushed my fork along the outer edges of the meat, moved the fork inward to where I guessed was about a centimeter, then cut. I raised my fork toward my nose, smelling pepper and charcoal, before biting into the most sumptuous, slightly-too-large piece of steak I'd ever had.

I took a gulp of wine. The darkness made it hard to concentrate on anything but going blind. Laughter, chatter, and the clanking of utensils was louder than a typical restaurant. Everyone seemed to be enjoying the experience, but only because they knew that once they stepped outside the doors, they'd see again. So, while I loved what Opaque represented—a heightened tasting experience created by the blocking of one's visual sense—I wasn't on the same tasting adventure.

"You're not saying much," Jeff commented.

"It's loud and unless they'll let us stay all night I need to concentrate," I lied.

Jeff laughed, "But it's good?"

"Best meal I've ever had," I said. This part was true, but I was on the fence as to whether the food was made better by my actual inability to see it or by the new experience of dining in the dark. "What do you think?"

"The food is great. I'm on the fence about the experience," he said.

"How so?"

"Well, it's interesting because they have successfully kept me from using my visual sense, but I'm still distracted—it's just by sounds rather than things I can see," he said.

"Right. Like instead of noticing a woman with too much plastic surgery I notice pitches in people's voices."

"Exactly, and I think we're annoyed by the same laughter," he said. He was right. Somewhere to my left was a high-pitched cackle. "Do you think blind people recognize voices the way we recognize faces?"

"Not. If. I. Talk. Like. This," Jeff said, using a robotic tone.

I laughed in spite of myself. Jeff was never one to take himself too seriously, and I found comfort in his presence.

With over a decade of friendship between us, we had tons of stories to rehash. Jeff brought up the time we worked the Houston Street Fair together and spent half the time eating corn dogs instead of selling them. I brought up the time we tried to build a tree house with sticks, twigs, and string—we were seven.

As we reminisced, I noticed that Jeff and I finished the entire bottle of wine, plus a glass each of Moscato, which came with our dessert. We were drunk.

As we stumbled home, we laughed hysterically about how angry the super-nice receptionist had gotten when we accidentally started to walk out the door before signing the final bill. I thought it was hilarious that Jeff was embarrassed because the receptionist didn't act like it was a mistake but rather that we were trying to dine and dash. Genuine by nature, Jeff always got flustered when someone accused him of wrongdoing. In turn, he fumbled his words, and it made him seem like he actually *was* guilty.

When we got to our room Jeff opened the door for me but grabbed my arm as we stepped inside. He closed the door behind us, pressing me up against it in a deep kiss. Finally. I pulled his faced toward me, kissing him back with a hunger I hadn't felt in years. He unzipped the back of my already loose-fitting dress. My gown fell to the floor and I pulled off his shirt as he unzipped his pants. I felt my heartbeat quicken and hoped he wouldn't notice as he moved away from my lips and traveled down my body.

When he came back up to kiss me again the gaze on his face was so intense that it rendered me speechless, and when he tilted his head and leaned down until his lips met mine, I felt my body surrender to him. Picking me up by the waist, he carried me to the bed, my legs wrapped firmly around his hips. Our clothes lay in a heap on the floor as he set me down gently. He hovered over my lips briefly, before moving lower to kiss my neck and breasts. Letting out a breath I didn't realize I was holding, I pulled his face up from my neck and kissed him deeply—I wanted to be connected to every part of him, an inch of space between us was too much. Jeff moved inside me. I wasn't sure if it was lust or love, but at the height of intensity my toes curled and I had to move my hands from his shoulders to keep from digging my fingers too deeply into him. Jeff finished soon thereafter, collapsing down next to me before rolling over to pull me into the curve of his naked body.

"Wow," he said.

"Yeah," I breathed, letting myself sink into the comfort of his embrace.

We fell asleep soon thereafter.

The next morning, I carefully slid myself out of bed and into a robe, grabbed my paints, and pulled a chair up to the window (the balcony was too small to paint on). Everything about Paris felt like a dream and I was afraid that if I didn't capture the moment quickly, I'd lose it when the sun rose and reality set in. Quietly setting up my easel and pouring out bags of pigment, I mixed the colors I wanted and sat back to fold a crane out of paper while formulating a new interpretation of *Midnight in Paris*.

By tilting my head to the side, I worked around the thickening RP line, which had become central to my vision. Doing my best to concentrate on my brush strokes, I changed the perspective to an omniscient one looking down from the sky. At the top of the Tower, I painted a couple holding each other as Jeff and I had. Using the space on the canvas to create distance, I painted another couple dancing far below. Dabbing my brush in the Mars pigments I'd picked up in India, I made the Eiffel Tower light up with a bright yellow hue against the deep blue night. The foreboding darkness in the first painting was all but gone and what remained was a kind of whimsical fairytale romance. I had no idea what any of last night meant, but I knew that, at least momentarily, it felt like love. While I moved my brush across the canvas, I thought about my parents and wished there was a phone line to the afterlife. I wanted to know if our stories were similar. I wanted to giggle and tell my mom how amazing it felt to be here with Jeff. *Hey Mom, do you think Jeff and I could be as happy as you and Dad?*

"It's incredible Aubs, better than the last one," Jeff said, rolling out of bed in his boxers and heading for the coffee maker to grab the pot.

"Thanks," I replied, smiling.

When I heard the sink turn on and the sound of his toothbrush scrubbing back and forth, I realized I hadn't yet brushed my own teeth and I quickly looked around for gum. I wanted him to think I woke up with fresh breath.

"It's early," he remarked, spitting into the sink before gargling and washing off the head of his toothbrush.

"It is. You should go back to bed," I whispered, my voice not yet ready to function at full volume.

Without a word, he took the coffee pot, now filled with water, back to the machine. With no gum in sight, I quickly darted into the bathroom, rinsed my mouth, and followed him back over to the window.

He studied the painting carefully, and I worried he might read too much into it. I had been working on autopilot and wasn't exactly discreet about who the gentleman was.

"Are my shoulders really that broad?" he asked with a smirk on his face.

"Would you prefer dainty shoulders?"

"No, no this is great. You made me look rugged and handsome," he remarked, regarding the tall, bright-eyed guy with chiseled arms in *Midnight in Paris II.*

I rolled my eyes and laughed as he kissed me on the cheek and walked back to the now-full coffee pot to pour each of us a glass.

"To traveling," he said, raising his glass in a toast.

"To traveling," I smiled, clanking my mug to his.

CHAPTER ELEVEN

Solitude

"Hello? Earth to Aubrey…"

"Huh? What?" I said, snapping to. Jeff was showing me a map of the Coliseum.

"I asked where you wanted to start."

I shrugged. "Wherever you want is fine with me." The truth was, I hadn't stopped thinking about our rendezvous in Paris.

Since sleeping together, things between us were incredibly awkward. On the quick flight from Paris to Rome, I put my head on his shoulder instead of sitting perpendicular to him with my feet tucked underneath his thighs. He sat stiff for a moment, and then rotated his shoulder with a casual laugh. "It's hard to type with your head there," he said. I moved. We sat in silence for the remainder of the plane ride, the walk through customs, and the short cab ride to our hotel. When he finally spoke it was outside of the Coliseum, and only to ask about our itinerary.

"Maybe we should get the English audio guide," he suggested. I agreed.

I popped in the earbuds but didn't press play. Sound of any sort blasting into my ears was the furthest thing from what I needed. All I wanted was silence. I looked up at the Coliseum before entering it. Was it huge? Yes. But it was also dilapidated and broken—like a national treasure that no one cared for. Even the arches, which were the fundamental reason the structure was so revered, were disappointing. Aside from the multiplicity and repetition of them, I saw nothing particularly interesting about the Coliseum.

Once inside, we were herded along the cement corridors with so many other tourists that I couldn't see a foot in front of myself. Tall enough not to have his face inches from the back of a sweaty body, Jeff wasn't quite as trapped as I was, but he looked like he was struggling. I tried to take his hand to soothe him but his fingers remained slack. I let go.

We passed through an archway and emerged at the center of the arena. Unlike the Staples Center or any modern arena I'd been in, the Coliseum showcased a walkway the length of a football field before it opened into a half-moon stage pushed to the far side. The spatial design made it clear the ancient Romans revered their entertainment. Sadistic as the games may have been, the architecture of the space suggested a high regard for those who fought. Standing at the center of it all, I imagined the roar of crowds instilling a sense of pride into the athletes as they stood in the limelight.

I followed Jeff as we climbed to the top of the arena for a bird's-eye view, but the farther away from the stage we got, the less excited I became. Jeff wandered a few hundred feet away from me and I quickened my pace to catch up. When I reached him, my stomach grumbled.

"You want to grab some lunch soon?" I asked. I needed a change of environment; we had spent nearly two hours in the sweltering heat looking at the exact same arches we'd seen coming in earlier.

"I'm not hungry," he said.

"Dude, we haven't eaten all morning," I said. He didn't respond. "You feeling alright?"

Jeff was silent for a moment before he said flatly, "I'm fine."

I took the hint. At least, for a few seconds. "Look, if it's about what happened in Paris…" I started.

"It isn't," he snapped, and I knew that it was.

"If that's what you want…but I'd rather just clear the air," I pressed, not at all wanting to clear the air, which was quickly becoming muddy with smoke.

Silence.

A hundred thoughts raced through my head but nothing came out of my mouth. Like a shaken up can of Coke, my emotions festered beneath the surface just waiting to explode. I wanted to yell at him for letting me believe there was something between us and I wanted to kick him for making me feel like more of a fool than I already did. Actually, I wanted to kick myself for not knowing better.

"It's not always about you, Aubs."

I was prepared for regret, maybe even embarrassment—but hostility? I turned away from him and waited.

"I'm sorry," Jeff finally said, cryptically.

"Tell me the truth," I said, turning back to him. "Whatever it is, I can handle it."

He hesitated and let out a long breath. More silence.

I dropped my gaze as my heart sank to the pit of my stomach. "You regret it," I whispered, just barely audible. Maybe it was masochistic, but I needed to hear him say it.

He said nothing. He looked exhausted—like he'd already had this fight in his head and was just now going through the motions with me. Then, just as I was about to walk away, he said, "Veronica e-mailed me." The way he let the words hang made it seem like they should have answered all of my questions.

"When?" I asked, staring past his knees at a block of concrete and keeping my eyes glued there. I physically couldn't look at him for fear that I'd cry.

"Yesterday."

"In *Paris*?!" I was stunned. Actually, stunned was putting it lightly. I was furious, or maybe devastated, which for me manifested as rage anyway. "After our night together?"

"Yeah," he said sheepishly, making me almost feel sorry for him.

"What did she want?" I stammered.

"I guess she saw all the pictures I've been posting on our trip and she just wanted to say 'hello'".

Bullshit, I thought.

"It's crazy…after all this time?" he said, as though he wanted me to agree with him. I said nothing. "Back in Jordan, you said you weren't looking for anything serious," he said, looking pained.

"I'm not." I remembered what I'd told him when he

questioned my attraction to Atef. "I just didn't expect the 'nothing serious' to be with you."

"Well…" he trailed off. The silence was deafening. "I still care about you, Aubs. I always have." His words were like ice-cold water being dumped on me in the middle of a blizzard.

I felt his hand on my forearm and jerked away saying, "Don't touch me."

"Aubs," he started.

I cut him off, "I need to be away from you right now."

"Uh, I'm not ditching you in a foreign country."

"Do you want to be with her?"

"I don't know. Look, I'm really sorry. It's complicated."

"It's not that complicated," I retorted.

"We were supposed to get married," he said.

"Just forget it," I said.

"So, what? You're just gonna run away for another ten years?"

"What?"

"You're so quick to write people off."

"Yeah, I am," I said as I spun on my heel and left. With cloudy eyes I stumbled through the crowd trying to process everything that had just happened. Dismissing the curious stares as I passed by people, I somehow managed to find an exit and wandered aimlessly through the streets of Rome.

Until five weeks ago, Jeff wasn't a part of my life and I was just fine without him. Wasn't I?

A bright building with robust columns caught my eye, and as I got closer I realized I had stumbled across the Pantheon. From what I could remember, the Pantheon was full of artwork, the perfect escape from my situation.

Inside, I walked down a short hallway before emerging in the famous dome. A streak of light, brighter than any I'd ever seen in an interior space, pierced diagonally across the room from a hole in the ceiling. From where I stood, the opening was about the size of my palm. An English-translated pamphlet I picked up at the door explained that the oculus was uncovered and, during storms, water literally fell through it. The architects of the Pantheon designed a drainage system into the floor below specifically for rainwater.

Priceless monuments and artwork of historical significance filled the room, yet dirty, polluted rainwater was allowed to fall in here as if it were the most natural thing in the world. I didn't know whether to be horrified or impressed.

At midday, the sun's rays were reminiscent of religious postcards I'd seen of Jesus descending from heaven, and even as a person of no religion I found the experience quite spiritual. Dust particles filled the beam of light and, as I reached my hand directly into it, the sun's warmth soothed me. For a moment I was connected to something larger than myself, and the idea of an external force watching over me or taking care of me eased the burden of fear, which had become a constant companion.

Past the streak of light was the Madonna del Sasso, a sculpture of Mary holding baby Jesus in her arms with one foot on a rock. Beneath her lay the remains of Raphael. He was the lesser-known of the holy trinity of Renaissance painters—third only to Michelangelo and Leonardo. A pioneer for painting women as they were, voluptuous and full-bodied, Raphael embraced the natural features of the female figure and painted them with realistic proportions. He was one of the few painters in history to admit to being heavily influenced by his contemporaries, and found success because he incorporated the things he learned into his own body of work. That I happened past the place housing the tomb of Raphael, one of history's most influential artists, was significant because his model of studying and interpreting before creating was similar to my own.

The Madonna del Sasso was lit by two recessed lights carved into the upper part of the niche. At first, the bright yellow light bothered me because it cast shadows onto the sculpture and altered the color of the stone. I cringed at the thought of Michael standing before it.

Michael was a huge fan of Edison Price, the great fixture designer of the twentieth century. He read every article and attended every conference about this man who spent his life perfecting the art of lighting. Renowned for his work in developing fixtures that lit a flat wall with no glare, he was like the Godfather of museum lighting, and Michael talked about him incessantly. He believed that the proper lighting of a picture was just as important as the picture itself.

On the eve of my debut gallery opening, Michael and I spent half the day discussing the difference between incandescent, fluorescent, and halogen lights, as well as proper recessed and track lighting techniques, task lighting, accent lighting, downlighting, uplighting, and LEDs. We talked about the fact that the viewer's attention should never be drawn to the lighting itself.

Our eyes were the lenses we used to see the world, and the

combination of our human eye and lambency was the foundation of every picture—photo or otherwise. "Hues, for example, only exist as an interaction between the optic nerve in our eye and the luminosity it perceives," he said, knowing he'd catch my attention by relating light to color.

I stood in front of the Madonna for ten minutes, observing the curvature of her face and the easy flow of her gown. Lorenzetto, Raphael's apprentice and the sculptor of the Madonna del Sasso, mimicked Raphael's style of grace and restraint. Raphael was known for being judicious in his compositions, technically skilled, and pure in his taste. Keeping that in mind, I studied the sculpture and changed my mind about the lighting. Yes, the yellow light cast an unnatural color onto the white stone, but it also created a shadow of a mountain behind the sculpture. Madonna del Sasso meant Madonna of the Rock, and the darkened formation looked like a stone mountain in the background. This contrast of dark and light was emblematic of the Renaissance Period and highlighted the softened edges of the Madonna's dress, which meant the lighting worked for the piece and not against it.

Michael would be proud.

Jeff, on the other hand, wouldn't have understood its importance, I thought. A pathetic effort to convince myself that my feelings for him were misplaced.

Whatever Jeff was dealing with was separate from me and I knew he was sincere when he said he hadn't meant to hurt me. I was, however, angry with myself, and that was quickly turning into self-pity. I was frustrated with myself for not accomplishing more, for taking for granted the time I thought I had to build a career, and for dedicating my life to an obviously frivolous job. It was hard for me to reconcile my part in the world as an artist who couldn't see. Every day that my eyesight worsened, I felt my personal value diminish with it.

I was damaged goods. The phrase entered my mind, followed by an avalanche of others. My questionable talent, my ever-fluctuating bank account, my inability to cultivate a healthy romantic relationship, and my stubborn nature. I was twenty-seven with no kids, no house, and now no career either. No wonder Jeff preferred to be with Veronica.

Coming on this trip was beginning to feel like a mistake. The dark rings that had begun to form around my periphery were subtle, but I couldn't deny their presence. Four weeks away hadn't gotten me any closer to figuring out what I was going to do with the rest of my life. Traveling held no answers to life's big questions. As far as I could tell, its only purpose was to prolong the actual process of moving forward.

It was evening when I noticed the gold crown of the Vatican in the distance. Walking alone, I was less a tourist and more a lonely soul wandering unfamiliar streets. Everyone around me seemed to have a purpose: talking on the phone, walking briskly toward a destination, chatting animatedly, or moving hand in hand with a lover. Then there was me, meandering aimlessly toward the Vatican with not the slightest idea of what to do when I arrived.

I crossed the Fiume Tevere River and passed along the backside of an old castle before coming to a halt in front of it. Castel Sant'Angelo, a massive fortress made of round, multi-tiered sections with a giant blue-green sculpture of a bird on top, had a fire hydrant at the entrance painted red, white, and green—the colors of the Italian flag. Finally, a country that appreciated the artistic merit of a fire hydrant. I took a photo for the postcard I'd later burn for my dad and thought about the message I'd write:

Hey Dad,

I guess you weren't lying when you said I was 1/16th Italian! Wish you and Mom were here. Love you both immensely. Missing you always. -Aubs

I kept all of my messages short and sweet. Nothing heavy, nothing sad, and especially nothing about RP. My parents would've blamed themselves and I couldn't stand the idea of them feeling sorry for me.

The postcard tradition was something I couldn't bring myself to give up. So, for the first few years after their death, I mailed the postcards home knowing I'd be the one to receive them through the forwarding service Eli set up. I switched to burning them after my good friend Stephanie's grandfather passed away—exactly two years after my parents. He and I never met, but Steph talked about him frequently, relaying stories and Chinese proverbs that he'd impress upon her whenever she saw him. She'd retell them to us with an air of passivity, but I knew they affected her. *A small hole not mended in time will become a big hole more difficult to mend* was one proverb that surfaced often when she argued with her mom, and unsurprisingly their issues were always resolved before nightfall.

At her grandfather's burial site, a pit was set up with

burning coal where the family placed Joss paper, a symbol of money, and other items like paper villas, cars, medicine, food, and top shelf liquor made of papier-mâché. In death, he was given all of the luxuries that had eluded him in life. For me, the burning of symbolic items opened up a portal to the afterlife. Fire, which before I had equated to destruction, now represented renewal. That same night I burned the stack of postcards I had previously mailed home.

Two blocks from the Vatican entrance I saw a sign that read "Migliori Spaghetti Carbonara in Tutta Italia." I had no idea what it meant, but Spaghetti sounded really good and the aroma of garlic bread sealed the deal. The restaurant was on a bustling street corner with a patio facing the Vatican. Small buildings obstructed most of my view, but I could see the crown dome topped by a golden cross. I ordered the carbonara special and a carafe of vino, and sat observing the flow of the city. My need for sustenance meant I wasn't going to make it to the Vatican.

As I waited for my food, it dawned on me that Jeff's absence was strange and at the same time liberating. Not because I wanted to get away from him, but because I was tired of pretending I wasn't afraid. I didn't want to admit that my relationship with Jeff had changed in the nine years we spent not being a part of each other's lives, but he was no longer the person to whom I could say anything. High school was a long time ago and I didn't feel comfortable bursting into tears in front of him now. That kind of emotional freedom came only with solitude.

My spaghetti carbonara arrived beautifully plated with the angel hair pasta covered in a creamy sauce, bacon bits sprinkled on the outer edges of the plate, and a raw egg yolk sitting on top. I pierced the yolk with my fork and watched the yellow insides drip over the strings of pasta creating a yellow river down the front of my plate. Swirling the pasta onto my fork, I took a bite. Surprisingly light for how thick the sauce appeared, I finished the entire plate and sat idly sipping my wine while watching pedestrians pass by—and occasionally hearing snippets of conversations from the diners nearby.

With quite a bit of alcohol in my system, the evening felt serene despite the crowds in the streets. I laughed to myself as Jeff's words rung in my ears. He might have had a point about me running away at difficult moments. I'd been gone for over four weeks and I still hadn't even told my closest friends the real reason behind the trip. But how much longer could I keep avoiding this?

Hailing a cab, I decided it was time to face the music.

When I opened the door to our hotel room, Jeff was nowhere to be seen. His bags were just as we had left them and nothing in the room appeared to have been touched. I flopped down on the bed and stared at the ceiling.

Jeff was definitely mad at me. Our very first fight had been in our freshman year of high school; Jeff had joined the wrestling team and was hanging out with the guys a lot more than with me. We argued about it, he disappeared for a few days, resurfaced with a giant bag of peanut M&M's, and we made up over some comedy starring Ron Livingston and Jennifer Aniston. The same went for the time I stood him up at the winter formal sophomore year because I thought I was having a creative breakthrough. Two days of silence, a bag of Sour Patch Kids, and a movie starring Ben Stiller made everything all right. I wasn't worried that Jeff wouldn't come back; what concerned me was whether a bag of candy and a funny movie could fix the situation we had created.

I rose off the bed and moved over to Jeff's computer. Signing in under guest mode, I logged into my Gmail account to send a mass e-mail to my friends. The letter was three paragraphs long: the first, a description of the lanterns in China, floating in the Dead Sea, and the Taj Mahal, with promises to send photos soon; the second, a moment of honesty about why I suddenly had to see the world; the third, a request. I asked that they not reply or send me anything telling me how sorry they were. I didn't want to pity myself and if they pitied me, I wouldn't be able to help it.

When I was done with the body of the letter, I started adding its recipients. Sharon and Alison: my Columbia roommates who now lived in Washington D.C. Jason, Michael, and Courtney: Houston-to-L.A. transplants whom I quickly befriended in a bar during an Astros-Dodgers game. Nicole, John, and Eddie, my hipster ex-coworkers at Blick Art Supplies—my first of many part-time jobs in Los Angeles. Bill and Lina, my adventurous, outdoorsy friends who let me tag along on group camping trips they planned. The three of us had had many an existential conversation under the stars with Kahlua and hot chocolate. I thought about adding aunts, uncles, and cousins, but I had distanced myself from all of them after my parents' funeral. Just thinking about the sorrowful looks on their faces as they read that I was going blind made me remove them from the e-mail. They were loving and always reached out to me during the holidays, but the pity and grief that lingered in their eyes made it hard for me to be strong. Michael already knew, but I added him anyway so he would know that I told Rusty.

I attached a link to photos I had uploaded to Instagram and clicked 'Send.'

Instantly, the computer started ringing. Rusty was calling me via Google Voice. I answered.

"Hello?" I said, hearing static in the background.

"I cannot believe you left for China without even telling me!" He had obviously not read the entire e-mail yet.

"I'm in Rome now actually," I said, suppressing a smile even though he couldn't see me. It was good to hear his voice.

"Rome? You get around, don't you?" he teased.

"How is everything back home?" I asked.

He didn't respond for a long time. "Is this for real?" he finally asked. He had obviously gotten to the second paragraph.

"Yes."

He didn't say anything for a moment. "How far along are you?"

"That sounds like you're asking when my baby is going to be born," I laughed, trying to keep the tone of conversation light.

"Are you okay? Do you need anything?"

"I'm fine. I don't need anything—I'm with Jeff."

"Jeff who?"

"High school Jeff."

"What? I'm confused. Start at the beginning."

I told him everything. Even about our ill-fated romance

and my misplaced feelings. Eventually, I tried to steer the conversation in another direction, and I mentioned how being at the top of the Eiffel Tower was similar to gazing over L.A. at the Griffith. I also told him that the natural red rock of Petra reminded me of his painting *Seasons* and promised to e-mail him a photo.

"Have you been painting at all?" he asked.

"Yes. I've been shipping some paintings to Michael, but he still hasn't received the one from China yet. Enough about me though, what's going on there? I miss you," I said.

"It's all the same."

"Are you working on anything?"

"Yeah, I've started a new collection."

"That's awesome! I can't wait to see it when I get back," I said. Rusty didn't say anything. "I'm going to be fine Rust," I said with false confidence.

"You just worry about yourself and making the most of your trip. Tell that Jeff kid I'm going to punch him in the balls," Rusty said as the electronic latch on the door clicked and Jeff walked in carrying a giant bag of mixed candies.

"Will do," I said to Rusty. "I gotta run."

"Alright, bye darlin'."

I hung up and moved over to the bed where Jeff was dumping the candy. "*Jesus*," I said, impressed by the amount that was there. Jeff was spreading it about like a kid assessing his loot after a night of trick-or-treating.

"Please don't be mad," he said sheepishly.

I made a face.

"I'm sorry about what I said—"

"We made a mistake," I cut him off. "You're sorry. I'm

sorry. Let's leave it at that." I opened a candy wrapper to try and mask the lingering smell of alcohol on my breath.

"Are you sure?" he asked.

"Yes."

Jeff smiled. "Have you been drinking?"

"Yep."

Jeff sat down next to me on the edge of the bed, just close enough for me to tuck my toes under him. He smiled.

"Are you going to tell me where you've been for the last twelve hours?" I asked.

"Walking," he said.

"Walking?"

"Yeah. What about you?" he asked.

"I walked to the—"

"Walking?" he repeated with a mocking smile.

I laughed. "I walked to the Pantheon and meant to go check out the Sistine Chapel and Vatican, but I got sloshed instead."

"The Pantheon is supposed to be pretty cool," he said. "Did you make any spiritual revelations or forge any divine connections?"

"No," I said. "Just did a lot of observing."

"Me too." He let out a long breath as he leaned back, lying on the bed with his face turned toward me. "My mom says 'Hi.' I kind of let it slip that we were traveling together," Jeff said.

"I didn't know it was a secret," I replied.

"It's not. It's just, you know my mom…" Jeff trailed off.

"She still holds a torch for our kindergarten romance?"

"The day I told her I asked Veronica to marry me, you

know what she said?"

"What?"

"Does Aubrey know?"

"Yeah right."

"I swear to God," he said.

"Well, can you blame her? I mean we did make a pretty cute sandbox couple," I smiled, suddenly wishing I'd kept in better touch with his parents over the years.

"You *were* the first person to ever break my heart, so by default one could say that all of my romantic problems stem from you." He headed for the bathroom to brush his teeth. I followed, unable to remember if I'd brushed my own earlier.

When I was done brushing my teeth and washing my face, I asked, "How did I break your heart again?"

"Wait," he said before I got into bed. He quickly tucked the sheets in, fluffed the pillows, and straightened the comforter on my side even though his side remained untouched.

"Feel better?" I asked humorously. Although, I had to admit, I was a little surprised at how much I liked pulling the sheets back and climbing into the freshly made bed.

"You didn't let me buy you ice cream. You always told me 'no' when I tried to do nice things for you," he said, heading for the shower.

"Huh?"

"That's how you broke my heart."

I gave him a quizzical look. He didn't elaborate and disappeared into the bathroom.

I laid in bed for a while before reluctantly peeling the covers off again. While Jeff was still in the shower, I unpacked my bag, stretched a canvas, mixed my colors, and spread out my brushes. Then, I sat down with the hotel stationary, which I tore into squares and began folding into cranes. I imagined a large pyramid with the Eye of Horus at the top covering most of the canvas. The center would mask a naked couple sitting on their knees and wrapped in each other's arms. Once I decided to have their embracing bodies form a triangle with their toes making up the two bottom corners, I set my seventh crane down and began to paint.

Jeff, meanwhile, emerged from the bathroom, remade the bed *again*, and sprawled out on top of the comforter to read a book. I thought about making fun of him and saying something about how old habits die hard. But I didn't because I wondered if the small act of rebellion was his way of getting back to himself after being lost in a relationship.

The painting was similar to my earlier works of juxtaposed images but without the dark humor. Just pieces of earth and fragments of life that wouldn't otherwise exist together. Borrowing from the Latin American artist Debra Hurd, I created them in abstract pieces. The way her *Blue Jazz* painting featured people had always inspired me. Individual faces were indiscernible because it wasn't about the musician—it was about the music. But where the paintings had similarities, they also diverged. *Blue Jazz* was loud, bursting with sound, and demanding to be heard, whereas mine was subtle, serene, and unassuming.

I hoped to convey unity—what could emerge when two forces became one. My characters were a representation of any two things meeting to form a unique outcome. I might have even gone so far as to say that one was me and the other was Retinitis Pigmentosa personified. It was my hope that when swirled together on a palette, we formed a one-of-a-kind point of view. What emerged was so different from my usual works that I didn't know if I liked it. The palate was monochromatic and two figures embracing in the center looked almost ghostlike. I considered adding more color, but found myself instead looking at the unintentional details found in the flowing brushstrokes and knew it was done.

CHAPTER TWELVE

Nature

When Michael sold *Ballerinas on Skid Row*, I received a bottle of 1996 Opus One, a red Bordeaux blend, from him in the mail. When he sold *Boy with Pigeons*, he showed up at my doorstep in Venice Beach with a bottle of vintage Chateau Margaux. The first I drank alone in my Harlem studio full of moving boxes—straight from the bottle. The second, he and I drank together out of champagne flutes I'd bought at an estate sale up the street. I'd just moved to Venice three weeks prior and still had no furniture, so we sat on the floor of my studio apartment having a drunken discussion about the perils of selling art over the $400 bottle of wine.

Just a year earlier, the Michael Sanders Gallery had been the butt of many art critics' jokes. "They said my taste was too commercial and lacking in depth," he confessed, referring to the work he exhibited. "So when I came across you peddling New York City skylines, I bought one just to stick it to them." I didn't know whether to be honored or humbled. "Don't get me wrong," he continued, "I loved *Ballerinas on Skid Row* and hoped you would be my crossover artist. And here you are."

"So how did you sell it?" I asked.

"I didn't."

I looked at him, not understanding.

"I had it up near the back for several weeks and I noticed that everyone who walked past it stopped to look; but, like me, they couldn't quite put their finger on what struck them about it," Michael said. "Then the Gibsons walked in, and..." he paused to laugh, "she schooled me on the art of technical painting."

"She's always told me that I'm a good technical painter, and I never knew whether to take it as a compliment or some sort of advice," I slurred.

"It's both," Michael replied. "Your paintings lack the vulnerability needed to connect with people in a broader sense. If you continued down the path you're on now, I'm sure I could sell the shit out of your work, because it's beautifully crafted and juxtapositions are always intriguing, but I wouldn't mind seeing something new either. You know how to paint, but how does your work define you as an artist."

I had always thought he wanted me to put more of myself into my work. To be like Rusty and wear my heart on my sleeve. For months, I tried to capture my fears and doubts as an artist. Then, on one of the days Eli's statements arrived, I forgot about myself and *Midnight in Paris* manifested. "It's good," Michael said as we hung it in the gallery next to my other piece, *Poverty and Gluttony*, the painting of a homeless child curled up next to a trashcan in an alley behind a row of the finest restaurants in New York. I really liked the contrast of the two pieces next to each other because it was a representation of my growth—or so I thought. "It's good," Michael repeated. "But there is more to you than your history. Don't be afraid to leap outside of the box completely."

Jeff and I spent our second day in Rome touring the Vatican and standing shoulder to shoulder in an international mosh pit of tourists, all trying to get the perfect photo of Michelangelo's famous Sistine Chapel ceiling. I, too, took quite a few photos, but when I discovered that by shifting a foot or two to my right or left I could align my ever thickening RP line with the edges of each segment, I stopped. It was like seeing normally again for a little while and I wanted to savor the time. Between the two of us, Jeff and I had a few uncomfortable moments of talking over and bumping into one other, but for the most part the awkwardness was fading. At least on my part, my anger subsided and I began falling back into friendship mode.

On the flight to Peru, Jeff was mentally somewhere else. His laptop was open with Cabana, Word, and BetaTesting, running and ready to serve, but for the most part he just stared at the bottom of the seat in front of him, zoned out. I was sure he was thinking about Veronica, but I was the last person he would open up to about her. And to be honest, I didn't want to know.

I opened my magazine to read an article on the history of

the airline, but focusing on the tiny print made my head start to pound. I tried really hard to get through the entire article but found myself re-reading the first paragraph over and over. Shifting my focus to the smiling flight attendant in the accompanying photograph, I wondered if the airline would ever consider hiring a blind flight attendant. I closed the magazine, stuffed it back in the seat-back pocket, and thought about my disease. The process of going blind was already different than what I was expecting. The thin rim that had formed in the center of my vision was like a bar that divided windowpanes, only permanently attached. My view of the world was literally changing and I pushed myself to think about collaborating with this newfound perspective. Being a blind artist would make me a minority among minorities and somewhere in that experience I hoped to find a craft. *Okay RP,* I thought, *if we're in this together then I can't be the only one working here. So what've you got?* I closed my eyes.

On the eighteen-hour flight, which included a quick layover in Madrid, I came up with exactly two benefits to going blind, and fifty-six drawbacks. One benefit was never having to drive and the other was my other senses heightening. Eating in the dark at Opaque enhanced my recognition of different flavors, which allowed me to describe what I tasted with nuanced detail. With only smell, touch, taste, and hearing, I was forced to evaluate what I was eating in a different manner than I was accustomed, and the words came from a vocabulary I rarely utilized.

I considered becoming a writer. Books were a favorite pastime of mine because the reader was such a factor in the equation. The author described the world, but it was up to the audience to complete the picture. But I knew nothing about writing. I'd been a B student at best when it came to mastering the English language, so it was something to ruminate on but far from a solution.

Looking past the sleeping woman in the window seat next to me, I watched as the wing of the airplane sliced through puffs of cloud. A continual river of white, dense-less condensation rolled over the plane's wing then disappeared downstream. Suspended above the earth, being in a plane was like being given a timeout on life; too bad by the time we touched down in Cuzco I had no answers and a million more questions.

As was required for all entry to the Inca Trail, we booked with a local tour company weeks in advance. Quince Tour Group, which looked to be the smallest outfit, had ten porters (not including our tour guide). Sebastian and Sabrina, an adorable European couple who, like their names, complemented each other perfectly, had been grouped with us. They were about our age, but their English accents and swanky Under Armor attire set them apart from us in our casual outfits of shorts and tank tops. We didn't talk much that first day because the hike itself required nearly all of our energy, and we'd all gotten up at 5:00 a.m., so everyone was understandably exhausted. I did, however, notice that Sebastian always made sure Sabrina walked on the side closest to the mountain and he often checked in on how she was doing while coaxing her to drink more water, something she didn't seem inclined to do. Cayo, our tour guide, was a short guy who wore a New York Yankees baseball cap, red windbreaker suit, and a matching, worn, two-pocket backpack slung over one shoulder.

The entrance to the trail was marked by a simple wooden arch, carved by hand and inscribed with symbols of valleys, mountain ranges, and rivers. Groups took turns taking photos in front of the arch as we sipped coca tea made for us by our porters. The green leaves were fresh and whole, unlike the dried tea we typically drank at home.

"Every day you drink this tea, good for you," Cayo said. "Help with altitude sickness."

We posed together for a photo, crossed under the entrance, and the trek began. One of the last groups to take off, we walked briskly; well, as briskly as we could with backpacks weighing about twenty pounds each. The air was humid but not hot, and shades of green and brown were everywhere. Light green stems connected to forest green flower buds, faded lime bled across fallen leaves on their way to turning brown, and moss green spread across the sea of trees. Perpendicular to us was the wide Urubama River, which moved with surprising ease considering its brown, clay-like appearance.

Every guidebook and online reviewer mentioned spending two full days in Cuzco adjusting to the high altitude; however, because of our schedule, Jeff and I only had about half a day before we set out on the hike. Big mistake. We drank lots of coca tea and made sure to stay hydrated, but the last couple hours of day one were a steady incline and I began to feel lightheaded. Cayo had one of the porters carry my things, and I moved at a snail's pace behind everyone else. Luckily, I made it to the campsite before any real symptoms kicked in.

After lying down in the tent for about an hour I felt pretty good, so I decided to join the group for a meal. I sat for about four minutes before my head started throbbing and the dinner tent started spinning.

"Are you okay?" Sabrina asked.

"Yeah. I'm just feeling a little dizzy," I replied, getting up. I got about six feet outside of the tent and the world went black.

"Jeff!" I shouted.

"Yeah," he said, his hands resting on my shoulders. "Aubs?"

"I can't see anything," I said, panicking. "I can't see anything, I can't see anything."

"It's probably just the altitude," I heard Sabrina say. "Let's get her in the tent and have her drink some coca tea."

I blinked quickly and moved my head about searching for something—anything. "I can't see anything," I whispered again. I didn't know what else to say so I kept repeating the phrase over and over again, waiting for a different outcome. *I can't see anything...*

Inside the tent, I felt the windbreaker material of my sleeping bag as I crouched down to sit. Someone gently pressed down on my shoulders to help me lean back, but I got about halfway down and panicked again. I had a sudden fear that if I leaned back any further I might fall into an abyss, or off one of the many mountainsides I'd passed earlier that day. "Stop," I said, breathing hard. "Sorry, I just need a minute."

"It's okay. Take your time," Sabrina said. "It's pretty tight in here. I'll be outside if you need anything."

"Thanks," Jeff said. I started a 'thank you' as well but it got caught in my throat and never came out. Reaching around in the darkness until I found Jeff's hand, I squeezed it tight, closed my eyelids, and concentrated on slowing my rapid breathing.

When I felt my heart returning to a normal pace, I slowly lifted my heavy eyelids and let out the breath I'd been holding. Things were fuzzy at first, just blotches of scattered colors and a few undefined shapes, until finally the opening of the tent came into focus and I could see the silhouette of mountains against the night sky.

Relieved, I let go of Jeff's hand and let myself fall back onto the plush sleeping bag.

"I'm okay," I said.

Lying down next to me, Jeff propped his head up with one hand and looked at me with such intensity that I shifted my gaze toward the flapping zipper of the tent's entrance.

"I don't think I've ever been that scared in my life," I said. "I mean, I know I should've expected it. I know what's happening. I just—the world went black." I was having a hard time articulating the fear I'd just experienced. My lungs burned from lack of air, and no matter how hard I concentrated, I couldn't seem to get myself to breathe properly. "I—"

"It's okay, Aubs," he whispered, cutting me off. The intense look in his eye was unwavering. But this time, I didn't look away. I held his gaze until his lips reached mine and I felt his hand on the small of my back pulling me close. His kiss was soft but strong and I melted into his protective embrace. Our bodies were pressed together and yet I felt as if he were still too far. I closed my eyes and let my hands explore the muscular definition of his collarbone. Making my way down his arms, I felt the flex of his biceps before grazing his chest to feel the beating of his heart.

He somehow managed to zip the tent while removing my clothes and we moved about exploring each other's bodies with slow, meticulous movements. Taking his time, he moved from my mouth, down to my neck, and carefully wrapped his lips around my left nipple while he squeezed my right breast in his hand. As he traveled down the rest of my body, the trail of wet kisses he left sent a tingling sensation shooting through me to the ends of my fingers and toes.

I was bursting with so much emotion that I was ready to climax the moment I felt him inside me. I kissed him hard as our bodies moved in tandem. Then, letting out a soft involuntary cry, I gave into my senses, feeling as if all of the blood in my body was rushing to meet with Jeff's. Intertwined with him as one, I'd never felt closer to anyone in my life.

We both lay silent for a long while, before I turned to him and said, "I'm going blind."

"No, you're not," he laughed.

"Yes. I am," I replied. "The doctors told me before we left."

Bolting upright, Jeff looked at me. His face was a mixture of concern, confusion, and resentment. "What?" he said.

"My ophthalmologist told me—" I started, but he cut me off.

"You've known this entire time?"

"Yes."

"Geezus Aubs!" he nearly shouted. It looked like he had a million things he wanted to say or yell at me, but nothing else came out.

"I'm sorry that I didn't tell you sooner," I said.

"Honestly, I don't know why I'm even surprised that you didn't tell me," he said.

"I wasn't trying to hide it. I had just found out when you invited me to come with you and I thought it would be my last opportunity to see the world. I didn't tell you because I didn't want it to interfere with the trip."

"You've never been one to face things, Aubs," he said.

"You're one to talk," I snapped.

"Right, I'm gonna take a walk before I say something I'll regret," he said, putting on his clothes.

When I awoke the next morning, it took me a minute to realize where I was. I could hear the other trekkers chatting outside and, like a freshman running late to my first final exam in college, I got dressed at lightning speed. I didn't want to be the one they were waiting on.

Clumsily stepping out of my tent, I zipped the entrance closed before turning around to put on my shoes, but the view stopped me dead in my tracks. We were perched at the top of a mountain so high the clouds were literally beneath us. I knew that Cuzco was high in elevation—my body still bearing the brunt of altitude sickness—and that we'd trekked upwards for most of the day before, but I had no idea just how high we actually were. It was a spectacular view; what I had imagined Earth to look like from Heaven. The air was crisp, the ground damp, and through the thin layers of cloud I saw a lush valley covered in a solid, dark green. The tree-to-person ratio had to be something like 2000 to 1, because I felt elated by partaking in the most basic of human activities: breathing.

"Aubs, you alright?" Jeff asked from underneath the breakfast tent. I looked up and realized I was standing in an awkward position with one sock successfully on and the other in mid-attempt.

"Great!" I said with a bit too much enthusiasm. "Just, uh, taking in a breath of fresh air."

"Did you sleep alright?" Sabrina asked.

"Good enough," I smiled, glancing at Jeff whose eyes were now locked to his plate. "What's for breakfast?"

"The most amazing spread," Sebastian said in his perfectly polite manner of speaking. Yes, I was one of those foolish Americans enamored by the English accent.

"Omelets and bacon," Sabrina finished.

"Bacon?! Seriously?" I sat down next to Jeff, taking notice of his shift to make room for me on the already-empty side of the bench. As if waiting for me to arrive, a plate of food was handed to me by a porter. "Thanks," I said as he smiled sheepishly and slunk away to the back where the rest of the porters sat eating their own breakfast. I had expected some kind of Peruvian dish with rice and alpaca, Peru's main source for protein, so bacon was a welcome surprise. I loved that we were having eggs in the morning for no other reason than that they were familiar. That's when I felt, for the first time in years, a pang of homesickness.

Not for my apartment in Venice, but for the home where I

grew up, in Houston. Cheese eggs were the go-to food in our house on nights we were all too exhausted to get takeout but needed sustenance. After they passed, I spent months avoiding eggs of any kind until finally, one drunken night, I had a hankering for them. I went about making myself a plate at 3:00 a.m. on a Saturday night, and as I sobered up I thought of all the times I'd had eggs for dinner with my parents. Raising my plate in a toast to them in Heaven, eggs became my go-to food for when I missed them.

Day two of the hike was the hardest. For ten hours we climbed stair after stair, after stair. I was tired after the first hour so the last nine felt like an eternity. As we trekked, I wondered if the ancient civilizations built the stairs in a feeble attempt to reach God. From the base looking upward, the mountaintops peaked above the clouds and I could see how one might come to the conclusion that God was sitting up there waiting. I could only imagine how disappointed they were when they reached the peak and all they found was a pathway back down the other side.

God or no God, the journey was the closest I'd ever come to having a spiritual connection. The high altitude meant oxygen was thin, and after my panic attack the day before I was focused on only one thing: breathing. Cayo walked beside me as the others moved about leisurely ahead, and he made sure I stopped at the slightest hint of rapid intakes of air. As far as I was concerned, he was the Incan equivalent of a Buddhist monk. My legs were sore and sweat poured out of every pore in my body, but I found a deep calmness within, which helped me continue moving despite my physical difficulties.

Even though the trek was considered hard and, by the very nature of camping, uncomfortable, it wasn't as 'hardcore' as one might think. Hired porters carried all non-personal items like tents, cooking supplies, sleeping bags, and food, and did it with an astounding efficiency. Once we had breakfast, we packed up our personal belongings and they packed up the rest. But twenty or thirty minutes later, we'd see them running past us on the trail! And lunch and dinner were ready to go by the time we arrived at our resting destinations, and they did it carrying twice the load in sandals made of used tires.

"What are you thinking about?" Jeff asked.

I smiled automatically—a natural defense mechanism—and said, "The porters' sandals. I was thinking about how amazing it is that they can hike this far in sandals that look like thrift store throwaways." Jeff had been avoiding me, and after sleeping with him again, I couldn't get myself to look at his face so I continued watching the porters' feet.

"I hadn't even noticed," Jeff said. He took a closer look as a group zipped past us. "You've always had a really good eye."

"And yet, I'm the one who's losing it," I snapped. I hated the bitterness in my voice—it made me sound like a petulant child.

"You are," he said gently, but also matter-of-factly.

"It's not fair."

"No, it's not."

"You're not being very helpful."

"You're not asking for help."

"No, I guess I'm not. Why would I, from where I'm

standing you don't really seem emotionally capable of being much help," I said.

"I can tell you're irritated so… I'm going to give you some space." He walked a little faster toward the happy-go-lucky couple before turning back and saying over his shoulder, "Let me know when you're ready to talk again."

I wanted to throw a rock at him. But he was right, I was angry, and the quickest way to calm me down was by not indulging me. Any other guy would have tried to fix the situation; Jeff knew to stand back.

It took me a full twenty minutes of walking alone and stewing in my frustration before I settled down. First I was mad at Jeff, then I was mad at the universe, and finally, I was mad at myself.

We walked by a small stone house where a little boy stood outside wearing a blue and gray striped t-shirt, dirty underwear, and yellow rain boots. His gray Labrador Retriever puppy chewed on a twig next to him and they both curiously watched the hikers trekking by. His yellow boots popped out of the scene as if the moment were a living Kim Anderson portrait. She was known for using isolated color in a photo to bring attention to a single object while fading the rest of the scene into a black and white background.

I smiled at the boy as my anger settled, but I was embarrassed and having a hard time breathing, so I didn't bother trying to catch up. The group was about a hundred yards ahead of me for an hour before they stopped at the Phuyupatamarca ruins. Perched on the side of the mountain were rounded structures that looked like old, abandoned castle corners. Roofs were gone, floors were covered by compact dirt, rock, and grass. Throughout the area, colorful flora could be found sprouting out of cracks in the concrete buildings. Peach fungi, similar in size and shape to enoki mushrooms, grew in small patches along with bundles of small, purple orchids and a long-stemmed lupin flower that reminded me of the Texas blue bonnet. My favorite was a drooping red flower, Caiophora andina, which, as it turned out, was beautifully poisonous. Held strong by a green peduncle covered in tiny clear thorns that permeated the drooping flower itself, the andina grew in the shape of a red, hollowed-out pumpkin, and was about the diameter of a quarter.

I took a macro photo of the flower with my camera and then turned a corner and saw the smallest stream of water. It trickled into a stone basin through a hole in the rock wall. Its flow was consistent and the shade of rock underneath the water showed that even seasonally the stream didn't change much. I reached my fingers in and watched it wash away the dirt on my hands.

"Hey," I heard Sabrina say from up above me, "Are you about ready? We're heading out." She, Sebastian, Cayo, and Jeff were all looking down at me.

"Ye-ah," I replied. I had no idea that my voice could crack while uttering a single syllable, but it did. Halfway through the word, I seemed to choke just enough for it not to go unnoticed.

"You look tired," Cayo said.

"A little bit," I replied, knowing it was less a physical exhaustion and more a mental one.

"Try this," he said, handing me a black substance. "Chew

on like this, then you let sit, and then you spit," he said. He opened his mouth to show me how he pushed the black rock into the space between his teeth and cheek and left it there.

"Tobacco?" I asked suspiciously.

"No. Black Rock."

"What's Black Rock?"

"It helps give energy for the walking," he said. I shrugged and took a bite. I could see that it turned his teeth a yellowish color, which was not appealing, and coupled with the fact that it tasted like garbage, I was inclined to spit it out. But I didn't want to be rude, and to be honest I needed the boost, so I kept it there until Cayo spit his out some fifteen minutes later.

Slowly, I felt its chemical compound race through my system. Was this what it felt like to be on steroids? My shortness of breath was gone and I was certain I could run up the steps until I reached the top. Red Bull had nothing on this Black Rock stuff. The added kick of euphoria was a bonus. I discovered later that the euphoria and energy were because Black Rock was a mild form of cocaine, grown locally in Peru, and used by most of the population with the same popularity as cigarettes in the United States.

"Hey, slow down there Rocky," Jeff said, catching up to me. I slowed down. "Can we talk?" he asked.

"About what?"

"You know what about," he said dryly.

"Okay, shoot," I said, not looking at him.

"I'm sorry about yesterday. I don't know what came over me. With Paris and then you telling me you were going blind I reacted really poorly. I feel like a dick. I'm not trying to hurt you—"

I knew I was as much to blame as he was. He had made it very clear after Paris that he wasn't available and I knew going into it that this was a possibility, but I had hoped for a different outcome.

"Takes two to tango right? I knew what I was doing," I said with a half-smile.

"Meaning?"

"Meaning we're twenty-seven, shit happens. So let's just drop it okay?"

"So, does that mean we're okay?" he asked.

"Yeah."

"Okay," he hesitated for a moment and then opened his mouth to say something but Sebastian interrupted.

"Hey Mates!" Sebastian yelled after us from behind. "We're filling up the jugs, do ya need any water?" They had stopped on the side of a stream and Sebastian was pumping river water into their bottles using a portable filter.

"Yeah, that'd be awesome," Jeff said as he started to head over toward Sebastian with our nearly-empty bottles in hand.

"What were you going to say," I asked.

"Never mind. It's nothing," he smiled.

Over dinner, the four of us became fast friends. They were both recent university graduates traveling on a one-way ticket around the world. Neither of them had any idea what their next step in life was going to be, and I found it comforting to be in their presence because they weren't at all concerned about their uncertain futures. Careful not to meet Jeff's gaze, I told them I was in the midst of a career change as well and had no idea where I would end up in a few years.

"What do you do, Jeff?" Sabrina asked.

"I used to teach high school, but now I'm creating apps."

"Like Instagram?" Sabrina asked.

Jeff laughed uncomfortably. "I develop games mostly. They're pretty much just rip-offs of games you already play like Bubbles or Angry Birds."

"That's not true," I jumped in. "He has a really cool one he's working on called *I Travel Better Than You*, and it's sort of like Instagram and Vine but adds a travel aspect to it with cool filters and video options."

"It's still in beta," Jeff added.

"That's pretty sick," Sebastian said.

"Yeah. But the name is kind of weird, isn't it?" Sabrina said.

"You don't think it's catchy?" Jeff asked.

"No," Sabrina and Sebastian said in unison. I laughed.

"So how long have you guys been together?" Sabrina asked.

"We're friends," Jeff quickly said.

"So were we before he started shaggin' me," Sabrina replied. I laughed at her blunt humor, but also because she said what I couldn't.

"We've actually been friends since high school," I said. "And randomly just ran into each other a few months ago at the DMV."

"Well, when the two of you get over this whole getting to know each other business, I expect an invitation to the wedding," Sabrina chided.

"We're headed for America in three months' time, so if

you could make it around then, it would be super-convenient," Sebastian said.

We all laughed. "I've got a couch and floor in my studio that y'all are welcome to crash on anytime," I said.

"Ditto," Jeff added. "But she has the ocean view."

"That would be amazing!" Sabrina exclaimed.

Sabrina had crossed her arms and squeezed her triceps only once before Sebastian had his coat off and wrapped around her shoulders. It was such a small gesture, not to mention one that I didn't need because I wasn't cold, but a pang of jealousy shot through me nonetheless.

"I'm jealous of all your traveling," I said. "I wish I had done this years ago."

"You're here now, right?" she replied. "That's all that matters. It was about fifteen hundred quid for our tickets, but we're spending six months traveling. I can't imagine cramming it all into six weeks."

"Did you just say quid? Why is it that you British people have such strange ways of saying basic things like money?" I joked.

"*We* British people?" Sebastian laughed. "Don't even get me started on the stupid things you Americans do."

"*Stupid* Americans," Jeff chimed in. "Could you at least be original?"

"I loved America. I don't think I've ever been as popular with the men," Sabrina said.

"Did I not just call them stupid Americans?" Sebastian countered.

Sabrina punched his arm lovingly. "Don't be a git."

"Don't be a what?" Jeff asked.

"A git. It's like an twat or a wanker," Sabrina explained. Jeff and I burst out laughing.

"I love it. I'm taking 'git' home with me. It's going to be my new favorite word," I said.

Somewhere during the course of our twenty-minute-turned-two-hour dinner, we crossed the threshold from acquaintances to friends. From that moment on, the floodgates of humor were rapidly flowing.

A long-legged girl from another tent walked by on her to way to the bathroom and I caught Sebastian looking before seeing Sabrina's gaze on Jeff. Sabrina rolled her eyes, "These boys have been camping for three days, they smell like armpit, and they think they've got a chance of sexing her? I'd pay twenty quid just to watch you get rejected."

Her confidence was magnetic. She took a situation that could've easily been a couple's spat and flipped it on its head. I admired the way she controlled the situation and I could tell Sebastian did too. He pulled her in tight, kissed her on the forehead, and said, "I was simply thinking that she's not as hot as my bird." Charmer that one.

"I didn't even see her," Jeff shrugged, almost believably.

"You're a terrible liar, mate," Sebastian laughed.

"Right, because you're one to judge," Sabrina said, rolling her eyes at Sebastian.

"All men, be it British or American, are pigs," I laughed, hiding the jealousy I now had for a stranger on our trek.

"Yet we love 'em anyway," Sabrina said, kissing Sebastian's arm.

Being around them was refreshing, especially coming on the heels of Rome, where I had spent so much time alone, but watching them as a couple was killing me. Objectively, Sebastian was the better-looking of the two because he had an athletic build and supermodel cheekbones. Not that Sabrina wasn't good-looking. Standing at about 5'7", she was slender with an athletic build, which made her more of a tomboy than a sex symbol. Looks aside, her easygoing and charismatic nature deftly trumped the A-listers of physical beauty and Sebastian knew it. I was sure they were a walking cliché of meant-for-each-other, but as I looked over at Jeff, I found I didn't subscribe to the concept.

CHAPTER THIRTEEN

Nurture

Sleeping that night was especially difficult. I found myself waking up every hour until finally it was so close to dawn I decided to give up. The ground was damp and cold, and all I could think about was how much I wanted to be Sebastian and Sabrina—cuddled together in a sweet and loving embrace. Jeff was lying next to me but he most definitely wasn't with me, and that was almost worse than being alone. Pulling a sweater over my head, I tiptoed out of our tent in search of some tea or coffee. Outside, the moist and foggy air was cool with droplets of water and condensation covering everything from the tops of our tents to the blades of grass below. As I made my way over to the breakfast tent, I noticed green algae partially covering many of the gray stones lining our path. These same rocks decorated our campground, making the entire area seem bathed in a meadow of green.

The sun had yet to rise, but our porters were bustling

about when I arrived in the dining tent and found Sabrina already in there.

"Hey," I said, pouring myself a cup of tea. "You're up early."

"Yeah, I'm not a morning person, so I have to get up super early and have my three cups of tea before speaking to anyone."

"That seems counter-intuitive. Shouldn't you sleep in as long as possible?"

She laughed and raised her cup, "This is number three. You should ask the porter who brought me my first mug."

I smiled. "Got it."

"What about you? What's your excuse?"

"Couldn't sleep." I left it at that.

She didn't pry as I had expected her to; instead, she turned her gaze from mine and said, "Life is so much simpler up here."

"Life can be simple anywhere. We choose to make it complicated," I replied.

"Did you see that little boy yesterday? Sitting on the front step of his house?"

"The one with the yellow rain boots?"

"Yes, he was so adorable with his filthy little puppy."

"Was he dirty? I thought he was just gray? Do labs come in gray?" I asked. I regretted not taking a photo of the picturesque scene of youth and innocence—but he seemed completely unaware of his bleak surroundings and I couldn't stand the idea of drawing attention to it with my digital camera.

"No, I don't believe labs can be naturally grey. He was

probably a mix. Cute as hell, those two," Sabrina said.

As we both went back to sipping our drinks, a feeling of loneliness crept back up on me. I thought about Lexi, who was my puppy for five minutes to and from school every day. Because we lived only three blocks away, my parents always walked me. "Walking frees your mind to be creative," my dad would say.

Lexi belonged to my neighbor, Mrs. Gottesfeld; she was a gift from one of her grandkids. The first time I saw her barking at the windowsill I let go of my dad's hand and bolted toward her. She was sitting on a child's chair, and as I approached I put my palm to the window and giggled loudly as Lexi pressed her paw to mine behind the glass.

"Come on squirt," my dad said, peeling me away. "We've got to get to school."

"Okay," I replied, full of disappointment.

We only got as far as the driveway before I felt Lexi's tiny paws bounding up my right leg. She had escaped out the dog door. My dad was horrified—concerned that Lexi might get run over by a car. Mrs. Gottesfeld assured him, though, that Lexi greeted her grandkids the same way when they arrived and would promptly come back inside once they left. "She's a smart pup," Mrs. Gottesfeld smiled as she handed me a small cracker.

"Make her work for it," she said. "She's a spoiled dog so she can only sit and shake."

Lexi didn't even wait for me to ask her to "shake" before lifting her paw. I giggled as I took the paw in my hand and gave it a firm shake. The connection was instant. In fact, that was probably the first time I internalized the power of our most basic form of introduction. As far as I was concerned, she was my girl. Occasionally I might've forgotten my math homework or English assignments at home, but I never left home without treats in my pocket. Twice a day, every day, we met for a little tussle that lasted eleven years. In fact, in college, on days where I was so tired I was running on autopilot, I'd sometimes find broken cracker pieces crumbling in my pockets.

The light, energetic way that the gray lab bounded about playing with his twig reminded me of Lexi. Life was as simple as a game of fetch.

Jeff and I were distancing ourselves from each other. Anything even bordering on the lines of flirtation was gone. Actually, he stopped making any kind of physical contact with me. Yet his banter and verbiage remained the same and, at times, I forgot that the boundaries of our relationship had shifted at all. Veronica was Jeff's Mumtaz Mahal, and I was crazy to think I could compete with that.

"This is going to sound crazy," Sabrina said, cutting into my thoughts, "but I feel like my life is consistently unbalanced. If my lovelife is in tact, then my career falls apart. When I get a lot of compliments on the way I look, my life seems to be total shit," she laughed.

"Where would the challenge be if you had it all?" I said. She shrugged. "Maybe the question you should be asking yourself is why you feel like what you have isn't enough."

"We're pre-programmed to always want more. I want to experience everything—I want to do everything before I die, don't you?"

"You want to know the real reason Jeff and I are here?"

She nodded. "I'm going blind." Sabrina was being so open with me about her fears that it felt insincere to not tell the truth at this point.

"Bullshit."

I laughed, "I keep hoping. But it's true."

"Well that explains your dizziness yesterday. Should you even be doing a hike like this?"

"It's not super bad yet. It's different than what I was expecting. I thought things would start to get blurry, like a camera going out of focus. But I'm starting to see dark rings around my eyes, kind of like looking through a set of binoculars, except right now my periphery is still pretty wide."

"How long before you're completely blind?" she asked.

"Six to eight weeks, they said…that was five weeks ago."

"Oh, bollocks. Well, that's really shitty, isn't it?"

"Totally *shitty*," I said, mimicking her accent. "Sorry. I don't know where that came from." *Holy cow I'm an asshole*, I thought. She laughed.

After a short silence Sabrina concluded, "I would be really angry if I were you."

"Believe me, I am."

"I'm trying to imagine what I would do if I were in your situation."

"And?"

"And I think I would be doing the exact same thing as you. Traveling around the world with the person that I love." I opened my mouth to deny the accusation of love, but she waved me off. "I don't know what the deal is with you two, but I know you love each other."

It didn't matter that she had no basis for making that statement; I loved her for saying it. I wanted to know why she thought it. Had he made some kind of gesture that I missed? Was it his body language? All I needed was a glass of wine in a private tent and I would've told her everything: my history with Jeff, how we had reconnected, his heartbreak, Paris...all of it. I wanted so badly to share my side of the story, to analyze and discuss the situation, and to have someone else confirm that my feelings were not misplaced.

Instead, I mumbled, "Bad timing I guess."

"Just remember, the man can't always be expected to make all the effort." I wanted to ask her what she meant by that, but Jeff emerged from our tent just then and walked over to make his own coffee. "Morning," he grumbled.

"Morning," Sabrina and I said in unison, before she continued on with the conversation. For a second I was worried she was going to ask him about our so-called "bad timing," but she didn't.

"Sebastian and I have been traveling for nearly six months now, and no matter where we are, whenever I see sprawling landscapes I always feel like I need to meditate. Like Mother Earth needs me to really take a look at her—to see something on the horizon, or in the trees. Maybe flowing in the river beneath me. It's like she's pointing me towards answers except I don't know the questions."

"That's very philosophical for six a.m. I'm going back to bed. Wake me up for breakfast," Jeff yawned as he lumbered off back to our tent.

"You got it, champ," Sabrina laughed.

"Have you tried meditation?" I asked.

"No," she said, as though offended I would even think that. She had pulled that entire monologue out of her ass. I was impressed. I felt like I had met my soulmate. Too bad she was a girl.

"I know you were just trying to get Jeff to go away, but I actually think there is a direct correlation between one's happiness and the amount of time they spend in nature every day."

"Oh, I'm sure there is. I mean, why else would a third of all paintings in people's homes be landscapes?"

"Is that true?" I was skeptical.

"Yea, I did a summer internship at the National Gallery in college," she replied.

"Don't you think most people, especially in large galleries and museums, walk by paintings too quickly?" I asked. "And because of that they see something static, but really great paintings are always moving. If you pay attention to the brush strokes and look at the details, the movement is always there. Every painting has a secret—layers that were brushed over, sometimes completely, to hide something the artist wanted to share at some point but then redacted." I had stopped talking to Sabrina and was really only talking to myself. In the twenty years I'd been painting, I never once stepped back to look at my process, notably my lack of an outline and my love of mistakes. Behind the couple dancing in *Midnight in Paris* was a swing set—my childhood swing set. I put it there to help me paint the expressions of joy on their faces. When I snapped to, I noticed Sabrina had her elbows propped up on the table and was listening to me. Embarrassed, I apologized for rambling.

"I can't tell if you're genuine or just another artistic hack," she finally said.

"Definitely the latter," I smiled.

"Good, because otherwise your condition might be a real tragedy. I've never heard such meaningful bullshit," she said with glistening eyes.

"Maybe this is the universe's way of telling me I was supposed to be an actress after all," I said.

Throughout our whole conversation, Sabrina never once offered up advice on what I should do or harped on the fact that she didn't think I deserved to go blind. She was honest about the fact that she was worried she might be acting overly sympathetic because of a subconscious guilt stemming from relief. She was glad to not be in my shoes. Her candor and dark humor made me trust her and I was grateful for the fast and easy friendship.

The ancient city of Machu Picchu was built inside a valley guarded by mountain ranges. We entered at the top of the southeast mountain range and stepped out onto a small platform. Once my eyes peaked above the crest, a wide space opened up and I walked to the edge of the cliff to discover an enchanted city. I looked back at the path from which I came: behind me were the thousands of steps I'd trekked up. I turned to face the thousands more I'd have to walk down before I reached the city. Four days of hiking led us to the Holy Grail of ancient ruins and stepping through the Sun Gate, which was little more than a rectangular stone hut containing six carved-out windows and an entryway, meant I had arrived.

Down below, the ancient city was crawling with people: other hikers who'd beat us there, and those bused in from Cuzco to explore without first traversing the hilly land on foot. Like the hierarchy of any society, the city was built in tiers, and at the bottom of its six or so ranks was the mighty Urubama River. A reddish-brown color similar to that of clay, the muddy water looked filthy, but it was responsible for the lush green hillsides and was the main source of hydration for the free-roaming alpaca. From our vantage point on the platform, we had an aerial view of the ruins, and it made for the perfect photo-op. I watched as others next to me took perspective trick photos of themselves stepping on, taking a bite of, or pushing the ruins. My own cliché photo was of me holding my hand out as if I were painting the landscape. Unoriginal, I know, but it was me.

I had walked over forty-one kilometers carrying only my personal belongings while struggling to breathe at times and feeling my heart beat mercilessly. How had the Incas found the strength and willpower to move enough earth and rock to build an entire city?

"This is incredible," I said, more to myself to than to anyone else.

"Here, give me your camera," Sabrina said to Jeff. "I'll get a picture of you two."

Jeff handed her his camera and we stood side by side for a photo. Sabrina had us shift a couple of feet this way and that. Then, a couple of times we had to wait for people to clear the shot. She took a photo, looked disappointed, and shouted her positioning demands all over again. After the fourth set-up, we caught on to her little scheme: initially her commands were for repositioning but eventually they were just to get us to stand closer together. Jeff and I rolled our eyes at her and she laughed. Ten minutes later we had our shot, or rather, twenty-seven of them.

Using Sebastian's camera, Jeff reciprocated and took a few photos of them while I looked at the ones of us on Jeff's camera. Even after four days of not showering, he looked as handsome as ever. I hit the back button and found that Sabrina had taken quite a few candid pictures of us. There was one of Jeff looking down at me with a smile while I was lost in thought looking off into the distance. We looked like a couple. We looked happy. I shut it off.

It took us about twenty minutes to reach the bottom, where Cayo gave us some basic information about the different areas in Machu Picchu. Then he sent us out to explore on our own. We took a group photo and exchanged information before parting ways in case we didn't run into each other back in Cuzco. As she hugged me, Sabrina whispered in my ear, "Go easy on him. Broken hearts don't always mend properly." I started to say something back, to tell her I wasn't the one he needed, but she had already backed away.

"We'll Facebook and Skype and then forget all about each other in six months," Sabrina waved. I laughed, knowing that it was probably true and hoping that it wasn't.

Machu Picchu sat on the crest of a mountain in the Andes, but instead of it being the highest peak, it was the lowest. All around us were lush green mountaintops, misty but pure air, and the remnants of a lost civilization. Even with maps, GPS tracking devices, and state-of-the-art technology, I was certain I'd never be able to find my way out of the valley had I stumbled on it on my own.

Jeff and I wandered about until we came across the Intihuatana Stone, which was thought by archeologists and historians to be the Inca equivalent to a clock. Its design, like all early indicators of time, used the shadows cast by the sun to delineate the hours in a day. The English referred to the stone as "The Hitching Post of the Sun" because of the Incan belief in the stone's ability to hold the sun in place during its annual rotation in the sky.

"Hey," I said to Jeff. "I'm going to do a little wandering with the iPod, I'll meet you back here in 20 minutes?"

"Sure," he said. "Don't you mean twenty degrees in shadow movement?"

I laughed, "Right."

I popped in my earbuds and turned on my iPod, which randomly selected the song, "Stronger" by Kanye West. Jamming along to the hip-hop song felt good, but I only got a couple of verses in when I heard local music somewhere on the grounds. The sound was wistful and full of soul and when I finally found the source, I was surprised to find two English musicians. Using the Quena, an Andean flute, and the Xampona, a wind instrument made of up a row of cane tubes in varying sizes bound together, they could be heard throughout the city. I closed my eyes and listened. Musical notes emanating from wind instruments always lingered in the air long after they'd escaped musicians' lungs, and in Machu Picchu that was even truer because the large mountains that protected the city reverberated the sounds.

They flowed outward only to come back in. The rhythm was tantalizing.

Lost in thoughts of spirits, earth, and whether or not there was a real connection between the two, I wasn't really paying attention to where I was going. When I reached the eastern edge of the city, I stumbled upon an image that pulled me back into the present: it was a large rock in the shape of two mountains that people were literally hugging, or trying to anyway. The sacred rock was an energy point, a place where one could get in touch with Pachamama (Mother Earth) and recharge one's energy. At any other time in my life I might have skipped joining in, but with nothing to lose, I found myself leaning against it for an exchange of ions.

The surface was smooth like glass at the bottom of the sea, and warm like a blanket fresh out of the dryer. One of our family traditions on holidays was to change into sweats, put on thick socks, turn off the central air, open all the windows to let in the fresh, chilling air, and sit in front of the burning logs of our fireplace playing games or watching movies. After my parents died, I carried on that tradition alone with an indoor electric fireplace and home videos instead of board games.

Afraid that my emotions might get the best of me, I backed away from the rock and went to find a secluded area. With the faint sound of music still lingering in the air, I sat down and opened my pack. Inside was a rolled up piece of canvas, my portable canvas stretcher, and a small box with paints and brushes. Using a large rock to prop up the canvas, I began to paint.

Without any paper to fold into cranes, I played with the

grains of color pigment, rubbing them between my fingers. Again, I asked myself, what difference would it make to me if the sea were red, the trees brown, or the dirt green? So I painted the piece to be a reflection of a world where color didn't matter.

I started with black, letting the brush move about the canvas freely until it was covered completely. The darkness was a backdrop for solitude. I wanted it to be there, burned into the canvas so that every layer of paint I added was automatically a little saturated. Only then did I slowly start to cover the canvas in color using the bags of pigment from India. A large mountain stood on the right side of the canvas with a zigzagging trail that ended somewhere off the frame. But I changed the colors. I made the sun blue, the leaves and grass brown, their trunks and stems green, and the earth violet. At the bottom, a lone pair of white sandals made of tire, like the ones our porters wore, sat facing the steps, ready to ascend. In the center of the canvas, black clouds hung low against a damp yellow sky. This was the first time I'd ever painted a landscape, so I was surprised that something so common could make me feel so lonely. Landscapes, void of people or animals, had always felt stagnant to me, and I wondered if people were drawn to them because they were a reflection of the loneliness inside themselves? No, the forlorn feeling was personal. Most people loved landscapes because, in nature, there was a place to look outward and discover something inward.

As I began to place a fire hydrant in the painting, I realized I didn't have a reference point for fire hydrants along the Inca Trail. In Cuzco, I saw a silver one outside of the

Cathedral of Santo Domingo in the Plaza de Armas, but along the Inca Trail, there were none. The city was built long before the conception of aboveground water plugs, but I found myself stunned nonetheless to have landed in one of the few cities of the world without them. And I liked the city more because of it. Incorporating a steel-cut object anywhere among the ruins would have been like taking Monet's famous *Water Lilies* painting and adding a rose bush off to the side. I left the fire hydrant out.

I wanted to show that color didn't matter, that it was simply a perception we created, but the opposite happened. Color became the central theme of the piece, posing the question of why we feel a certain way with certain colors and how the tone of the piece changes with our personal connections to blue, green, yellow, or any other color. My mom was laid to rest in a yellow floral dress, so for me, yellow signified transition and Heaven. In the painting, the yellow sky doubled as metaphor for going blind. As the finishing touch, I blurred the edges to reflect the progression of Retinitis Pigmentosa. If the painting was going to be a world that I hoped to cultivate, then it was only right to show it as I really saw it.

Jeff approached me as I waited for it to dry. "When you said twenty minutes, I didn't realize you meant twenty Incan minutes."

"Oh my god! I'm so sorry, I just got caught up in the moment, and I stopped…"

"To paint," Jeff finished.

I nodded sheepishly, "How long did you wait?"

"About an hour. Then I started wandering," he said,

checking out the canvas. "Think it's going to dry by five?"

I remembered the last bus out of here was at five. "I hope so. I didn't exactly think it through when I started. Maybe the high altitude will speed up the process." Standing up, I walked to the edge of the mountainside and looked down at the briskly flowing Urubama River below. Jeff followed. "If you asked me in high school where I thought I'd be at the age of 27, I never would have guessed I'd be here with you."

"Me neither," Jeff said.

"Didn't you miss me after high school?" I asked, referring to college. He knew what I meant.

"Sure," he said. "Did you miss me?"

I had cut ties with everyone from high school, not because I didn't like them but because I didn't want them to judge me. I wanted to be free to make mistakes: smoke weed, drink myself into oblivion, sleep with someone I didn't love, and rid myself of any preconceived notions of who I was. "Yeah, but I think we needed to grow apart in order for us to grow up," I said. "It's hard to change who you are, or to reinvent yourself. I honestly don't think I would've stuck with painting if I had stayed."

"I think I still would've been a teacher. The difference is, I'd also probably be content," Jeff said.

"You'd probably be married to someone from class who also never left home. You never would have known heartbreak."

He nodded. "I could probably do without that experience."

"Do you think all of this being ruins means it was a mistake?" I said, gesturing around us. "That they never should've built it?"

"What are you getting at?"

"Everything that's broken was beautiful at one time. And our mistakes make us better people," I said.

"I'm still not following."

To be honest I wasn't entirely sure I knew what I was getting at. "I guess I'm hoping that the loss of something we love doesn't have to mean that it was all for nothing." Most people yearned to love just once in their lifetime and he was lucky to have experienced it already. Just as I was lucky to have had any success at all in the art world. Artists were a dime a dozen, and very few of us were lucky enough to see our work displayed for a large audience—or *any* audience, for that matter. I had to remind myself of that.

"I won't pretend that I understand art the way you do," Jeff said, "but I've watched you connect and disconnect from it over the past few weeks and I'm certain you'll figure it out."

"Thanks," I said, genuinely touched. I didn't need his approval, but the authority in his words was encouraging and I was grateful for the positive reinforcement. "I'm sure you'll find what you're looking for too."

CHAPTER FOURTEEN

Fear

Getting from Cuzco to Rio de Janeiro took an entire day because we had a layover in Lima as well as São Paulo, but I didn't mind. Anything to postpone the eventual plane ride home was fine with me.

On the three-hour layover in Lima we scarfed down Bembos's Peruvian-style burgers, loaded with a fried egg, plantains, and white onions, while scrolling through the 1000+ photos from Jeff's camera as he imported them onto his laptop.

"Oh, that one was my favorite!" I exclaimed at the sight of my red, prickly flower.

"I stuck a leaf in it thinking the flower would devour it," Jeff said.

"And?"

"It didn't," he replied.

"Why would you expect it to?"

"Wouldn't you?" he countered. He had a point.

"Why do you have so many of this one?" I asked, stopping at a red trumpet-looking flower.

"Did you not listen to anything Cayo said? That's the national flower, a kantu."

"As a matter of fact, I did not," I replied. "I was a little distracted by my altitude sickness." Jeff looked at me with concern. "I'm going to be fine. You have like a million photos—are they all for your app?"

"Yeah, I think so. It'll probably take another six weeks to sort through them, but I'll definitely show you it when it's done…" he said, letting his words trail off. By the time he sorted them, I wouldn't be able to see anymore. I didn't say anything.

I spent the short plane ride to São Paulo flipping through moments that seemed both recent and distant at the same time. We'd only been traveling for a little over five weeks, but the Great Wall and the night market in China seemed like ages ago. My peripherals had definitely been impacted, but not nearly to the extent I had thought they would, given Dr. Rostin's estimated timeline. Things were blurry in the corners of my eyes, but my depth of field and central vision were not significantly impaired yet. I was grateful for Retinitis Pigmentosa's unexpectedly slow progression but resentful about the hope it gave me for a miracle recovery.

In São Paulo, Jeff and I had a seven-hour layover. We ate dinner and quickly ran out of souvenir shops and duty free stores to entertain us, so we rented a computer station to help pass the time and reconnect with the outside world. There was only one available so I stood next to him as he checked his e-mails, and my heart nearly skipped a beat when I saw an unopened message with a cryptic "Hey there ;)" subject line.

I shouldn't have been looking but a couple of words caught my eye: "Italian Spaghetti"…"great to see you"…"back in America". My mind was reeling and I told myself to look away but I couldn't.

The e-mail was signed:

Ciao bello,
Veronica

He closed it without replying and said, "All yours. I'm going to get something to read, you want anything?"

"No, I'm good," I said, knowing I'd have enough to think about without any extra reading material. Pushing the many questions I knew he wouldn't answer out of my mind, I told myself I needed to focus on me. I had no control over his feelings but I did have control over my life, and I needed to steer the wheel back onto the main road.

Checking my own e-mails, I found one from Michael. He was ecstatic about receiving the first three paintings I had shipped to the gallery. I sent them back as I finished them because I didn't want to risk ruining or losing any, yet somehow they all arrived at the same time. I braced myself for Michael's favorite question: "Is that really the deepest you could go with that?" It never came. He was wholly encouraging and positive about the direction of my new work.

I wrote him back saying another two were in the mail and

my most recent one would be coming back with me. He wanted to have a gala in my honor when I returned to showcase this body of work, but I was hesitant. These last six were a departure from my other work. They were personal; they didn't have the humor or candor of juxtapositions I had become known for. I wasn't sure if people would understand how these paintings emerged. Moreover, I wasn't sure I could handle the criticism if they were poorly received.

I also had several e-mails from my friends, all asking when I would be back and if they could help in any way. Rusty sent me a photo of the Griffith Observatory with two red cups Photoshopped into the foreground and a note saying a "vent session" was in order immediately upon my return.

On Facebook, I read the seventy-two comments people had left beneath a few photos I had uploaded from the Great Wall, Taj Mahal, and Petra. People I hadn't spoken to in years resurfaced, leaving comments about how jealous they were of my globetrotting. I wanted to reply, "It's easy. Have your doctor diagnose you with RP and then all of a sudden hopping on a plane seems like the least of your worries." Instead, I closed the window and signed out of the computer.

Back at the gate, I found Jeff sitting off to the side alone; behind him were large, paneled windows and beyond that, the runway. A plane sped down the tarmac and lifted off the ground. All these people constantly moving and shifting about the terminal was fascinating. I wasn't a jetsetter, but something about being a passenger headed towards possibility felt great.

"I got you a *National Geographic*," Jeff said, handing it to me as we moved over to the boarding area to get in line.

"Thanks."

On the plane, I sat in the window seat with my knees up to my chest so Jeff could stretch his legs into my area if he needed to. Once we reached 10,000 feet, he lifted the armrest and looked at my feet, waiting for me to stuff them beneath his thighs. I smiled and obliged.

The pilot's voice announcing our descent into Rio woke me. I yawned as I lifted the window shade to find that from above, Rio de Janeiro looked like the very definition of the word 'vacation.' Situated on the southeast coast of Brazil, its inhabitants built the city on a lustrous landscape. The mountain ranges were a rich green, with a shoreline that faded from deep blue to a light aquamarine like the center of a geode.

On foot, the city was as busy as any other metropolitan area. It was known as the 'party capital of the world,' and the people were like walking advertisements for 'fun.' Women were voluptuous, tall, tan, and confident. Less was more in terms of clothing, with bikinis, short shorts, and sundresses dominating the fashion trends. Vibrant colors filled the city, making it feel lively and full of energy. And laughter was so common that I wondered if it wasn't automated.

It was paradise. A place where happiness was priority and problems were waved off as trivial chores to be taken care of at a later date. At least it seemed that way to me. It should've been so easy for me to immerse myself in the welcoming atmosphere, but it was the complete opposite of how I was feeling. There was nothing for me to celebrate because I'd spent six weeks traveling around the world hoping for some kind of revelation, and all I had was a vague notion that, blind or not, somehow I would still create art.

We checked into our hotel, the famous Copacabana Palace known for its close proximity to the beach and top-notch spa amenities. In our room, I immediately walked into the bathroom, turned on the shower, filled the tub with bubbles using the free shampoo, and took a bath. Everything about the atmosphere was wrong so I basically hid out in the tub until my fingers and toes became raw and pruney.

When I emerged from the bathroom an hour later, there was a note from Jeff saying he was hungry and had gone to look for food. I didn't know why, but I was relieved he was gone. I looked at the clock—it was nearly 4:00 p.m. Flipping the paper over, I left him a reply saying I would be on the beach directly in front of our hotel. *Look for the only fully clothed person on the sand*, I wrote.

The beach felt like home. "You are a true Pieces, always wanting to be near water," I remembered my mom say when at the age of ten I suggested we install a pond in our front lawn. Just past the gate of our backyard was a huge, man-made pond, around which the houses in the neighborhood were built. But a Vietnamese couple who lived three doors down had one with koi fish in their front yard, so I was obsessed with having one too. My mom suggested I take care of the fish in the giant pond, and I argued that they weren't mine. I came home from school the next day to find a fish bowl on my desk.

Digging my toes into the sand, I felt the wind whoosh across my body. I closed my eyes and listened to the waves crashing into the shore before receding back into the sea. Crashing and receding. The repetition was both numbing and soothing.

When I opened my eyes I looked to the west, where the sun hung low in the sky. I had always been told not to look directly at the sun, but I did it anyway. Part of me hoped that the sun would have remarkable healing properties—that it might infuse light into my eyes and reverse or at least stop the damage. In any case, it couldn't do any harm.

Jeff appeared beside me. When I looked at him, I saw that he was holding a bag with what I hoped was food. "What's that?" I asked.

"The world's greatest beef and pork cutlets. As accredited by the handmade sign on the old man's charcoal-burning cart," he said, pulling out a box full of sliced meats. Without even asking for a fork, I reached in, picked up a piece of pork with my fingers, and gobbled it down. Salt, garlic, and lime were the only seasonings I detected. What made the meat delicious was not the flavoring, however, but rather how juicy each bite was.

"Either I'm really hungry or the old man is the greatest chef du churrascaria in the world," I praised. Jeff laughed, dropping the forks back into the bag and joining me as I savagely ate without utensils.

"You might want to slow down," he said. "I bought it from a street vendor, so your stomach might need some time to acclimate."

"Too late," I said, my mouth still full. "If the D is coming, it's already well on its way. Might as well enjoy the final hour."

"Can we at least sit?" he asked. I laughed and we plopped down onto the sand. Jeff looked out at the water.

"It reminds me of Venice," I said.

"Homesick?"

"No. If anything, I'm afraid of going home. I knew six weeks wasn't a lot of time but I thought I'd be coming back with something—a spiritual awakening or a sign pointing me in the right direction. Instead, I feel like I'm landing in a minefield because when that plane touches ground at home, whatever changes are coming, they're gonna come fast."

Jeff took a while to respond, choosing his words carefully, "You do have to face that reality, Aubs."

"I know."

"Do you? I can't tell. You don't need to be so proud, especially not with me. You know I'll be there for you."

I wanted to tell him that my mind had been a little preoccupied with other thoughts and that he was partly to blame. Instead, I said, "I doubt that would go over well with Veronica and I don't need your pity."

"Why is it so hard for you to accept help?" Jeff said.

"Because I don't want to depend on people."

"Oh, come on."

Watching public arguments was one of my favorite pastimes, but I never wanted to a part of one so I didn't say anything until I'd had enough time to level out my tone.

"I don't want to become dependent on someone and then have them disappear."

"What are you talking about?" He didn't shout, but anger will still permeated his words.

I felt ashamed for resenting my parents' deaths…but I did.

I resented them for abandoning me even though logically I knew it wasn't their fault.

"We're not kids anymore. Why pretend like staying friends is even possible?" I asked. Jeff didn't say anything.

We sat there in silence for a long while.

Finally, he said. "You know I care about you."

"I know," I said, getting up to head back to the hotel. I didn't know what I knew, but I did know sitting there wasn't helping either one of us.

Our dinner consisted of salgadinhos, deep-fried snacks shaped like pointed eggs, filled with corn and cheese, and a Kuat con Laranjas, an orange soda, to go with it. Unlike most of our dinner conversations, which flowed freely, this one was stilted and full of silence. So when Jeff chose to work on his program that first night in Rio, I took a walk.

Outside, Rio was in full-swing party mode. I found myself surrounded by beautiful women in barely-there dresses and heels with arches so high they were practically en pointe, along with suave men in fitted jeans and muscle shirts. Colorful drinks with tiny umbrellas littered surfaces like red cups at a college frat party. And less than a hundred yards from my hotel, a crowd had formed on the beach to watch three chiseled Brazilian men and their two Sports Illustrated swimsuit-model assistants perform tricks using glow sticks tied to the end of a thin rope. They performed side by side, creating bright streaks of light against the night sky in the shapes of a Venn diagram, glowing angel wings, a primrose flower, and a mesmerizing tornado that was nothing short of hypnotic.

I stood there for an hour watching the glow sticks streak through the air and leave a momentary imprint before disappearing. The light moved and shifted, creating images in the darkness while simultaneously highlighting bodily features of the performers—a constantly shifting art installation. No two moments were exactly the same, giving the dancers' fleeting images a sort of artistic urgency. I was entranced.

The next morning a cab dropped us off at the base of Corcovado Mountain, where we hopped on a red train. Winding through the forest, both sides of the train were lined by greenery and poorly camouflaged electric poles along the railway. Jackfruit hung from treetops, butterflies were scattered about, and occasionally when the forest opened up there was a slanted view of the city below. From the train we climbed an additional 220 steps to the top—all in relative silence. After hiking in Machu Picchu, this steep incline was nothing more than a light stroll through the park, but the awkward interactions between Jeff and me made the journey anything but relaxing.

"Sorry," I said, running into him accidentally as he stopped to take a photo of the train from a distance.

"Do you—"

"I think—" I started at the same time.

Silence.

"Go ahead," he said.

"Never mind, it was dumb. What were you going to say?" I asked. The truth was, I was so flustered by how strange it felt being around him that I had forgotten what I was going to say.

The speaking over and bumping into each other was bad, but the absolute worst was his politeness. Jeff had never been polite on a casual level with me—our relationship was built on and sustained by his sarcasm.

So when he said, "Do you want the last carrot?" I lost it.

"Are you kidding me?" I said, glaring at him. But I stopped short, and for some reason I didn't know how to complete the thought. It was ridiculous—of course I didn't want the last carrot. He looked horrified.

"Yes," I sighed, chomping down on the vegetable that just so happened to be my least favorite.

When we finally reached the top, we emerged just beneath the feet of "Christ the Redeemer," a 120-foot statue of Jesus standing with open arms. Made of stone, he seemed oddly condemning for a man standing with his arms outstretched to the world. His solemn expression was more sad than regal.

"Are you mad at me?" Jeff asked

"No," I sighed. "I'm just tired."

He moved to put his arm around me and said, "I've got something that should help with that." He produced chocolate bar from the side pouch of his backpack.

"No thanks," I said as I slid my shoulder out from under his grasp.

"Aubs—" he started.

"When we get back to the States I don't think we should see each other anymore," I said, cutting him off and hearing the words as I said them.

"Really?" He looked hurt.

"Yes." I, too, was surprised by own certainty. "It's the best thing for both of us and you know it," I added, trying to hide how hard it was for me to say this. "Look, I gotta do my thing. I'll meet you back here in an hour or so."

I didn't wait for a response before turning on my heel and walking away. My eyes stung, but I blinked back the tears.

Even though I knew I was right in severing ties with Jeff, a part of me hoped he would disagree. That he might assuage my concerns and tell me I was the only one for him, and then we would ride off into the sunset toward a happily-ever-after-world where RP didn't exist.

I laughed at the irony: The guy who didn't love me had converted me into a being a believer in love.

Breathing in deeply, I calmed my rattled nerves, popped in my ear buds, and scrolled to Beyonce's "I Was Here." A really morbid friend of mine had mentioned that it was the song she wanted played at her funeral. Rio was the end of so many things for me, and the overall tone seemed appropriate.

The words floated around on repeat in my ears as I circled the enclosed platform on which Christ so benevolently stood. The song had a sorrowful melody, but Beyonce's fierce and strong vocals added a power to the ballad that made it more than just about leaving an imprint behind. She captured the universal fear we face with our own mortality and did it in a way that made me believe I had the power to shape my own destiny. It probably sounded corny, clichéd, and far-fetched, but I was relieved, albeit only for a moment.

Twenty feet from Jesus was a gray cement wall about waist-high, which outlined the base area and covered the rest of Corcovado Mountain's plateaued top. The area wasn't large and I had some time, so I walked the perimeter starting from the back. My fingertips brushed against the rough, sandpaper-like surface. Slowly moving parallel to the wall, I stared up at the gargantuan figure and thought, *In this moment, Christ is here, and so am I.* I looked up at him I said, "Okay, now what?"

No answer.

My paintings were an unfinished legacy—an image only partially complete. I hadn't yet reached my full potential, but deep down I knew my days wielding a paintbrush were almost over.

"If I believed in you, would you give me back my eyesight?" I asked aloud. His expression remained stone cold and I badly wanted to punch the rock he was made of to get him to look down at me, to pay attention, because I was losing it.

I moved toward him, tears already running down my face, and when I reached the dark plinth upon which he stood, I pressed my body to the stone. With my cheek flush against the cool surface and my hand balled into a fist, I cried.

My sobs were manic. I couldn't breathe, it hurt so badly. Pressing my forehead to the platform, I looked to the ground, afraid to make eye contact with anyone. I knew they could see me, but I ceased to care. Exhaustion outweighed embarrassment, and I just couldn't be strong anymore.

I didn't want to go blind. I didn't want to go home. I wasn't ready for any of the changes that were coming my way. And I didn't want to be alone. Darkness had emerged as a phobia, which I had no choice but to cope with. The tears had blurred my vision completely, so I didn't see the hand that reached across me, gently guiding my cement-indented forehead into his chest. Jeff pulled me into his arms and hugged me tighter than he had ever hugged me before. I was still sobbing heavily and my body must have given way, because he turned around and leaned against the wall for support.

When my breathing finally slowed to normal pace, he stroked my hair and said, "You're gonna be okay."

"I need to sit," was all I could muster. Jeff guided me to the side, out of the pathway of tourists who no doubt wanted to take photos of Jesus *without* the hysterical girl crying in front of it. A few women handed me handkerchiefs and napkins, nodding in understanding as they moved past me. It wasn't until later that I realized they must've thought the tears were the result of my being in presence of Jesus Christ. Too bad Jesus was about as real to me as Santa Claus. I admired those who could trust so completely in someone who felt the need to constantly test them and who time and again disappointed them. Of course, many could argue that perhaps my disease was a direct result of not believing.

Without letting me go, which I was grateful for because I might've just fallen, Jeff slid with me to the ground.

He sat with me in silence, and I cried for a long time. The uncontrollable repetition of hysterical breathing calmed to a few sharp intakes of air, followed by longer inhales and exhales, until finally I sounded normal again.

"Thanks," I cracked.

He didn't say anything. Instead, he hugged me tight and kissed the top of my head.

When we finally stood up, I leaned over the edge to look at the sprawling city beneath us, and Jeff stood beside me with his arm ever-so-slightly grazing mine.

Agreeing that Jesus was probably strategically placed facing the best vantage point, we scouted for a spot directly in front of him. When a little girl, her parents, and her grandma vacated a space, we slid in. I scanned the landscape by literally turning my body 360 degrees in place. The topography seemed to be a kind of paradise with beautiful beaches on one side and huge mountain ranges just beyond the sprawling city. Corcovado Mountain was the tallest point around, so the panoramic view was crisp and unobstructed, save for the statue of Jesus himself. Directly beneath, green foliage spilled down the mountainside and expanded to the smaller mountains nearby. In between the pointed ridges of green lay the city. White and gray buildings covered every flat section of Rio's terrain, making it one of the most beautiful areas of industry.

Directly in front of us was the Atlantic Ocean, and the sun behind us cast an orange glow over the darkening horizon. I didn't know which God I was praying to, but as I studied the landscape, I silently begged for a miracle cure.

The morning before our flight home, I painted my last piece: my eyes. I had to look in the mirror while doing this, because they were pretty nondescript. They were neither beautiful nor ugly, and because of this I hardly paid attention to their detail. People always said that the eyes were the windows into the soul, but I was hoping to paint a window into the world. Like the *Mona Lisa*, my eyes connected back to the viewer. I wanted to have a conversation with my audience. I wasn't known for being a minimalist painter, so I had to resist the urge to paint the beautiful things I'd seen around the eyes. *Seeing Black* would be my most simplistic and bold painting to date.

The darkness was an allusion to the Rothko Chapel in Houston. As the place where my imagination first began to flourish, it was a nice bookend to my career. Designed by Mark Rothko in 1964, it was an octagonal room with dark canvases painted in dark colors, ranging from deep black to velvety purple, covering the walls. A sacred space, a sanctuary for people of all beliefs, the room was used for everything from personal meditation to small church services. It was the only place I'd ever been that gave me insight into the world using only the knowledge I already possessed in my mind.

My dad took me there when I was young because he liked the *Broken Obelisk* sculpture that sat in the open plaza in front of the Chapel. I regret never asking if he knew that the sculpture was dedicated to Martin Luther King, Jr. as a symbol of his broken dream after he was assassinated. As a kid I never thought much about the problems that plagued my parents. I wondered if he came there to ruminate on the difficulties of his job, marriage, or even dealing with me. It was also possible that he may have just enjoyed how its structure challenged him mathematically. The obelisk, snapped in half like a broken pencil, stood upside down so that its tip met the zenith of a pyramid. Two points of minimal substance met in a geometrically impossible center. It looked like an optical illusion, yet there it was in all of its dimensions.

My dad didn't much care for the Chapel, but because I loved it so much he would sit with me for as long as I wanted. He and I probably visited the room a hundred times, but my most vivid memory was when I was six years old. It was a week after my sixth birthday and I was mad because he and my mom wouldn't let me have a bounce house at my party. I was so angry with them that I didn't speak for four days. He took me to the Chapel knowing I wouldn't be able to contain myself, and that I'd want to talk, as I always did when we visited my favorite place. Begrudgingly, I sat down next to him and watched as the sneaker he had crossed over his knee bounced up and down while he patiently waited for me to give in.

We sat there for what seemed like hours but was probably only fifteen minutes. Finally, I couldn't take it anymore and I stood up on the bench to press my small hands against his eyelids. "Daddy, what do you see?" I whispered.

My fingers, which now rested on my thighs as I waited for the paint to dry, tingled at the memory. I didn't know the chapel was a place of prayer or meditation—I honestly thought we were supposed to stare at it and then close our eyes and see images. I thought it was a game. "*I* see a unicorn standing in front a waterfall. What do you see?" I urged.

He paused for effect and then replied, "I see my daughter growing up too fast."

"Am I pretty?" I asked him, taking his words literally. I thought he could see the future.

"The fairest in all the land," he smiled, looking back at me as I dropped my hands from his face.

I remembered feeling relieved, as if being beautiful were tantamount to my success in the future.

I noticed a few places where the white canvas beneath peeked though the black and I added touch-up strokes.

"That's creepy-looking," Jeff said, coming up behind me.

"And you wonder why I disregard your artistic opinions," I replied, still analyzing the black.

He took a seat across from me on our balcony overlooking the Atlantic Ocean and said nothing for a long while. The impending journey home was uncertain for both of us, and I think we found ourselves reveling with nostalgia at the difference six weeks had made in our lives. I appreciated what the path represented and I thought Jeff grew in many ways on this journey as well, but he was such a private person it was hard to guess what changed for him, if anything at all.

Picking up my iPod, which was resting on the table beside me, he asked, "What have you been listening to this entire time anyway?"

I looked up at him. "What do you think?"

"Tupac, Eminem, Kanye..."

I laughed, "Kanye actually did pop up, but it was mostly random. I don't believe in God or love, but I do believe in the art of music shuffling."

"The art of music shuffling? That sounds like some sort of Venice hippie bullshit."

"Oh come on. You know what I'm talking about. You'll be feeling so shitty and having the worst day, and then the perfect tune comes on the radio and makes you burst into song."

"I never burst into song, but yes, I know what you're talking about."

"There you go," I said. There was nothing new age or hippie about it.

"Then by default you believe in fate."

"I believe in real fate, not the ideal one. Things happen that we can't control, but I don't think everything happens for a reason. They just happen," I corrected.

"You're a pessimistic fateist."

I laughed, "If that's a real thing, then yes, I guess I am."

Our final descent into Los Angeles was surreal. From my window I could see familiar landmarks like the 405 freeway, the Santa Monica Pier, high rises clustered all along Wilshire Boulevard, Venice Beach…home. A mixture of relief and fear gripped me as the wheels of our plane hit the tarmac. My journey around the world was over.

CHAPTER FIFTEEN

Acceptance

"Woof," Tig barked.

"I know, I know," I whispered. "Gotta work on the whole getting up thing." I blinked my eyes, waiting for the small amount of light that I could still see to surface, but there was nothing. Dr. Rostin's estimation of how long it would take for complete blindness to set in was wrong by about six weeks. Considered legally blind at eight weeks, I had my license revoked two weeks after returning from Brazil. I had been seeing virtually nothing for about a week, so the fact that today was the day I lost all ability to see was inconsequential.

The physical act of going blind was less dramatic than I had anticipated. What began in Italy continued gradually as my field of vision became smaller and smaller, like looking through a set of binoculars as the objective lens shrank little by little. Tig's trainer, Tracy, had a cousin with Glaucoma, who described it as being able to see a paperclip clear across the room but tripping over the elephant in front of you trying to get to it. He was spot on. I thought it would be like clicking through a View-Master, except that every day the images would become progressively blurrier until eventually the blur turned to black. Instead, I had remarkably clear but narrow vision in the final few weeks. Depth perception, or lack thereof, was the root of my frustration—nothing was safe around me. I tripped or bumped into furniture, walls, signposts, newspaper boxes, and people—the latter being the least forgiving.

Falling off my bed was a morning ritual I didn't bother to adjust. For some reason, I liked the physical jolt of falling, which separated my dream state from reality every morning. Two and a half months after making my way from Rio to Los Angeles, I had only just begun to figure out a system for my tiny studio apartment. But the place was a mess. I knew this not because I could see it, but because I couldn't recall the last time I'd put anything away. Luckily I ate prepared foods with paper plates and plastic silverware, so at the very least the place didn't smell. And, somehow, I usually knew where I'd last left things.

I knew that on my nightstand was a postcard of the Kemah Boardwalk from 1997—a memento of my weeklong visit to Houston shortly after returning from Brazil. Sorting out my parents' affairs wasn't something I could put off any longer. So, I was back for only three days before booking a ticket home.

I stood on the front lawn of my house, thinking it was smaller than I remembered. A quaint, one-story home with three bedrooms and a study held all of my adolescent memories. Almost as soon as I entered, my mind became inundated with them. I noticed, hidden at the foot of the couch, the wine stain from a glass knocked over when I was eight. They were watching a scary movie, my mom's favorite genre, when I came running out of my room shrieking at the noises I heard. Just like the stupid characters in the horror movies who headed toward danger instead of away from it, I walked in on someone's finger being severed off with a butcher knife. Never again would I sleep with my fingers and toes anywhere but neatly tucked beneath the blanket. My mom wasn't thrilled about the stain, but it did earn me two weeks of sleeping between them in their king size bed.

Perpendicular to the couch on the wall closest to the door was the space they designated "Aubrey's coloring area." The second I learned to walk, they surmised that they couldn't keep me from marking up the walls, so they decided to give me one and hope I'd stay confined to it. Oddly enough, for the most part, I did.

I was obsessed with the color green, though I can't remember why, so almost all of the drawings were in varying shades of lime green, blue-green, green, and neon green. I remember hogging—and stealing—the green crayons from preschool because I loved the color so much. The wall was a four-year-old's version of the view from our backyard porch. Perspective and proportions were completely out of whack, but my parents loved that wall. When I got older they punished me by refusing to paint over it, even though they knew it embarrassed me to have my friends see it.

"You should've thought about that before you went decorating our walls," my mom would smirk.

I stood in the doorway remembering my mom and dad like characters in a movie. While my mom cooked, my dad would sit on the sofa reading some boring analysis of angles in relation to pressure and how it affected the structural integrity of whatever. When he got stuck, they would orally work out the answers to complicated math equations while I colored the wall. Had I not been the spitting image of the both of them combined, they probably would've gone back to check to see if I'd been switched at birth.

On a Tuesday afternoon, while I was waiting for a 3:00 p.m. meeting with my parents' attorney, Eli, I stopped in at my favorite vintage store, Miss Daisy's Shoebox. Thumbing through the postcards, I was pleasantly surprised to find that I had been to many of the destinations on the cards: the Statue of Liberty, Eiffel Tower, Colosseum, Venice Beach, San Diego, the Hollywood sign, and Kemah.

I stopped.

It was a photo of the Kemah Boardwalk circa the 1990s and to the left of the frame, standing in line to buy ice cream, was Jeff and me at the age of twelve.

Our backs were turned away from the camera but I recognized my iron-on "peace" and "love" patches glued to the back pockets of my French-rolled jeans. Almost as a reflex, I jammed the card back into the stack only to instantly regret letting it go. My hands shook and my breathing accelerated as I searched for a couple of minutes before finding it again. The message on the back read: *A beautiful Spring day in Kemah. Wish you were here...*, and it was sent to a Gunnar White in Nashville on March 11, 1997.

Finding the postcard was like finding a piece of home, and

it was one of only a few things I brought back with me before putting my parents' house up for sale.

I had gotten several voicemails from Jeff since I'd returned. In them he said he missed me and asked if we could have dinner or even just grab a coffee, but I ignored the messages. Things were difficult enough without his added complication.

Knock knock. Michael was at the door.

"Just a minute," I yelled, reaching for my walking stick and purple cotton robe, both of which hung at the edge of my bed. I felt ridiculous using Tig inside my tiny apartment, so even though I had dozens of bruises from running into furniture and door jams, I stubbornly guided myself to the door.

"Hi Michael," I said as I let him in.

"How did you know it was me?" he asked, taking my hand and leading me to the sofa. I heard the door close a few seconds later.

"Because you're the only person crazy enough to come to my apartment at 8:00 a.m. on a Saturday," I replied.

"I really wish you'd let me get you a maid."

"Is it that bad?" I asked. "I woke up this morning with every intention of cleaning."

"To be honest, I've seen worse, but that's not the point. You really should let us hire you some help," he said, his voice having moved away from me. I heard the refrigerator door open and close, then the freezer door, followed by footsteps walking back toward me. "Water and gelato. No wonder you're so thin," he said. I had lost a significant amount of weight, fifteen pounds, which was easily noticeable on my 5'2" frame, but it wasn't for lack of food.

"I was never big on cooking," I said, as if that explained the empty shelves in the pantry and fridge.

"I brought you three different dresses," he said, laying them across my lap. "Try them on. Oh, and there was a box on your doorstep so I slid it in, it's on the right side of the coffee table, okay?"

"Thanks," I said.

My gallery opening was less than four months away and I was in a perfect state of denial. How had the last few months passed so quickly? When I agreed to have the opening I had just come back from Brazil, and I was certain that by March I would have my life organized. But being organized was the least of my problems.

Every day was a new adjustment. Things like dressing myself and taking a shower were a Sherlock Holmes investigation of feeling my way around my clothes for unique details and recognizing the bottle shapes of shampoo vs. conditioner. I did my best to feel for the seams on clothes but often wore tank tops inside out.

For the most part I knew where everyday things like plates, utensils, toothbrush, combs, and clothing were, but I dreaded looking for anything I hadn't used since going blind. I didn't attempt to put on makeup and ate store-bought food for every meal. The only people I saw with any sort of consistency were Rusty and Tracy. Tracy came every day to work with Tig and me, and after two months of mapping out Venice Beach we'd covered a six-block radius around my apartment. This meant I could walk six blocks in any direction and not get lost. Progress was painstakingly slow.

"What color is it?" I asked Michael, feeling the silk fabric of a tube top dress that ran the span of my arms, indicating it was full-length.

"Midnight blue."

Going into the bathroom I took off my robe, stripped down to my undies, unzipped the dress and stepped into it before pulling it up. With effort Michael got it to zip. "Wow that's tight."

"It's elegant," he said.

"I've never really been a big fan of tube tops," I said, feeling the lining with my fingers and praying that my next breath didn't cause the seams to burst.

"What about this one," Michael said, putting a chiffon dress in my hands as he undid the tube top. I put on the new dress and he helped me with the belt. The dress hung heavy on my shoulders, had a deep structured V-neck, and where the dress stopped at my knees in front, it continued to my ankles in the back.

"What color is it?" I asked.

"Champagne gold and it looks amazing on you, Aubs," Michael gushed.

"It's not too deep?" I asked. The V-neck plunge made my chest feel bare and I worried about a wardrobe malfunction.

"You look like you belong on a red carpet," he said.

"Do you think it'll match my walking stick?"

"Funny," he said. "Look, I gotta go finish setting some things up, but I'll see you later, okay?"

"Yeah, of course," I said, putting my pajamas back on. He gave me a hug and kiss on the cheek and I heard the door close behind him.

"C'mon, Tig. You hungry?" I asked, reaching down to where he sat nestled at my right ankle. Using my walking stick, I felt my way to the kitchen and poured Tig a bowl of dry food from a container placed on the far right side of the counter. After setting it down, I listened to make sure I'd given him the right stuff. His first couple days with me, I accidentally poured cereal in his bowl and he sniffed it but refused to eat. Good dog.

Moving my fingers along the counter I made my way over to the coffee pot, which was timed to produce coffee every morning at 8:45 a.m. I poured myself a cup and sat at my kitchen table in silence.

The sale of my parents' house bought me time, but I didn't want to squander their money doing nothing. I refused to believe I was meant to stop creating. In death, as they had in life, my parents protected me—they gave me the means to stretch my creative muscles and I'd be damned if my career ended here.

So I painted. Using only black on large blank canvases, I painted with free flow. There was no structure or design, just carefree brushstrokes on an empty canvas. I hoped that by getting back to the basics I might tap into my inner child. If Picasso could develop cubism after a ten-year search for inspiration found in his youth, then I could come up with something too. I did my best to use blindness as a challenge —to see it as an obstacle meant to make me better. The struggle was having no idea what I was looking for and no guarantee that my efforts would amount to anything. I constantly reminded myself that Picasso was a classic example of someone who perfected a craft only to inspire a movement by breaking with convention, and I needed to do the same. Innovation was born of creativity and I was frantically searching for a place where the two might converge.

In the span of a single week I painted sixty-seven pieces that were strewn about my apartment, and not one of them was worth the canvas it was painted on. A craft could be learned, but intuition and creative instinct were born from the artist. After the fiftieth painting or so, it became quite clear that my precise hand-eye coordination, which once came so naturally to me, was gone. I couldn't conceptualize anything that I painted. Take distance, for example: unless I planned on never lifting my paintbrush, I found it impossible to pick up where I left off and even then I had no idea how far my brush had traveled from point A to point B. At one point, out of desperation, I even ditched the brush in favor of my fingers, hoping to find a connection with the fabric— anything to act as a launching point into something not only artistic but also original. When that didn't work I launched the canvas across the room in anger.

Sliding off my stool, I moved to the couch and knocked my shin on the cardboard box Michael mentioned bringing in.

"Jesus!" I yelled, kicking it.

I wanted to kick some more things and scream at the top of my lungs, but I was afraid my neighbor might call the cops, so instead I grabbed a pillow and yelled into it. When my voice was hoarse and my body exhausted, I moved to the box on the floor. Inside, I found picture frames, a plastic Rubik's cube, salt and pepper shakers, my mom's abacus, a few Christmas ornaments, and my dad's old Mamiyaflex camera. Almost all of our family photos, even the most recent ones, were taken with this camera. "Digital is the lazy man's photography," he'd say as he paid for the film to be processed. "There's no art in automatic, right Aubs?" he'd smile.

I moved my fingers along the frame, careful not to touch the lens. Made of steel, metal, and glass, the camera was fairly heavy.

"Knock, knock. Hey, it's Rust," Rusty said, opening the door, which I had neglected to lock after Michael left.

"What's up?" I asked, unfazed by his brazen entrance. He stopped by every single day to check on me, albeit at different times. Sometimes his visits were brief and other times we'd stay up so late drinking and talking that he'd pass out on the couch.

"What happened here?" he asked.

"I'm not sure, you'll have to tell me."

"It looks like a Goth thrift store tore through your apartment. You've been working on these for weeks. When are you going to add color?"

"I was experimenting." He didn't say anything more, his lack of enthusiasm proof of what I intuitively knew: they were shit.

"Aubs, do you remember that Dali that we saw in New York?"

"*The Persistence of Memory*," I recalled.

"We spent hours discussing the philosophy of time——"

"——and the faculties of the mind," I finished. The famous image of melting clocks had been studied by the world over and there were many theories about the landscape representing immortality and the clocks representing time's relativity.

Rusty laughed, "It made us feel like time was malleable, insignificant even. It gave us a way to intellectually circumvent the grip that time seemed to have on life."

"Ahh to be young again," I mused.

"*Not* to be young again. That's the point. It's that you don't have to have all the answers right now," Rusty said.

"What do you mean?"

Rusty paused. "Come to my studio with me," he said.

"And do what?"

"Practice, explore, test theories, whatever. I have a huge space and from the looks of it you've got tons of pigment being wasted as wall decor."

"Thanks, but I think I'll pass," I said.

"Oh, come on. You can't expect a new art form to emerge overnight. It took you twenty years to be the painter you are. If it takes you six months, a year, or even five to figure out your element, then so be it. Time is relative remember?"

"You know what I think? I think Sharon just finished a Supreme Court clerkship and is moving on to a big firm. Bill and Lina just broke ground on a new sporting goods store, and Chad and Elise are getting married. Even John got his shit together with that Fry Heaven food truck. But me, I'm supposed to frolic around with art students relearning the basics so in six months I can wow everyone with my blind rendition of a bowl of fruit? Time might've been relative for Dali, but from where I'm standing it's pretty straightforward," I snapped.

"Your opening is going to be huge. I'm not bullshitting you when I say it's your best work to date," he countered.

"Rust! I can't see anymore!" I shouted. "Why is that so hard for you to understand? Without sight there is no connection, there is no more art, and no matter what I do it's not coming back."

"You're an artist. Your job is not to copy, but to create," he said matter-of-factly. "So Monday, at 7:00 a.m. sharp, I'll pick you up. We'll work, have lunch, work some more, bitch about things, have dinner, and work again. Do not mess with my mojo by making me late, Johnson. I'm not like those laissez-faire people who wake up at noon and wait to be inspired." Like Jeff, Rusty knew how to calm me. By keeping his tone even, he didn't engage my dark moods.

I let out a sigh. "Do you really start at 7:00 a.m.?"

"Sharp." Rusty shoved me lightly in jest.

"You're ridiculous," I said. I didn't see the point in going, but I saw even less of a point in arguing about it.

"I have no freaking clue how to operate this thing, Aubs," Rusty said as he fiddled with the camera. Rusty's workspace, an open loft with large windows overlooking Venice Beach, was always immaculate. And because he kept furniture to a minimum, our voices echoed and bounced off the walls. "Why can't you just use a digital camera like the rest of the world," he complained.

"You can't do what I want to do with a digital camera," I said. Click. Something swiveled and I heard the tiny screech of a hinge turn.

"So that's how you open it," Rusty said. "Oh, good God,

you're going to have to manually wind film into this thing."

"Aren't you supposed to be encouraging?" I asked.

"Hang on a sec," Rusty said, standing up. I heard a beep and the faint sound of his phone ring before he said, "Hey man, what's up?" Pause. "Oh cool." Pause. "Yeah man, of course. Well I kinda need a favor." Pause. "Uh huh. Cool. Yeah. Bye."

"Who was that?" I asked.

"Patrick. His studio is just downstairs so he——" Buzz. "——is already here."

Rusty shuffled across the room, opened the door, and said hello. I heard patting, and two kisses, then they made their way back to where I was sitting. I sat up straight and tensed. "Patrick, this is my friend, Aubrey," Rusty said.

"Hi," I replied, reaching my hand out and waiting for him to shake it. It took him a moment and I imagined he shot Rusty a questioning look, but he didn't ask the obvious question of "*Are you blind?*"

"So you're the famous Aubrey," he said. "Oh man, this is a beauty."

"Thanks," I said, knowing the compliment was meant for the camera, but jokingly acknowledging it as a compliment for myself. Both he and Rusty laughed. I remained tense. I was worried he would laugh at the idea of me being a blind photographer.

"I seriously hope this is why you called me," he said.

"It is," Rusty said, and all of a sudden I became shy. It was one thing for Rusty to watch me fumble with a camera and a whole other for a stranger to scrutinize my efforts.

"What do you want to know?"

"I don't know...maybe this was a bad idea," I said.

"Why?" Patrick asked. There was a sincerity in tone that made me certain his question was genuine and not just a rhetorical gesture of kindness.

"I don't really even know where to begin," I replied. "All I know is I want to be able to use it without assistance."

"Okay," he said, sitting down beside me. "Let's start with you telling me what you know about photography."

"She's a painter," Rusty said.

"Right," Patrick replied. "Well, that makes things a little easier."

"How so?" I asked.

"For starters, I don't need to teach you about composition. But," he said, taking the camera from my hands, "there is still a lot to learn. Tell you what, why don't you meet me in my studio in twenty minutes?"

"Sure," I hesitated. "I know how ridiculous my request is, so I honestly won't be insulted if you have better things to do."

"Tomorrow I have a shipment coming in, but today I've got nothing. So I'm all yours."

He left and I listened for movement before asking, "Are you sleeping with him?"

"We're dating, thank you very much," Rusty said.

"Based on his overzealous willingness to help me I'd say you've been dating two months?"

"Three."

"Three?! How come you never mentioned him?"

"With everything you're going through it didn't seem appropriate to flaunt a new relationship."

"Don't be crazy. If he makes you happy then of course I'm happy for you," I smiled.

"Thanks."

"Besides, you produce your best work in the midst of heartbreak so this'll give me time to get my shit together," I smiled.

Rusty and I often joked about sabotaging each other's careers, but Rusty had been careful not to take any potentially hurtful jabs at me since my return from Brazil. That I could finally poke fun and laugh at myself again meant time was doing its job and I was healing.

Trumping whatever jealousy I might have harbored for Rusty's ever-booming career was a strong desire for normalcy. I wanted to move past the hushed tones and awkward silences that invariably followed the accidental use of words like 'see' and 'look.' I was blind, but I refused to be defined by it.

In Patrick's studio, our voices echoed, either because he had even less furniture than Rusty, which I doubted, or his space was substantially larger. From the door, I walked forty-three paces before reaching the couch and, based on the direction of Patrick's voice, I knew he was sitting across from me. As a way of protecting myself, and others, I typically did a 360-degree feel of any new surroundings. The couch was stiff with an equally stiff tweed sham, which I accidentally sat on. In front of me at arm's length was a glass coffee table with cold steel legs.

"If you have any valuable lamps or anything you may want to put them away," I warned him.

He laughed. "I think you'll be fine."

My Mamiyaflex was traded for a pinhole camera, which was basically a Quaker Oaks Oatmeal container wrapped in black paper. As far as I could tell, the idea was pretty basic: Point the hole at an object, open the cover for fifteen to thirty seconds, then close it.

With me, he focused more on accuracy than creativity, stressing that everything within my frame be intentional. And for better or worse, he held me to the same standards as his seeing apprentices. Every inch of my frame was mapped out beforehand and the photo was taken over and over again until it looked exactly as I described. Only after I mastered framing with the pinhole camera did he gave me back the Mamiyaflex. Guiding my fingers around it to each of the twenty-nine knobs, buttons, screws, and latches, he explained how each component affected the image. Photography, I discovered, was analytical and required an intermediate level of mathematical proficiency. No wonder my dad preferred analog to digital.

With Patrick's help, I practiced loading and unloading dummy rolls of film in daylight so he could correct any mistakes I made. Once I was able to load a spool of film on my own, we started taking photos. We modified a light meter to include braille markings so I could calculate my exposure time and aperture. When he set me up for my first solo shoot in Rusty's studio, he gave me a corner of the room and told me to explore what I wanted within my frame. I moved about carefully, though most of the space seemed empty. When I came upon a podium, I felt along the top until my fingers touched a wicker basket filled with fruit.

"Very funny, Patrick," I said.

"What?" Patrick asked, feigning innocence.

As I learned about f-stops, focus, and processing, I found that photography mimicked my new life. Every step involved counting, structure, and memorizing. Slight adjustments affected the outcome of the image greatly, and before creativity was ever part of the process, I had to understand these functionalities. Learning to operate without sight was one thing; actually living a full life despite RP was another.

In Patrick's darkroom, I learned about the different solutions the film and prints needed to pass through. "A lot of it has to do with the timing," he explained. "If you take it out too soon or leave it in longer than necessary, it'll make the image lighter or darker." Using the roll of film containing my images of the basket of fruit, we practiced developing the same image with different timings. And, as with the framing of my shot, he had me describe the difference in sharpness, contrast, and brightness to see if I was right.

When it became clear that helping me was more than just an afternoon tutorial, I offered to pay him for his time and the use of his space. He surprised me by asking for a 1% commission on the net profits instead of an upfront fee. A good faith gesture in the form of an investment. I agreed, humbled by his support.

For the next seven weeks, I was Danielson and Patrick was Miyagi. Working twelve to fourteen hours a day kept my mind busy, but the framed postcard of Jeff and me in Kemeh, which I knew sat next to my alarm clock, made him my first and last thoughts of the day. I could have thrown it away, but I knew that wouldn't help. He had called several more times, asking me simply to call him back, but I still couldn't being myself to return the call. Jeff wanted to be friends, and to a certain degree I did too. I missed him, but my feelings toward him had shifted and I didn't think I could sustain a platonic relationship. I was also, most definitely, not ready to meet Veronica.

CHAPTER SIXTEEN

Innovation

"I'm not going to call him," I said, clutching my phone tight in my hand.

"Fine, then give me your phone and I'll call him," Michael reasoned.

"No," I refused.

Michael and I stood on the corner of Washington and Park Place in Marina Del Rey after yet another rejection to lease commercial space. My budget was only $750 and I needed a month-to-month lease because if my experiment failed I didn't want to be stuck in a yearlong contract. This was our thirty-seventh appointment and out of pure frustration I made the mistake of mentioning Shawn's basement.

"I told him I didn't want to see him anymore, I can't now turn around and use him for his basement," I said.

"Yes. You can. It's called reaching out to a friend when

you're in need. I remember Jeff from your opening, he's a cowboy. Cowboys love to help to damsels in distress." He couldn't help the jab. "If anything is stopping you right now, it's pride."

"You're telling me that if you were in my situation you'd have no problem calling your ex and asking for help?"

"He's your ex now? I thought you just slept together."

"Same thing. We have a history—"

"I'd do it. It'd be hard, but I'd do it," he said, his tone finite and full of conviction. He wasn't backing down.

I hesitated for a long while, then decided to leave it to fate. "I'll give you the address. We'll drive there, if someone is home I'll ask, if no one is home we'll leave and never speak of this again."

"Deal."

I handed Michael my phone so he could navigate, and we headed to Hawthorne Heights.

From the driveway, I could hear music blasting and the sounds of a party. When the door opened, loud laughter and chatter blasted us in a gust of drunken fury.

"Hi," I said, competing with Miley Cyrus's song, "Wrecking Ball," which reverberated in the background.

"Aubs!" I heard a male voice shout from across the room. I was about to ask if it was Shawn when I felt myself being lifted off the ground in a giant bear hug.

"Hi Shawn," I smiled. One thing he and Jeff had in common was their larger than life hugging. "I never would've taken you for a Miley Cyrus type of guy," I said.

"She's my best client!" Shawn laughed, as someone yelled his name from outside. "One sec!" he yelled back. I felt

Michael's gentle arms pull me backward a few steps before the door closed and the music dampened. "Sorry about that. Are you looking for Jeff? Because he moved out about a month ago."

"Oh," I said, surprised at how disappointed I was. "Well, actually, I kind of have a favor to ask of you?"

"Me? Anything. What can I do you for?"

"When I came here last I remembered there being an empty room in the basement. I was wondering if I could rent it out from you. I need a space that's completely dark and basements are an anomaly here."

"Yeah. Absolutely. Of course, whatever you need," he said. "Tell you what, I don't have an extra key right now, but I'll have it made and ready for you tomorrow morning."

"That would be great!" I said.

"That's fantastic, thanks so much for helping her out," Michael added. In my mixed-up jumble of thoughts I had forgotten he was standing there.

"Oh god. I'm sorry," I said. "Michael, this is Shawn. Shawn, Michael. Michael is the owner of the gallery that showcases most of my work."

"Gotcha. Nice to meet you," Shawn said. "You two want to come in for a drink? I didn't mean to be rude and not welcome you in, but as you can tell it's pretty hard to hear once you cross the threshold."

"Maybe next time," I laughed. "I'm sure I'm underdressed."

"You know he's been trying to reach you right?" Shawn said.

"I know. It's just...you know, been a rough transition.

Maybe in a couple weeks," I said. "Should I come by in the evening?" Suddenly I couldn't get off his doorstep fast enough.

"Whenever. I'm an early riser. Anytime after eight should be fine."

"Eight in the morning?" I asked, incredulous. "You did say tomorrow right?"

He laughed. "I'm an old man now Aubs, this party started at noon, it'll be over by midnight and if it isn't, well, my bed is just upstairs."

I smiled, "Okay. See you tomorrow."

In a single Sunday afternoon, Patrick, Rusty, and Michael arranged the room to my specifications. I asked that they hang black fabric everywhere to cover the white walls and then build a few tables in varying heights. Off to the side, they set up a playpen for Tig with a daybed and some toys.

I remember thinking my first art class at NYU, Art Fundamentals II, couldn't have been more of a cliché, but now, having come full circle with photography, I chose to use the same subject: a basket of fruit. For learning purposes, the basket was perfect because it utilized varying colors, lent itself to dark shadows depending on the angle of light, and didn't move. Testing exposure times and different lighting techniques, I recorded all of the changes I made to each exposure so Patrick and I could discuss everything later. This repetition of trial and error helped make the process automatic and each subsequent exposure bore just a little more creativity than the last.

Like a pianist who played the same song over and over

again until the muscle memory of his fingers learned all of notes and chords, I repeated the process of photographing that basket of fruit using sound and touch. In my mind I held an image, in the dark I set the frame, and slowly, using the careful brushstrokes of light, I built an image for the camera. When I was ready for a real subject, I hired a ballerina to pose for me.

"I've never worked with an artist," Katrina rambled excitedly as Tig led us into the house and down to the basement. She hadn't stopped talking since greeting me at the door and discovering I was blind. "It's amazing how you get around with such ease. I mean really, kudos to you. I don't know how I'd do it."

When we reached the room, I opened the door to let her in before undoing Tig's harness, letting him know he was off duty. He scampered off toward his playpen and I heard the shake and squeak of a toy as he did whatever dogs do with their stuffed prey.

"There's an 'X' on the floor, do you see it?" I asked.

"Yes."

"That's your mark. The bathroom is two doors down to your left, or you can change here if you'd like. When you're ready I'd like for you to stand in Attitude, with your bent leg behind and en point."

"Okay," she said, unzipping a bag. "The traffic getting here really wasn't all that bad. I expected it to take way longer from Hollywood."

"That's good," I replied, only half-listening.

Inspired by the Brazilian street dancers who created fleeting images in the air using glow sticks, I came up with a photographic concept involving the controlled use of light. I wrapped a blue gel around my flashlight and turned it on. Pressing my finger to the gel, I waited to feel the heat that would confirm the power was on.

"Ready," she said. The girl clearly wasn't shy about her body considering she hadn't even bothered to close the door before changing. This was a good sign because my fingers were about to get pretty personal.

I moved toward her and ran my fingers along the silhouette of her frame. From her feet upward, I adjusted her body to be just slightly askew. In Attitude, she stood on one leg with the other lifted and bent at the knee. Her two arms were shaped like an "L" with one out to the side and the other stretched upward. Once I had it all set up, I shut off the lights and opened the shutter of the camera. Then, as she stood still, I used the flashlight to move around her figure, creating the dance.

Katrina was a trooper. Because of the long exposure time, each photo took about ten minutes, and if her legs hurt, she never once complained. When we were done, she changed and waited while I packed up my things so we could walk out together.

"Where are you headed? Do you need a ride?" she asked.

"No thanks. I take the bus, but thank you for the offer," I said, holding Tig's harness in one hand and reaching into my bag with the other for the pre-filled-out check I'd stuck in the outermost pocket of my purse. "I'll call you in a few weeks if you're interested in seeing the final result."

"Absolutely. That would be great," she said, taking the check from my hand. "Thanks."

"Thank *you*," I said, opening the front door for her to exit.

"I seriously don't mind dropping you off. The bus system here is terrible," she offered again.

I smiled. "I'm okay, really. It's good practice for Tig."

"Okay, well it was great meeting you, Aubrey," she said, pulling me into a hug like we were old friends.

"Yeah, you too," I said.

Getting to Hawthorne Heights from Venice required two buses and a combined twenty-minute walk, but Tracy mapped out the route with Tig and me during our training sessions and pretty soon, the bus drivers greeted me by name. Once I got over the initial fear of missing my stop and getting lost, the bus was actually a welcome commute. I was rarely ever in a hurry anymore and the time alone allowed me to reflect on and set goals for the work I intended to create. Tig loved coming to the house because Shawn let him run amok in the backyard and, surprise surprise, he loved to swim.

As I unlocked the door to Patrick's studio with the key he'd made for me, Tig and I were greeted warmly. "Aubs!" both Patrick and Rusty said, giving me hugs and Tig treats.

"Good boy," Patrick cooed, giving Tig a pat as he took his harness from me. I pulled out my walking stick.

"Is the lab free?" I asked.

"Yup, all yours," Patrick replied from across the room.

"Sweet. Try not to have too much fun without me out here," I smiled.

"Yes, ma'am," Rusty said. I laughed.

I counted twenty-six steps and made a left using my

walking stick to make sure I didn't trip over anything. Once inside the darkroom, I closed the door behind myself. I double-checked the light switch to make sure it was off, and then I got to work. In a lightproof bag, I popped open the film reel and rolled it gently onto a spool, which fit snugly into a tin canister. Once the canister was sealed, I took it out of the bag and brought it to the sink, where I poured in pre-measured developer. I set a stopwatch and agitated the film every thirty seconds for three and a half minutes. Then, wearing gloves, I poured the developer back into its container, added the Blix solution, set a timer for six minutes and twenty seconds, and waited. The process for developing was full of timed-out steps, the last of which took the longest. Once the film was done developing, I opened the canister, carefully shook out any remaining water, separated the film reel, and then, using a clip, unrolled the film and let it hang dry.

I had repeated this process thousands of times before, but this was different: This was my first creative roll. I imagined for a moment that I could see the filmstrip coming into focus, blurry images crystallizing into solid visuals of my dancer. The first exposure was done with a single blue gel, but the next had layers of orange, and the one after that had green, red, and yellow. How beautiful it must have been to see the progression, to watch the dance unfold on still squares of film?

Thoughts like this occurred to me all the time—sometimes as keen observations and other times with an emotional gust that made me want to cry. I couldn't deny that I missed my ability to see. On my best days, I accepted blindness with courage and grace; even if my sight returned, I would never look at the world the same way again. But anger was always just a shin-bump away, and I had to actively participate in the fight against my own negative thoughts. Usually, this was accomplished by focusing on a project, so I prepped my workstation. To adjust for my blindness, Patrick had containers of ambient temperature RA-4 chemicals pre-measured and labeled in braille. As a result, the words 'color developer,' 'stop,' and 'fix,' were the first words I learned to read.

Using the enlarger was challenging, but we kept things simple by creating only 8x10 prints. This way, the focus knob could be preset. After that, I needed Patrick's help. There was no way around having to ask him to cut the film negatives for me so that they would fit into the negative holder for enlarging.

I opened the door and heard them laughing. "Hey Patrick, can you help me cut the negatives?" I asked.

Rusty came along, and the three of us moved back into the darkroom.

I listened as Patrick used an air bulb to clear off any dust from the negative. After several quick pumps, he slid the negative back between my fingers, moved across the room to close the door, and said, "Ready."

Pulling a sheet of 8x10 photo paper out of a black bag next to the enlarger, I carefully lined the paper with the edges of markers Patrick and I had pre-set. Then, moving my fingers along the upper ledge of the machine, I found the button for red and pressed it down for twelve seconds. I repeated the process for green for fourteen seconds and blue for twenty-four seconds. Sighted people created test strips to gauge proper color and density of contrast, but I didn't have that option. Patrick started me off with concrete measurements of time and tested me on the resulting image, and once I became comfortable, I began timing things by feel.

"How does it look?" I asked.

"Uh-uh," Patrick stopped me. "How do *you* think they look?"

"Well, hopefully it's in focus and there's a dancer in the center. Again, hopefully she's in frame. If I did this properly, she should be illuminated by streaks of blue light. Of course, if I pulled the wrong negative, it could just be a bowl of fruit."

I wasn't looking to make something 'cool because it was created by a blind person;' I wanted to create something universally interesting and I knew Patrick wouldn't lie to me. His opinion mattered most to me, not because he had become my mentor, but because he himself was a photographer.

"It's slightly out of focus, but I kind of like it like that," he said with seriousness. "When did you come up with this?"

"It's out of focus?" I asked, disappointed.

"Just a little," Patrick assured me. "Aubs, I have an idea. I know you wanted this to be your process, so if you don't like it I won't bring it up again, but hear me out."

"Okay," I smiled.

"There's this new printing process on metallic paper that I think would make these pieces look stunning. There's a guy Peter Lik, who uses a similar method is his landscape photos and, because of the reflective nature of the paper, the image changes with the intensity of light."

"But that would mean someone else processing it for me?" I wanted this to be my process, something that I crafted and honed in the blind world.

"It would mean a collaboration," Patrick corrected. "Not unlike what we've been doing together. You'll have total creative control. And, Rust and I will be with you."

"I know your style better than anyone, Aubs. I won't let them change your vision," Rusty said.

I hesitated, but ultimately agreed. "Let's give it a whirl."

"First, let's celebrate this amazing milestone," Rusty said, giving me a hug and kiss on the forehead.

"My little apprentices. They grow up so fast," Patrick choked.

I laughed, "Oh, shut up."

"I have the perfect bottle of Dom Perignon for this," Rusty said. "I'll be right back."

Taking the print out into the main studio, Patrick and I sat on the couch. He hunched over the portrait, his voice echoing off the glass coffee table, and I sat back listening.

"The color, the movement, and the way she pops out at you is really cool. She's a static dancer and using your flashlight you created her movements. The eye travels across your strokes of light almost involuntarily. I find myself swaying back and forth to a visual rhythm," Patrick said. "The more I look at this the more I like that it's slightly out of focus."

"You're not just saying that because I'm blind?" I asked. "I don't want people cutting me slack because I can't see."

"It's not cutting you slack. It's acknowledging that that's the detail that makes the portrait unique to you. I heard once that Pink, the singer, breathes extra hard into the microphone so people will know that she's not lip-syncing and this slightly out of focus detail is proof that this photo was manifested fully in the blind world; yet, it's an image clearly meant for the seeing one. This piece is transcendent."

Just then the door opened and Rusty walked back in, saying, "I have been waiting a long time for an occasion to open this."

"Isn't that the really expensive stuff rappers spray all over the walls and the floor," I asked.

"It is," he replied. "And because we're middle class, we're going to drink every last drop."

CHAPTER SEVENTEEN

Foundation

It doesn't matter what they say, I told myself over and over as Carmen removed a clip from my hair and quickly rolled a thin strand along a hot roller. From the moment she sat me down her hands moved like quick fire, and I could only guess what they were doing.

"You have great hair," she mused. "I know women who would kill to have natural hair like this."

"Thanks," I said. "My dad was part Italian so I think I inherited it from his side."

"Close your eyes for me," she said, powdering my face. "Are you excited about your opening tonight?" she asked.

"I'm nervous," I admitted.

"Yeah. I could see that. My boyfriend designs skateboards and he's been doing it for like fifteen years, but he says he still gets nervous when showing them. Look up for me?"

I tilted my eyes upward and felt the cool brush of liquid

eyeliner. "Will he be coming tonight?" I asked.

"No, he's in Atlanta visiting family, but he told me to tell you that he's a big fan."

"Thanks," I said.

When she was done with my make-up, she took down the rollers from my hair, tossed the curls, added a little hairspray, and squeezed my shoulders. "This might be one of my best looks yet. Do you mind if I take a photo for my portfolio?"

"Sure," I said, smiling as naturally as I could. I tried not to think about how long it had been since I'd felt the thickness of lipstick on my lips.

The idea of standing in a room full of critics, all there to judge my new work, made me sick to my stomach and the car ride wasn't helping. Anxiety and regret clutched at my chest as my body shifted forward with the brakes. Luckily, Carmen rode with me to the gallery. "We're here," she said.

My hands shook as they moved across the door in search of the latch. When I found it, I pushed the door open with so much force that I heard it bounce on its hinges. A cool beach breeze filled the car instantly and I carefully placed one foot outside before lifting myself out of the seat. This was my first time wearing heels since going blind and my rattled legs made it difficult to find a solid footing. I told myself to act confident and lifted my body from my seat, only to bump my head on the roof of the car.

"Fuck," I whispered.

"You okay? Take your time, there's no rush," Carmen said, sliding her wrist into my right hand.

"I'm fine. Happens all the time," I said, rubbing the raised bump I felt forming.

Inside, high heels clacked on the ceramic flooring, chatter bounced across the walls, and a violin concerto lightly played from somewhere in the back. There was nothing quite like standing in such a familiar place only to hear it for the first time.

"Would you like a drink, miss?"

"Yes, please," I replied, slowly reaching into space so as not to accidentally knock over his tray. A thin champagne flute found its way into my hand. "Thank you," I said, taking a large sip and begging the fizzy bubbles to work their way through my system quickly.

"Aubs, you look beautiful," Michael said, giving me a kiss. I traded Carmen's elbow for his.

"Thanks," I said, squeezing his arm tight.

"Aren't you glad I made you do this now?"

"Glad is not the word I'd use," I smiled.

Shifting in my strappy gold heels, I felt goosebumps covering my legs, and suddenly the risqué choice to wear a low cut dress seemed like a bad idea. Did it look like I was trying too hard? And what if the tape came loose and I flashed everyone without even knowing it? The image of Janet Jackson at the Super Bowl crossed my mind and I quickly brought the hand holding my champagne to my chest to make sure nothing had shifted. Carmen had taped the edges to my body and as far as I could tell it was still pretty secure.

"Are you hot?" Carmen asked. Apparently she was standing on the other side of Michael.

"The opposite actually," I said.

"Then you might consider moving the cold champagne glass away from your skin?" she suggested.

"Ah, right," I replied. "Just checking to make sure the girls are still secure." I took another gulp of liquid courage and relaxed. If I was going to get through this night in one piece, it wasn't going to be sober.

"Are you ready to mingle?" Michael asked.

I took a deep breath. Ready or not, I couldn't just hide behind them. I released the air in my lungs and said, "Let's do this."

Swapping elbows once again, Carmen would be my eyes for the night. I asked that they do this because I wasn't particularly great at using my walking stick and I didn't want to draw any more attention to my blindness than necessary. I wanted to appear strong and able-bodied; to elicit triumph, not pity; to appear confident and happy. The room was quiet, too quiet, and I could feel their pitying eyes watching me. "Why is it so quiet?" I asked. The sudden lack of movement and chatter was disconcerting. My body mechanically pressed forward, ready to bolt even though I had nowhere to run. I had no idea where I was spatially in the room, because I hadn't been paying attention to how many steps I'd taken or how many times I'd turned.

Suddenly I heard a clap, and then another, and before I knew it the whole room was whooping and whistling.

The applause wasn't just a polite acknowledgment of talent but a fierce acclamation that rang proud. I had expected the event to be somber and quiet, like a funeral. Respectful praise for the pieces I created and sympathy for my situation. Their thunderous support was so unexpected that I did something I swore never to do at an opening: I cried. Carmen handed me a tissue, which I used to quickly dab my eyes as the noise died down. "It took Carmen three hours to make my face look this good and y'all ruined it in thirty seconds," I laughed, and the room laughed with me.

"Thank you," I smiled, straining to control my trembling voice.

"We love you, Aubs, and we're looking forward to many more works to come," Michael said from somewhere beside me.

"Right," I replied under my breath, before addressing the room. "Well, thank you all for coming. I always worry that no one will show up for these things." They laughed. "I'll make this quick: I just wanted to talk about the work you see at the end of the exhibit." I paused—just the mention of it made me choke up. Swallowing hard, I continued, "As most of you know, I was recently diagnosed with Retinitis Pigmentosa. Which is why, when you talk to me, it may seem as if I find something behind you far more interesting." They laughed politely. "Anyway, I went on this journey around the world looking for answers. Downloading all these images and memories to store as reference points so that when people mentioned things like the Eiffel Tower or the Taj Mahal, I'd know what they were talking about." My voice threatened to crack so I quickly rushed though the rest of my rehearsed speech. "These last six, they're a break from my usual work, so be prepared for that. And the seventh, the large photograph of the dancing ballerina, is my most recent piece and umm, I hope you enjoy them. Thank you all again for coming." I raised my glass and they all replied, "Cheers," in unison.

I turned toward Carmen, ready for her to lead me around, but she squeezed my wrist and stood stoic. There was another eerie silence. To release the tension I could feel building, I circled the top of my now empty champagne flute with my finger and waited.

"Aubs, I've known you since you were a nineteen-year-old kid peddling New York City skylines to tourists on a sidewalk." He was crying. The silence that followed my speech was everyone waiting for Michael to gather himself. "I remember haggling with you for the first piece I bought from you. I think I paid $500." I laughed, along with a few others. "Everyone here knows that I am a hard businessman. When I bought *Ballerinas on Skid Row*, I had no idea how talented you were. I only knew that your work made me feel something." He laughed to himself. "So when it sold for $5,000 to the Gibsons, I had no choice but to pick up the phone and call you."

My eyes were glistening. "And two days later I showed up in Venice."

"And two days later you showed up in Venice," he repeated.

I shook my head, "You steered me down this path, when I could've become an accountant." That got a few more laughs, including one that made my stomach flutter. His high-pitched, single syllable 'Ha!' was a sound I hadn't heard in months, but I thought I recognized it immediately. Jeff?

"You're gonna forge a new path and blow us all away. I know you are. And until then, there is always a place for you at The M. Sanders Gallery," Michael finished.

"As a sales rep?" I chided, trying not to think about Jeff being in the room. "Thank you, Michael." I felt his arms wrap around me. "I owe my career to you. I'll never forget that," I whispered in his ear. He hugged me tighter and then let me go. Raising my hand in a toast, he clinked glasses with mine and said, "To dancing on an empty canvas." He and I were the only ones who knew what that meant. Attached to the portrait in Petra, I had written a letter to Michael telling him all about Atef's blind tourist.

"To dancing on an empty canvas," I repeated, and we drank.

"May I?" Michael said, from somewhere on my right. He took the empty glass from me and rested my hand in the nook of his elbow. We walked twenty-six steps before he said, "Mr. and Mrs. Gibson were eying this second painting of Paris at midnight. It goes with the one they purchased earlier this year." I had no reference point for where the artwork was; Mrs. Gibson must've sensed it because she slipped her arm through my left arm and turned me slightly, toward what I assumed was the painting. Like a choreographed dance, Michael slipped his arm from mine and disappeared.

"Thank you for coming," I said.

"What you've done with these last six—it's astounding," Mrs. Gibson said.

"Thank you," I smiled. "Were you thinking of picking up *Midnight in Paris II* as a set?"

"We were, but it looks like someone already snatched it up!" Mr. Gibson said.

"Oh," I said. "I'm sorry."

"It's quite alright, dear. I quite like this new one. What's the story?"

"Well, I went to Paris for the first time this summer—"

"Oh no, I'm sorry. I'm talking about the *Dancing Ballerina* photograph," she interrupted.

"Oh," I said. Initially I was surprised by their interest, but then I remembered they owned *Ballerinas on Skid Row*. I smiled. "When I was in Petra, I met this tour guide who told me he had a guest once who was a blind photographer. When asked why he took photos that he couldn't see, the man replied, 'Just because I can't see the stage doesn't mean I don't want to dance on it.'"

"To dancing on an empty canvas," Mr. Gibson recalled.

I smiled again, "Exactly. Well, not long after that I came across these street dancers in Brazil who created all kinds of beautiful images by dancing with glow sticks. Again I didn't think much of it; that is, until I couldn't see anymore."

"I'm sure it wasn't easy," Mrs. Gibson said, squeezing my hand.

"No, but when I found my dad's old Mamiyaflex camera, everything kind of came rushing to me at once and the idea of painting with light emerged. It's a blind expression for the seeing world."

"And you do everything yourself?" Mrs. Gibson asked. I could tell she was impressed.

"All of my chemicals are pre-measured for me, but for the most part, yes," I replied.

"Michael's right. Art is engrained in your soul. You're not going anywhere."

I opened my mouth to say something, but another voice interrupted me.

"Aubrey, what a fantastic exhibit," a male voice said as he shook my hand.

I felt Mrs. Gibson's arm slip from mine. "Congratulations again, dear," she said, and then she was gone.

"Thank you, uh…" I started, unsure of who was standing in front of me.

"It's Beth and Eli," Beth interjected, giving me a hug.

"I'm so glad you could make it," I smiled. I'd had a total of two dinners with them when I was in Houston finalizing the paperwork on the sale my childhood home. Eli's firm, Kingston, Garber & Mitchell, managed my parents' trust, but since I was an old friend, he and Beth insisted I come over for dinner before talking any kind of business. Over roasted turkey, mashed potatoes, and corn, they told me about my mom and dad before they were a mom and dad. It was the first conversation I'd had about my parents that wasn't about their untimely deaths.

"I can't believe you guys flew all the way out here," I said, genuinely moved by their efforts.

"We're glad to be here," Eli said.

"Are you kidding me? A trip to California? I'm in heaven," Beth gushed as she slid her hand down my forearm to grip my palm in a comforting squeeze. "You look absolutely stunning in this dress," she said.

Beth was my mom's college roommate, and my dad became good friends with Eli through the marriage. She told me that my mom was super-independent, saying that she would never just be a stay-at-home mom. My mom had big plans for traveling and opening up her own school in Middle America. My mom loved her job as a mathematician, so I was surprised she had these earlier philanthropic aspirations.

They told me my dad's cameo role in Wes Anderson's cult hit *Rushmore* was because he just happened to be walking by the mathematics building while they were filming and they liked how "academic" he looked. Not because he was the best looking guy on campus, as my dad liked to tell it. Hearing about the things my parents wanted in their late thirties and realizing their lives were full of uncertainties was both comforting and sad. Sad, because these "growing pain" conversations I thought were reserved for adolescence were actually lifelong topics I wouldn't get to hash out with the two people whose opinions I valued most. Comforting, because it was nice to know that somehow, even without their guidance, I was living a life that in some ways paralleled theirs.

"Hey, listen. Eli and I have been debating for the last half hour about the meaning behind *Girl in Petra*," Beth said. "Because of its muted tones and fragmented design, I feel like it's about how we're all just trying to keep the pieces of our lives from scattering, but Eli thinks it's simpler than that —that it's about how the world is already fragmented and at different times in our lives we see the same images differently."

I smiled, "I would say you're both pretty spot-on. I was feeling like the portrait of my life had been whacked by a large mallet, cracking the paint that I had so carefully layered throughout the years. So as I was sitting at the top of this Monastery for hours, looking at these shades of pink that made up the landscape, I felt myself melt into it. But I was also at a crossroads and seeing the world from two different perspectives, so the cubist aspect of the painting is representative of time."

"It's a conversation piece," Beth said. "And it's going right over our mantle. I love it. Aubs, this opening is fantastic and I know it's bad form to say this, but I'm going to anyway. I wish you could see yourself, you look absolutely stunning."

"Thanks," I said. "Do you think I can top my dad's cameo? Like, actually get a speaking role?"

"Honey, in that dress I'd give you the lead," she replied.

I was left alone for a few minutes while Carmen ran off to grab me a champagne refill. I stood somewhere in the back room with the corner of a wall as my only point of reference. Everything sounded as I would have expected, light chatter, shuffling feet, and the tap tap of heels with occasional laughter. The room was full of people, yet I felt utterly alone. I was certain I'd heard Jeff's laugh, but the night was almost over and I had yet to hear his voice again. *Stop it*, I scolded myself. *Stop thinking about him.*

To distract myself, I imagined the layout of the room. I knew Michael had an eight-foot wall installed to separate a small space in the back for these particular pieces. On the front of that wall, I was told, was the collage of the world's most famous places that I had made out of one of my travel books. Having seen it on my wall when he picked up the painting from Peru, Michael insisted that it be transferred to the studio for my opening. "It's the thread that ties not only these six works of art together, but also bridges the gap between your previous work and your most recent," he said, more as a statement than a request for my consent.

To be honest, I wasn't entirely comfortable with a preamble to my new collection. I firmly believed that each piece should stand on its own in its ability to provoke and engage. What did it mean that these six needed a preface before their story could be understood? I wasn't sure. As for *Dancing Ballerina*, Michael insisted that she have a wall of her own in the center of the room. Professionally enlarged and reprinted onto metallic paper, the image was given an added reflective quality, which created greater depth and contrast. I imagined it to look ethereal, and thought it interesting that the common catchphrase referencing the image was 'magical.'

"I like her early works and I love the ballerina, but these six I don't get," I heard a voice say. The speaker had a feminine timbre and was either unaware or apathetic about the fact that I was standing nearby. Artists learn early on to let negative comments roll off, but my self-esteem was fragile and her words stung.

"*I* love them. They're dark and painful," someone else whispered in my ear. It was Rusty—the rasp in his voice was unmistakable.

"Twice in one day. You just can't seem to get enough of me," I smiled.

"Aubs. This dress is…wow," he said, pulling me into a tight hug. He kissed me on my cheek and the familiar fumes of cigar smoke from his beard moved through my nostrils.

"Tell me the truth, are there actually any people here? Or just playback devices designed to trick me?"

He laughed. "Get over yourself. No one has the time to plan that kind of elaborate scheme just for you. The place is packed. You're like a living Basquiat, Siddal, or even Giorgione."

"I knew I kept you around for a reason," I replied with a wide smile. His hands rested on my hips as he gently walked me a few feet to my right, adjusted my body forward, then stood beside me with his arm wrapped around my shoulders.

"These last six paintings. Do you know why they're amazing?" he asked.

"You know better than to ask me that," I said.

"They're you," he stated. "This is the first time you've put yourself into your work. Your other paintings are a reflection of your thoughts, and they're great too because you're a smart person, but these are like a window into you. Take this one for example: Just looking at it, I know you fell in love in Paris."

I shifted uncomfortably and began to protest. "How could I—" but he covered my mouth with the hand that hung lazily on my left shoulder.

"Don't bother. I'm not going to press you about the details tonight." I could tell he was smiling. Rusty was the kind of guy who fell in and, consequently, *out* of love very quickly. Critics often likened his work to music's greatest love songs on canvas. So I knew he would make good on his word to come back for a full discussion.

I rolled my eyes. "It's a little late for *I told you so*, don't you think?"

He squeezed my shoulders. "Art, from a place of vulnerability, is the kind that transcends age, gender, culture, and generational boundaries. Your intuition has always been spot on. Pay attention to it." He was quiet for a moment and

,then said, "I don't know how you're going to do it, but based these six paintings and the ballerina, I know that this is not the end of you Aubrey Johnson." Rusty kissed me on the forehead, slid my hand into the nook of his elbow, and led me to find Patrick, who he said 'was single-handedly marketing my new medium.'

"How about taking the day off tomorrow? We can drive up the coast, hang out at Griffith, whatever," Rusty asked as I opened up my walking stick and stepped out of the car.

"Take a break? Are you sure that won't mess with your mojo? Wouldn't want you turning into one of those laissez-faire artists," I smiled. "Thanks for the ride, Patrick," I called out, hoping he could hear me.

"Anytime, Aubs," he replied.

"Do you not trust me?" Rusty asked. "Why do you need the walking stick?"

"I need the walking stick for lips in the sidewalk that seeing people ironically, don't see," I said. "I also feel more in control with it."

"Right, because you don't trust me," he said as he walked me to my doorstep.

"If you were me, you wouldn't trust you either," I said, stumbling slightly because Rusty had stopped walking. We still had about ten steps before we reached the door. "What is it?" I asked, beginning to panic. Had someone broken into my apartment? Where was Tig?

"There's a dude in cowboy boots standing in front of your apartment," Rusty said.

"Hi," a voice said from somewhere in front of us.

I didn't say anything.

"Ah. You must be Jeff," Rusty said, leaning forward, presumably to shake Jeff's hand. "Rusty."

"Nice to meet you," Jeff said in a tone that suggested it was anything but.

"Right. Well, Aubs, Patrick is waiting for me in the car so I'm going to head out. You okay here?" he asked.

I nodded. Rusty gave me a customary kiss on the cheek before I felt his arm fall away from my hand. Jeff came toward me and led me the rest of the way to the door. Reaching into my purse, I dug around for my keys. Just through the threshold, Tig brushed past my leg, letting me know he'd gone out, and I left the door open so he could come back in.

"You wouldn't answer any of my phone calls," Jeff said.

"Were you at my opening?" I asked. It was the first question that sprang to mind, followed by a slew of others.

"Yes."

"I thought I heard your laugh. Why didn't you say anything?"

"I didn't want to chance ruining your night. Am I ruining your night?"

"No. Look, I'm sorry I didn't call you back, but—"

"No, I'm sorry, Aubs. About everything."

"It's okay," I said. "You don't need to feel bad about being with Veronica."

"I'm not with Veronica," he said.

"I don't understand. You were going to marry her."

"I thought I was, but when we got back together I realized, and I think she did too, that we wanted different things."

"I'm not a consolation prize," I said, my defenses rising.

"What happened between you and me had nothing to do with Veronica."

"Jeff, you chose her. We were together and then we got off the plane and you went to be with her. I don't know that I can just forget that," I said.

"Love isn't a game show where you put two people up on pedestals and break them down by pros and cons. This isn't about me choosing her over you, or even you over her for that matter," he said. I could tell he was trying hard to formulate his argument properly and thinking carefully before giving me answers. There was a pause, and then he said, "It's about me asking you for the opportunity to show you what we could be." He slid a folded envelope into my hand. "Come with me."

"What? Where?" I wasn't understanding.

"You came on a spontaneous journey with me once. I'm asking you to do it again. In your hand is a plane ticket. All you need is your passport and comfortable clothes."

I heard the eagerness in his voice and I wanted to go—of course I did. Jeff was saying everything I imagined he would at a reunion, but it was all too sudden and I wasn't sure I was thinking clearly.

"I'm not sure this is a good idea. Can I think about it?"

"Of course. Our flight leaves in a week. I cleared it with Michael at the gallery. He assured me you have the time."

"I'm gonna pretend like that's *not* creepy," I replied, trying hard not to smile.

"If it were anyone else, it would be. Lucky for you it's me."

There was a long pause before I asked, "Shouldn't you

take some time to just be by yourself?"

"And do what? Party hard? In case you forgot, Shawn's house is like a never-ending frat party. Check. Travel? Check. Think about what I want? Check. I know what I want. I want someone I can have a fifty-year-long conversation with and that's you. And I'm gonna go out on a limb here and say you want me too."

I smiled in spite of myself. "I don't know. Go on yet another trip where I can't bring my stilettos?" I said, feigning disappointment.

"You can bring whatever you want! Is that a yes?" he asked.

I shook my head 'no' and said, "It's a maybe."

"Maybe is good. Maybe is basically yes," Jeff said.

"Maybe is maybe," I corrected. I'll admit it was nice being in Jeff's presence again, but, still, I was hesitant. The past six months were a constant roller coaster of emotions and I wasn't sure I wanted to hop on another ride just yet.

Tig brushed past my leg letting me know he was back inside. "Who's this?" Jeff asked.

"Tig."

"Cool name, Tig," Jeff said, his voice sounding further away. "Good boy," he cooed, scratching Tig. "Listen, I'm gonna go before I say something stupid that makes you change your mind, but you'll call me this week?" he asked.

"Yeah, I'll call you," I replied, knowing what I should have said was 'Yes, Jeff, I want to go with you,' while he was still standing at my door. But my feet stayed planted and my lips silent as I listened to his footsteps fade away.

CHAPTER EIGHTEEN

Blue

John Sekoff and Gary Gibbs, a writer and photographer respectively from the *LA Times*, came to interview me at the Sanders Gallery the next morning. John asked me about RP, what this new art meant to me, how coming from a blind perspective shaped my worldview, and how I came up with the concept. The answers were pretty simple. Going blind was really hard, art was my world, and being blind meant creating in a blind world. Once I latched onto that idea, the concept of blind photography emerged. I told him how I found the camera in my dad's old things, and as I learned to use it I discovered I could feel light. I told him it was important to me *not* to have the input of seeing people in my work. I wasn't a part of the seeing world anymore, so my process couldn't be either.

He told me my story would appear on the front page of the Arts & Entertainment section. This was huge. Michael could barely contain his excitement as he moved about in a frenzy making sure the entire gallery was in tiptop shape. Being on the front page meant the art community, whether they liked my work or not, accepted me as an artist. That same evening, John e-mailed me a rough draft of the article. His prose was full of praise and admiration, and I couldn't help but grin from ear to ear as Jeff read to me.

"United Flight 6825 to Cancun will begin boarding at Gate 62A," a voice announced over the loudspeaker.

"That's us," Jeff said. We were at the airport and still, a part of me didn't believe that I was about to fly to Mexico.

"Do you need a kidney? Is that what this is about? You're taking me to Mexico because you need a transplant?"

Jeff smiled, "We're not even the same blood type."

"How do you know?" I asked.

"How could I forget? When you crashed your bike into that parked car junior year you swore up and down for like an hour that you needed a B-positive transfusion."

"Right," I laughed.

Being blind had its perks: we were allowed to pre-board with the passengers in first class. As the plane took off, I pulled my legs up to my chest.

"Nice socks," Jeff laughed.

"What?" I asked. Socks were the hardest for me to distinguish and at some point I gave up trying to match them by anything other than shape.

"Right one is Kermit the Frog and left is hot dogs."

I laughed, turned in my seat, and inched my toes beneath him. "Much better," he said. At times it was like the old days, an easy friendship with a long history of sarcasm and trust, and at other times he was a romantic stranger I'd met long ago and never quite forgotten.

After a moment, his tone turned serious. "I got a phone call today," he said.

I waited. "And…"

"Well, I don't want to jinx it, but I got a call from the Instagram guys and they want to have a meeting. Could be something, could be nothing. Could also be them suing me for plagiarizing their idea," he said.

"Oh my god. What if they want to buy your program?"

"We'll see what they say. I'm meeting Kevin and Mike when we get back."

"Kevin and Mike? So you're on a first-name basis with them now?"

He laughed, "I thought I'd try it on for size."

"That's amazing. I'm really happy for you Jeff," I said. "Is that what this is about? You're gloating?"

"Maybe," Jeff said. I could tell he enjoyed being cryptic.

Jeff booked our flights, hotel, and itinerary to Mexico—exactly what he'd done for our around-the-world trip. He even arranged for Tig to have a vacation of his own at the Rover Oaks Dog Hotel. After quickly checking in and unpacking at the hotel, we met with Miguel, our tour guide, in the lobby. I noticed he had soft hands as he gave me a firm, two-handed shake and helped me pile into a car that smelled of dust and pine seed.

"I was thinking about it and I realized we hit six of the Seven Wonders of the World," Jeff said as we rode down bumpy roads on our stiff pleather seats. "Chichen Itza is the last of the seven."

I smiled. "I've always wanted to see the Seven Wonders of the World. Why didn't we think of that six weeks ago?"

"Because then you wouldn't get to experience this last one with your new heightened senses," Jeff said.

"What if it just feels like being in Venice Beach?"

"I don't think it will."

"You really didn't need to do any of this, but thank you— for everything."

"You're welcome," he replied, squeezing my hand. His palm was probably twice the size of mine and its protective grasp was comforting.

"Only ten minutes more," Miguel said from the front. "May I—do you have a special request? I have not give tour for someone who…"

I chimed in, "Is blind?" By now, I was used to people asking me how they could adapt.

"Yes."

"Just do it like you always do and if there's anything I need, I'll ask," I smiled.

The bumpy rumble of the moving car stopped and I fumbled for the door handle. After opening the door, I unfolded my walking stick and stepped out of the car. I placed one hand on Jeff's elbow and used the walking stick to survey the floor for bumps, and walls for that matter. I still wasn't very good at detecting the different surfaces, but the rumble beneath my stick as it was dragged from side to side in front me indicated I was on a gravel-like surface. Small pebbles rolled beneath my covered flats. Different than the cement I was used to walking on, the ground was unpaved and my steps were slower than normal. Jeff kept my pace. The air was thin and smelled of leaves; there was a breeze coming from my left, and I heard a variety of languages being spoken.

"Are you okay?" Jeff asked.

"Yeah. I'm good," I replied.

We walked four hundred steps or so before stopping. "This is the base of El Castillo," Miguel said. I tried to imagine what they were looking at. I knew from photos I'd seen that the structure looked like a stepladder pyramid with a large plateau at the top.

"Fuck, really?" Jeff said, more to himself than anyone else. He sounded disappointed.

"What?" I asked, but before he could answer, Miguel continued with his tour.

"It is believed Kukulhan is a boy who is born as a snake and cared for by his sister in secret. But when he becomes too big for her to feed, he is running away to the sea, making the earth move. So when we feel the earth move under us, we know it is Kukulhan," Miguel explained, and we walked some more. When we stopped at a new location, I bent down and rubbed my fingers along the ground. I was right—sandy dirt with a few spurts of grass brushed under my fingers.

"It's roped off for some reason, but I swore you could go up it," Jeff said. I stood up.

Disappointed and joking—well, half-joking—I asked Miguel, "What would happen if I went up it?" Jeff guided my hand to a rope barrier so I would have something to hang on to, and I heard his camera start clicking away.

"Nothing. If you wish to go up you have only to step over

rope," Miguel replied.

"What?" Jeff exclaimed. "No way. You're joking, right? It says they closed it to preserve it 'cause it's eroding."

"Yes…and no," Miguel said. "My people believe El Castillo is full of magia, so anyone who goes up will be protected by Kulkulhan."

"I'm not worried about going up," Jeff said. "I'm worried about going to jail when I come back down."

"I think we should do it," I cut in.

"No," Jeff replied.

I have no idea what compelled me to lift my leg over the rope, which came up to my thigh, but I carefully stepped over the barrier and, using my walking stick, I headed toward what I hoped were the steps.

"Aubs!" Jeff called after me.

I stopped, partly because my stick hit something hard—the first step—and also because I expected a guard to stop me.

"Go. Go!" Miguel shouted. He was either proud of my boldness or thrilled to be sending another stupid tourist to jail—I could only hope it was the former.

I didn't really want to go up alone, so I turned back and said, "You can stay down here if you want, but I don't want to spend the rest of my life wondering what it would've been like at the top. Do you?"

When Jeff answered me, I could tell he was right beside me on the steps. "Oh come on. This isn't your life dream, Aubs, and it's not mine either, so if you're asking me to choose between seeing the top and not going to jail, I'm going to choose not to go to jail." But even as he said no, his footsteps continued following mine.

"There aren't any railings are there?" I asked, taking my first step up. I already knew the answer.

"No."

I was only on the first step when I began to feel vertigo. Stopping to gather myself I folded my walking stick, tossed it in my small backpack, and bent down to crawl.

Neither of us said much. Being on all fours was a hundred times more stable and we ascended rather quickly—or so I thought.

"You're doing great, Aubs, we're halfway there."

"Halfway?" I thought we were nearing the top.

Down below, Miguel shouted after us, "Don't rush, enjoy the Chichen Itza!" His voice reminded me of a *Cirque du Soliel* host because his assurances of safety only served to arouse more suspicion.

By the time we reached the top, I was panting. Standing up caused a surge of fear to rush through me as it dawned on me that walking around an unguarded platform blind was dangerous.

"How high up are we right now?" I asked.

"We just climbed up ninety-one steps, the plateau we're standing on makes ninety-two."

"I feel like that number is symbolic of something," I said.

"It is. There are four sides to the pyramid and each step represents one day of the year."

"We just walked up a quarter of a year—an entire season," I breathed, steadying my shaking hands. "I think we're in better shape now than when we climbed the Great Wall. Don't you?" I said, winking in Jeff's general direction.

"You winked at my chest. You know, there's a crowd forming down there," he said, sounding worried.

"And yet, the guards haven't come after us. Look, we already broke the rules, so let's just enjoy it."

Jeff was silent for a moment, but then he laughed out loud.

"What's so funny?" I asked.

"Miguel just gave us a thumbs up. It looks like there are two guards behind him. Probably discussing our impending arrest," Jeff said. The threat of jail only served to make me more audacious. When I was finally stable on my own two legs again, Jeff guided me to the structure at the top, which he described as an empty, square fortress with an opening in the middle.

We walked until our voices started to echo and I knew we were inside the structure.

"There isn't really a whole lot in here. Just a couple benches shaped like—God, how do I describe this?" He thought for a moment and then said, "Okay, imagine you're laying on your back, propped up by your elbows with your legs bent. It's a stone solider resting like that with his head turned to the right."

"Cool," I said, running my hands along the bend of its stone knees and up along the stomach.

"On the other side is another similar-type thing, but it's even more blocky and it looks like a tiger," he continued.

"Do you hear that?" I asked. The sound of clapping could be heard outside. We moved back outside, where the clapping was even louder. "What happening? It doesn't really sound like applause," I asked.

"I'm not—I don't know. They're all clapping and smiling, but you're right, it's not applause. I don't know what it is."

"Can you help me sit?" I asked. I didn't feel comfortable standing so close to an edge.

"Sure," he said, leading me back toward the building and helping me squat down. When I was comfortable he said, "I'm going to take a couple shots on the other side. I'll be right back okay?"

"Yeah, no problem," I said.

I reached inside my backpack for my iPod but realized I didn't need the distraction of music. People were still clapping in non-rhythmic patterns, but it didn't bother me. The concrete make-up of the infrastructure left a lot of loose gravel beneath my feet and hands and the thought of moving sent chills down my spine. Still, I boldly scooted forward until I felt my foot drop off the edge and touch the top step.

The wind brushed across my face and the sun warmed my back. I imagined the foliage and tried to create a picture in my mind of the treetops that I knew from photos were sprawling before me. Pulling out my clunky Mamiyaflex camera, I took several photos. I pictured a sea of dark-green pointed tops swaying in the breeze and had the urge to race across them like a vampire in Stephenie Meyer's *Twilight* saga. In my fictitious world, I was able to run forward and backward in time. The superpower even had a bonus of coincidentally curing my disease by giving me super-awesome-mega-power seeing capabilities. It was a nice thought.

"What are you smiling about?" Jeff asked, sliding down next to me so that we were shoulder to shoulder.

"I was thinking about what it would be like to be a vampire," I replied.

He laughed, having no idea what I was talking about. This was the closest we'd been since I my meltdown in Brazil. "Can you describe what's in front of us?" I asked.

A few moments passed while I heard him rifle through his backpack and flip quickly though a book. "According to my map, directly in front of us is the Temple of the Warriors, and to the right of the temple is a Group of a Thousand Columns."

"What do they look like?" I asked.

"Uh…" Jeff started. "I guess the Temple of Warriors looks like a giant multi-tiered wedding cake. There are a bunch of columns in the front, which I guess could've supported a roof of some kind, and then a set of super-wide stairs spanning about half the width of the entire structure that lead to the top. At the top is a stone structure with more columns inside. The whole thing is really massive. Like taller than all the trees around it, and the people look like little figurines in a giant's playground."

"What color is it?" I asked.

"It's kind of an off-white with a lot of black mold or dirt stuck to it. Maybe algae of some sort?" he said.

"What about around it? Are there other structures?"

"There's a building to the left, another ruin-like thing, but beyond that it's all trees as far as I can see. Trees and sky."

I smiled and was silent for a long time. "I can't believe they're still clapping."

"Oh. It's a revolving group of clappers. They come, clap a few times, laugh, and then move away. It's really weird," Jeff replied. "It says here that the Temple of Warriors looks like plain columns but back in the day they were covered in bas-reliefs and had a lot of color."

"This is nice," I said.

"Does it feel like Venice?"

"To be honest, Venice doesn't even feel like Venice to me anymore," I said. "When I learned that I was going blind, I was so certain that my world was about to shrink. And in some ways it has. Being independent requires a lot of repetition as opposed to exploration, but all that means is that life is experienced in nuanced detail rather than grand moments. I can't stand at the top of a mountain and see for twenty miles in every direction, but within a six-block radius of my apartment, I know where every stop sign, traffic light, and crack in the sidewalk is. So my world simultaneously expanded and shrunk at the same time."

"So what would you say the here and now feels like?" Jeff asked.

"It feels monumental. Beneath my fingertips I can feel the concrete edge of the step I'm sitting on. On my cheek I feel the flutter of a strand of hair being pushed around by the wind blowing from the left. My face and shoulders are warm, which tells me the sun is high in the sky, and the airs smells of treetop leaves and pine."

Jeff's hands found mine and moved them to cup his face. "Hey," he said, tilting my chin up toward him. "What do you feel?" he said.

"You're smiling," I laughed.

"I'm grinning. I'm grinning so wide my face hurts, and it's all because of you," he said.

Before I could reply I felt his cool lips on mine. The kiss was slow, but my heart was beating so fast I had to come up for air far sooner than I wanted. He took my hand and rested it in on the nape of his neck; I couldn't see his face but I knew he was looking directly at me. Kissing him blind was like being a teenager again and nervously making out with someone for the first time. His breath was shallow and rapid and I felt his throat swallow hard as I moved my fingers through his hair, enjoying the moment.

"With any luck," he said. "I'll be as famous as you one day."

"Luck," I said. "You don't need luck."

"Is that right?" he said, sounding sexier than I'd ever heard him.

"Yes," I smiled. "I have it on good authority that your travel app is quite popular."

"Aubrey Johnson, have you been social media stalking me?"

I laughed. "Stalking is such a strong word. I like to think of it as networking research."

He laughed deeply and I could feel the joy in his reverberating neck. "Right," he said. "We should probably head down." I didn't want to go, but I knew he was right. He stood, took my hand, and slowly guided me down the steps.

"There's no way Miguel could have such amazing reviews if all of his tourists ended up in jail, right?" I asked, while planting my feet carefully on the steps. Without railings, that first step gave me vertigo again, but I tried to keep moving.

"Well, he's still there. And both thumbs are still up—"

"Stop," I interrupted, having only made it down two steps.

Walking blind down a set of stairs with no hand railings was quite possibly the scariest thing I'd ever done. "I can't do this."

"I've got you, Aubs. Trust me," Jeff said reassuringly.

"It's not you I don't trust, it's me," I said as I slowly lowered myself so my hands were on the ground. "This is really embarrassing, but I crawled up and I'm crawling back down."

Jeff laughed. "We're never going to see these people again, so who cares."

"I can't see them now, and I care," I replied.

"Good point," he laughed.

Thankfully, he followed me down the steps with a hand on my back to guide me. Coming up I could tell they were steep, but crawling backward down them felt like rock climbing without the protective gear.

After about twenty minutes we reached the bottom, and Miguel greeted us. "It is worth it, no?" he asked, cheerily.

"Ask me that again after you bail us out of jail," Jeff said as I waited for my hands to be cuffed. Jeff whispered in my ear. "Just follow my lead." Like I had a choice. "Wave," he instructed.

"What's going on?" I asked as he led me forward with his hand on my back.

"Nothing. The guards stepped aside and are letting us pass. Everyone's looking at us and whispering like we must be somebody special. I wish you could see this," he said.

"Bad for tourism if American goes to jail at Chichen Itza," Miguel interjected.

"I don't think that applies when said Americans are clearly

breaking the law," Jeff replied, suspiciously.

Miguel laughed. "Ten years I have been a tour guide. I offer that to everyone but you are first to go up."

"Who *are* you?" I asked, confused. I would've felt much better if the police at least carted us off, fined us, and then let us go. But nothing at all?

"My family owns the land. Well, used to. We sold it a few years ago, but we still go up it whenever we want. Part of the deal," he confessed.

"Really," I said, letting myself relax a little. "So why don't you just tell your clients that?"

"This way is special. Remember the 'magia'? When you believe it and you go up, it's special," he explained.

He had a point. The experience was unique because taking charge made the moment ours. By seizing the opportunity, we became part of an elite group of people who got to climb the steps after it was closed to the public. Being up there by ourselves without the noise of tourists snapping pictures and crowding us—that was a trademark of Chichen Itza that no other place I'd been to could rival.

"You know your business would skyrocket if you advertised exclusive access to the Temple," Jeff added. "*And* you could easily charge triple."

"I can't charge. Also part of the deal. And I don't need money."

"How much did your family sell it for?" Jeff asked, apparently having lost his manners.

Miguel laughed, "More than enough. Check your statements when you get home, I never charge for the tour, only deposit."

"So do you tell your tourists eventually that they are allowed to go up it?" Jeff asked.

"I do not," he replied seriously. "You are the only ones who trust in Chichen, and so the prize is yours. Most people come to Chichen to look, few come to *see* with their real eyes," he said.

There was something very genie-like in his voice, and I wondered if maybe he wasn't human. He could've been a figment of my imagination or some kind of elaborate ruse that Jeff devised. But Jeff wasn't that good of an actor and I could hear the genuine surprise in his voice as Miguel explained the situation.

As if reading my thoughts, Miguel said, "I meet new people everyday. The world comes to me." He paused for a moment, as if searching for the right words. "You know why I don't tell them it's okay? When I was a boy, I was good. Never do anything bad. But why? Because I do not know how good it can be. You see?"

"I don't quite follow, no," Jeff said.

Miguel thought about how to explain it again, "Sin riesgo, no hay ninguna apreciación."

"Without something…there is no appreciation," Jeff awkwardly deciphered.

"Risk—Without risk, there is no appreciation," I concluded, and I knew exactly what he meant.

As we walked toward the car, I didn't bother using my walking stick. I trusted Jeff. Tilting my head in toward his arm, I gave him an affectionate squeeze. In return, he kissed me on the forehead and said, "Hey Aubs, guess what color the fire hydrants are in Mexico?"

Acknowledgements

This book would not have been possible without the help of so many people. My parents Richard and Nancy Hoang first of all, for pushing me to always do better and want more. My sister Kimberly who gave me the opportunity to *be* a writer rather than just call myself one. My younger siblings Andrew and Lillyan, who keep me hip to social media and all things "cool."

I owe an enormous amount of gratitude to Ryan Eslinger, who edited every variation of this book—without you this book would still just be an idea. And to my editors, Sara Taylor, Gina Hendry, and Jenny Pritchett, who made me look like a pro.

To my readers and friends: Mai Nguyen, Indigo Wilmann, Eric Batchelor, Shawn Muttreja, Ellen Burns, Michael Ngo, Amechi Ngwe, Bill and Lina Wood, Divi Ramola, Katie Suh, Mark and Laura Simpson, Khanh Thai, and Sally Felt. You all inspired me to keep writing when I had doubts and gave me the courage to release it into the world.

A special thanks also to my favorite Houstonians who made my two years there unforgettable: Dr. Ed and Chi Thuy Rhee, Kenny and Elena Marks, Jilly Marks, David Burns, Laura Burns, Sharon Graham and Alison Lott. Thank you all for your unconditional support and love.

About the Author

Jamie Hoang lives in Los Angeles, but does what she can to leave as often as possible. She is a certified diver, world traveler, food taster, and explorer of life. In her mid twenties she discovered she had a horrible allergic reaction to work and had no choice but to earn a living doing what she loves—writing. Jamie blogs about writing and her life at www.heyjamie.com, tweets at @heyjamie, and posts pretty pictures on Instagram at @heyjamiejo.

Jamie Jo Hoang

CPSIA information can be obtained at www.ICGtesting.com
Printed in the USA
BVOW08s1111060515

399250BV00004B/135/P